Killing Paparazzi

by

J H Ainsworth

Published by

MELROSE BOOKS

An Imprint of Melrose Press Limited
St Thomas Place, Ely
Cambridgeshire
CB7 4GG, UK
www.melrosebooks.com

FIRST EDITION

Cover designed by Sophie Fitzjohn/Tom Brennand

ISBN 1 905226 74 8

Printed and bound in Great Britain by:
CPI Antony Rowe Ltd.,
Chippenham, Wiltshire

Dedicated to my beautiful daughter Sarah who has been a great inspiration throughout the project.

Also special thanks to Val, Eileen, Ginny, Andy, Fiona and Linda for their input, enthusiasm and advice in shaping the style of my writing. The ideas and contents of the book have come from the general observation of life itself.

Prologue

The distinguished-looking man in his pinstriped suit stared at his computer screen. He was on the Internet. He typed several key words into the computer and waited for a few seconds as the electronic wizardry searched the World Wide Web. A list of possible entries appeared and he selected the one marked 'conspiracy theory'. He clicked on this and waited for a few seconds more before the website opened up. A coloured photograph of the couple appeared. The story was based on eyewitness reports and from CCTV footage. It made for uncomfortable reading. The man swivelled in his leather chair and looked out towards the River Thames. He had some thinking to do.

1

Paris

The private jet rolled to a halt at Le Bourget before the twin engines were killed, silencing the high pitched whine of the aircraft. The solitary customs officer clambered on board and smiled cheerfully, remembering that his cushy job depended on it. The red tape still had to be cleared, regardless of who the VIPs were. The small executive airport was only six and a half kilometres from Paris, which was perfect for their needs. They wanted no fuss, no hassle, as the holiday in the Med had been a complete nightmare. The paparazzi there had excelled themselves, snapping away like lunatics with their powerful telephoto lenses, devouring every inch of coverage like some seedy voyeur watching a peep show. They had stolen sneaky shots of them on board the yacht as craftily as the Artful Dodger would have done. The world now knew about the blooming romance as the cat was truly out of the proverbial bag.

The most iconic woman in the world was not Mother Theresa but a blond with a body to die for. She had clearly not gone unnoticed as the swimsuit had said it all. Her image may have graced *Vogue* but the coy smile had kept secret a deep-seated unhappiness, her soul craving for happiness in whatever shape or form. Her new image now looked totally different, as if immersed in some ethereal chemistry which had transcended through the grainy images. She appeared to be happy at last and the race was on to get the money shots, especially when the new man was stamping on dangerous turf. Beauty and fame had its price. It was a warm welcome to hell. The black limo with darkened windows pulled up before the customs officer had even finished his job. It was to keep the hoi polloi out, especially the paparazzi.

The limo swung sharply out of the airport and headed towards the centre of Paris, followed by the 4 × 4 carrying the luggage. The journey was only short-lived but they had been joined by another car just outside the airport, which went unnoticed in the Paris traffic. The driver in the 4 × 4 spoke on the mobile phone. The paparazzi were already waiting by the time they reached the hotel, as clearly the word had spread faster than a bush fire. The British boys in London became frantic; they were in the wrong place. The English Channel now proved to be a bloody nuisance and they had to get to Paris à tout vitesse. Once there, they needed powerful motorcycles with riders for the inevitable chase ahead. Being able to zip through the Paris traffic was going to be essential; too slow and the birdie gets away. The hardened professionals needed to shoot from the backseat for what must be the most important photo-shoot of the decade.

The hotel itself was an opulent building situated in La Place Vendôme, an elegant square which also housed the Justice Ministry, several banks and prestigious shops such as Cartier and Boucheron. The original square had been inaugurated in 1699 to show off some equestrian statue until Napoleon had had other ideas. It was replaced with a far grander monument, the Colonne de la Grande Armée, in 1806 to celebrate his military exploits. The ostentatious structure was removed in 1871, only to be replaced by a replica when Napoleon, the most potent symbol of France, could not be ignored. The paparazzi scarcely gave it a second look as they focused their attention on something far more interesting. The prize was just a stone's throw away and it could be worth hundreds of thousands, probably more if they were caught *in flagrante delicto*. It was worth waiting for, no matter how long it took.

The couple had already been hounded like foxes in a hunt and they simply wanted to unwind, to relax in the Imperial Suite, but the gathering maelstrom outside made it difficult. The buzz was on after she had taunted them about some big revelation, without giving any disclosure. It was a dangerous game to play. The paparazzi had lapped up every scrap of morsel thrown at them but every dog had its day. They knew theirs was just about to come and the cameras were primed to go. It was just a question of when. Like soldiers in any war, the ninety per cent boredom factor was matched by the ten per cent gut-churning action. They could snap away from the back of the motorcycles, dismount and follow on foot if necessary. But for the most part, it was a waiting game, like watching for the elusive yeti which never appeared on cue for the camera. Time itself could be measured by the numbers of cigarettes smoked, just like the local natives did in the Amazonian jungle. The cigarette ends mounted outside the hotel in the nervous anticipation but they were ready. The question remained: was she pregnant?

The couple suddenly emerged from the foyer and walked the short distance to the waiting limo. In that brief moment, the flashbulbs lit up the hotel entrance like the blitz on Baghdad, temporarily blinding them. They headed off to Les Champs Elysées for a shopping trip but the large number of waiting paparazzi had clearly rattled them. Shopping was meant to be fun but this was worse than the first day at a Harrods sale. The surging mass of photographers had made the situation far too dangerous and heading back to the hotel was the only sensible thing to do. Just like the seagulls which followed the trawler in the hope of a meal, the paparazzi did the same. The papers had to be fed with something, even codswallop.

The night security manager became alarmed at the developing situation outside the hotel. The milling paparazzi had already caused some disquiet amongst the other guests, especially those on an away day with their mistresses. He thought of asking them to clear off in a polite way but there was more chance of getting hit by an icicle from the lavatory of a passing jetliner. It would have to be Plan B. The couple had to be relocated to another venue and it was a relief when they agreed to do so. The discreet apartment belonged to the hotel, situated just west of the city, but it was necessary to run the gauntlet. Instead of using the main entrance, they would leave by the back door using a different car, a powerful saloon without the benefit of darkened windows. An experienced driver with advanced driving skills would ferry them across the city but with a bodyguard for their protection. The limo would now be used as a decoy to confuse the paparazzi. The plan was simple but flawed.

The saloon tried to escape into the Rue Cambon from the back of the hotel unnoticed, but the paparazzi spotted them without any difficulty. The whole pack scrambled into action quicker than a Spitfire squadron, amidst a cacophony of motorcycle engines starting up, which shattered the nocturnal peace. The powerful motorcycles sped off after the saloon as the witch hunt began, waking the dead from the catacombs down below. The car turned into Rue de Rivoli and headed towards the Place de la Concorde with the intention of heading down Les Champs Elysées towards L'Arc de Triomphe. It was the shortest route to the apartment and logic dictated this was the way to go. The traffic was light by now and the saloon could easily be followed as it streaked away under the canopy of street lamps. The paparazzi jockeyed for position but the leaders were already pulling ahead, totally committed to the chase.

Just as the saloon was about to turn into Les Champs Elysées, another car suddenly pulled in towards the right and deliberately blocked the route, forcing the driver to stay within the Place de la Concorde. It was the same car which had followed them earlier from the airport. The driver chose to drive on towards the river, instead of going around the Place de la Concorde once again. This route would take them further out but he had made his decision. It was the wrong one. They suddenly found themselves being closely followed by the car and two sinister-looking motorcycles. Unlike the chasing paparazzi, there was only a single person on each of these motorcycles. The chase had become more aggressive in a short space of time and the driver knew the game had just gone up a notch. They had been forced to cross the bridge and head for the tunnel runing alongside the Seine. The car sped up in an attempt to shake them off and approached the tunnel at sixty-five miles per hour, which was way too fast. They had to pull out into the fast lane to overtake a small car ambling along within the speed limit. The fear was palpable as the tension mounted. The bodyguard uncharacteristically clipped on his seat belt, something he never did on duty in case of any immediate necessary action, but self-preservation had taken over. The two cars raced into the tunnel, closely followed by the two motorcycles. Another car had foolishly tried to enter at the same time but was prevented from doing so by one of the motorcycles. The female driver swerved violently and was nearly pushed off the road. Something was obviously wrong, very wrong. The electricity supply to the tunnel had also failed just minutes before, plunging the whole place into darkness. Crucially, the video cameras had also stopped working.

The scant illumination only came from the headlights of the vehicles. With so little room to manoeuvre as they hurtled through the tunnel, a crash would be instantly catastrophic at that speed. The saloon remained in the fast lane, travelling dangerously close to the metal support columns which whizzed past in a blur. All of a sudden, there was a small nudge on the right rear side of the car. The driver knew immediately they had been hit and tried desperately to correct the steering as the car swung sharply towards the left. He couldn't control the saloon and felt it hit the metal pillar with a colossal impact, causing a severe deceleration. The front left side crumpled instantly, setting off the multiple airbags in the car which inflated within a micro second, the exploding propellant forcing gases at speeds of 20,000 metres per second into them. The momentum of the car had generated a massive force, spinning it around like a leaf in the air such that the right side also ploughed into the metal columns, completing the total destruction of the front end. The wreck now faced in the opposite direction, coming to a standstill in a hail of shattered glass. The human body was just a biological machine but ill-designed to withstand the massive forces put upon it. The internal organs would rip apart within the body cavity, tearing the blood vessels supporting them, causing death by haemorrhagic shock. A head strike would have been more merciful, causing death instantaneously. It was difficult to know who was dead or alive in the carnage.

The pursuing car drove away without stopping, followed by one of the motorcycles. The second motorcycle hit some debris and spilled onto the road, throwing the rider off before crashing into the wall. This had not been part of th eplan. The first motorcyclist stopped at the exit of the tunnel and waited, but nobody came out. He turned around and headed back in.

The other rider had not been critically injured and managed to hobble over to the crashed car. He looked in and found the driver slumped over the twisted steering wheel. The other occupants looked dead too. He quickly removed a syringe from his leather jacket and injected a clear liquid into the dead driver's jugular vein. The alcohol slowly diffused through the dead man's blood, which had not coagulated yet although his heart had stopped beating. The first motorcyclist roared in from the exit end and screeched to a stop. The paparazzi had already started to arrive on the far side of the wreck. It was time to go. The engine was revved up as he let the clutch in, racing off towards the exit after his injured friend had climbed onto the back of the machine. The tunnel had now filled with black dust with a heady smell of car fluids, scorched rubber and vaporised metal from the sparks. The gathering paparazzi and their riders climbed off their machines and gingerly approached the crashed vehicle, not knowing what to do. It was clear that everybody in the car was either dead or dying, but the enormity of the incident took a few seconds to sink in.

Other people had started to arrive and stopped to look. Somebody shouted for help but there was little the paparazzi could do. They stood there with their cameras, staring at the tangled mess, initially unsure of themselves but the pressure was mounting for somebody to take the first picture. One flashbulb lit the dark tunnel momentarily. The moral decision had been taken and hounds were free now to join in the feeding frenzy. The whole place lit up. This was not Ethiopia where a well-taken photograph of a young starving child could kick-start aid relief. It was some dark tunnel where the grim reaper had done his work. Many of the paparazzi had already gone by the time the police arrived, to get the exclusives onto the tabloids. The material was undoubtedly sensational just as they were repulsive. It was a winning combination but no sensible editor would dare print them without committing political suicide.

The first paparazzo to arrive had just been a few hundred metres away when the crash happened. He was too shocked to even think about taking any photographs, but found himself surveying a surreal scene. He could see a leathercladded motorcyclist doing something to the driver in the crashed vehicle. The helmeted figure had then jumped onto the back of another motorcycle before racing out of the tunnel.

The police seemed to have taken for ever to arrive as their radios had also suddenly failed. It had been a complex operation, conducted by professional assassins but one of them had screwed up. Crashing the motorcycle had been careless but as rear gun charlie, his job had been to make sure everybody in the saloon was dead. The saloon driver also needed to have enough alcohol in his body to take the blame for the incident. Leaving the crashed motorcycle was unfortunate. It was evidence. The botched operation was a near success and the targets had been taken out but only perfection would do. He vowed never to make a mistake again; it was bad for his reputation.

2

North London

Nick Forbes was a specialist orthopaedic registrar, working in a large district general hospital in north London. He had obtained his membership to the Royal College of Surgeons a few years previously, but had another year to go before finishing his training. The next step was to become a hospital consultant, to wear a smart suit and to give the orders. It was something he badly wanted after all the hard work and sacrifice but the smart suit thing wasn't his style, neither was giving orders. Spending five years at medical school had been tough, until he qualified as a junior doctor, when the going got a lot tougher. Working up to 120 hours a week became a walk in the park but he hated doing more than that. He had earned only a small fraction of the normal rate of pay for the enormous mandatory overtime, but all newly qualified doctors had to go through the sadistic rite of passage. The average trade union representative would have been reduced to apoplexy if their members had to work under these inhumane conditions, but doctors were a breed apart. Nodoby cared. Nick and others like him had been cheap labour for the National Health Service for too long. The introduction of the European Working Time Directive had resulted in a huge reduction in doctors' hours, which also ended the abuse, but it had peeved the health ministers and NHS executives, who now struggled to keep costs down.

Nick was working on yet another Sunday, when most people would be out abusing their plastic friend at the local retail centre, or eating dim sum in Soho. Even after passing his membership exams, he had to keep up to date by reading surgical journals and attend post-graduate meetings. The medical profession was not for the feckless airheads who wanted to play at being God because the rigours of medical school soon put pay to that. Many dropped out because of it. Those who got going when the going got tough would eventually be rewarded. Nick promised himself a lot of things when he became a consultant, but for now he would just stay focused on his career. Having the weekend off would have been heaven but at least he wasn't the only one working.

It was usually a good craic down in A & E, where most of his business was going to come from that weekend.

The Accident and Emergency (A & E) department in any hospital was the first port of call for traumatic injuries. The A & E, and the adjacent GP walk-in centre dealt with over 120,000 patients a year, making it one of the busiest in London. Sundays were usually busy times when people hurt themselves from pursuing leisurely activities or simply from tripping up on pavement when out shopping. Some people were happy to wait several hours to have their bee stings seen to, whilst others came in with serious, life-threatening situations. That was the nature of the work done in A & E and it required a certain type of person to work in there. Trauma was often distressing to deal with, especially when bodily fluids started to seep out. These unsung heroes of the health servicewere frequently abused, either verbally or physically, by the drunken and drug-fuelled idiots who had no respect even for themselves.

Nick's pager went off and a well-known number came up. He was in the middle of a ward round on the orthopaedic ward and excused himself before walking to the nearest telephone at the nurses' station. As the registrar on call, he took all the referrals, especially from A & E.

'Hello, Nick Forbes,' he said.

'Hi, Nick. It's Meg. I've got some business for you.' The reply was curt.

'Go on, what have you got?' He knew instinctively it was something significant by the tone of Meg's voice.

'It's an eighteen-year-old chap with a nasty tib and fib fracture. He was playing football and took a bad tackle. He's comfortable at the moment but his leg looks rather nasty. Could you see him soon?' she asked. It was now September and Sunday league football had started up again.

'Yes, sure. I'll be down in a short while. Try to keep the place quiet as I'm really not in the mood for a busy day!' He always said that as a joke but it was the providence of God which determined whether he was going to be busy or not.

'Yeah right! We have had over thirty people in already this morning. See you when you get here,' she said with some encouragement.

Meg Wallis was the Casualty sister on duty that day. She was a smart, slim blond, who didn't suffer fools easily. She had a sharp mind which some people found too formidable to handle. Her good looks attracted bucket-loads of men, but they usually wilted away after receiving a clipped comment as to their ape-like status. To Nick Forbes, she was putty in his hands, and her green eyes always lit up when he was around. They had a great deal of mutual respect for each other and seemed to be on the same intellectual planet, unlike some of the more moronic senior nurses who went about with a permanent growl on their faces. They were the ones who never got lucky and remained unmarried. These archetypal battleaxes had to do it by the book and would absolutely insist on waking up the tired junior doctor even to sign for a couple of paracetamol tablets. Thankfully, modern nursing protocols had seen to the demise of the Jurassic matrons and life for the junior doctor had suddenly become more pleasant. Nurses could now use their initiative and give out paracetamols. It was a sign of progress.

Nick returned to the ward round briefly before indicating to the consultant that he had to go to A & E, which was situated towards the east side of the hospital, a short walk away from the ward. The hospital had been built in 1910 to cater for the local population but it had been taken over by the War Office in 1915 and used as a military hospital, before reverting back to civilian use in 1920. Much of the original hospital still remained, including the medical and surgical blocks, operating theatres one, two and three, the mortuary and the administration block. The former kitchen block had been extensively modified to house the current A & E department, with the new kitchen moved to another location. The north pavilion, housing the main x-ray department and GP walk-in centre, had been severely damaged during the Second World War when it was bombed.

Nick reached A & E and headed for the Casualty office, which was the hub of the department. A large white board on the wall showed all the patients who were currently in the department, indicating the problem and what action needed to be taken. The patients had been 'triaged' on arrival, a system which involved an experienced nurse taking a brief medical history before deciding who should be seen first. The more important cases were given priority, but life-threatening conditions were always given immediate attention. An electronic notice board in the patient waiting area gave the approximate time before being seen. This was usually around four hours and it was no different up and down the country. It had something to do with the lack of resources despite having more managers around.

On this particular Sunday, the atmosphere in the A & E department was jovial as the workload was still relatively light. With laughter being the best medicine, a quick joke always helped to relieve the tension during times when the department resembled a battleground. No jokes were needed just now, unless is was just for fun. Nick glanced up at the

Casualty board and quickly found his fractured tib and fib. The tibia was the main weight-bearing bone in the lower leg. The fibula was its sidekick, the outer bone in the same leg. They extended from the knee down to the ankle, where they formed the ankle joint with the talus bone, which sat above the calcaneus, or the 'heel' bone. The young patient had essentially broken his leg above the ankle.

Meg caught sight of Nick, who was being his usual breezy self, exuding more confidence than he should as a specialist registrar. He was thirty years old and came from Edinburgh. He worked out at the gym regularly and had a good physique on his 176 cm frame, or five foot ten inches in old measurement. His likeable personality and handsome face often melted the hearts of the pretty nurses, even the male variety.

'Nick! Just the person I have been expecting. Your chap is in bay four. He looks a little miserable now with the pain. The x-rays are on the box, ready for your attention!' Meg said that with a cheeky quip, mocking his status.

'Hi, Meg. I can see you're rushed off your feet. The place looks empty so where have you hidden them all?' he said sarcastically, but in a friendly manner.

'People or chocolates?'

'Preferably chocolates.'

'Buy me some and I'll give you one!'

Her sharp mind was always ready with an innuendo, but in reality, she was always careful with what she said. Nick was different; he could cope and play the game, whereas most men would read something from nothing and make a complete balls of the situation. Despite getting plenty of offers, Meg had not been on a date for quite sometime out of choice. She had been hurt by a previous love affair, the usual excuse, but even at thirty-six years of age she was very much the single girl and had no notions of wanting to change nappies. This may seem a strange state of affairs for an attractive woman, but it happened even in London, where the opportunities were greater for meeting people. Meg could have a good-humoured banter with Nick and would know she was safe, without having to endure that awkward moment of wondering what was coming next. She wasn't interested in having casual relationships, it just wasn't her style and besides, he was already spoken for. It was a shame about his girlfriend.

Nick had a good look at the x-rays and he could see that the fracture was badly displaced. This raised the possibility that there could be some underlying soft tissue damage involving the muscles, blood vessels or even the nerves as the fractured ends of the bones dug into the soft flesh. There would certainly be a lot of blood leaking from the shattered bone and this would have to be removed, a mixture of clotted blood mixed with the fatty bone marrow. The patient would need an open reduction to assess the extent of the damage before the bones were pinned and plated together. This aspect of the job required great skill and it was the part that Nick enjoyed most, especially if the patient could return and play football again soon. The patient's future mobility and ability to play football depended on the skills of the orthopaedic surgeon who usually earned less in a year than some professional footballers made in a week.

Nick went to bay four and disappeared behind the curtain. The young amateur football player had a couple of his mates with him. He looked sweaty and was in obvious pain. Nick introduced himself.

'Hi. I'm Nick Forbes, the orthopaedic surgeon. I gather you broke your leg playing football.' The patient nodded weakly. 'Your x-rays showed that you have a displaced fracture of both the bones in your lower leg. I just want to have a quick look at your leg, okay?'

It was more of a statement rather than a question. He glanced down at the patient's leg and then the foot. The football boots and socks had already been removed by the A & E staff and the leg had been placed in a leg brace, supporting the broken limb. It was quite obvious that the leg was slightly shortened and bent. The discolouration around the break site and the bluish looking foot were not good signs, especially when the foot felt cold.

He needed to get the patient into the operating theatre as soon as possible in order to explore the leg with the consultant, although he was sure he would get to do the metal work, inserting the pins and plates.

'We need to get you into the operating theatre to fix that leg of yours. What time did you last eat?' Nick asked.

'I had breakfast at eight o'clock. What are you going to do?' the patient asked nervously.

'We will have to make a cut into your leg and see exactly how much damage has occurred inside. The bones have broken in a difficult way, so we will need to fix them with some metal plates and screws. You will need a general anaesthetic to put you to sleep, but we can't do this just now if your stomach is still full. However, looking at your leg, I think we will need to get you into the operating theatre fairly quickly.'

'Is it really bad, doc?' one of his mates asked.

'The colour of the leg isn't too good. I don't know if there has been some blood vessel damage. That's why we will need to have a good look inside.'

'He can play football again, right?' the other mate asked.

'There's no reason why not, if the bones heal up well. Okay, I'll go and make the necessary arrangements to get you set up for the operation. Do you have any other medical problems, such as diabetes, asthma, or any allergies to any medications or to general anaesthetic?'

'No, but can I get something for the pain? It's bloody sore. Just do what you have to do, doc,' the patient muttered under his breath as the pain intensified.

'Sure, I'll arrange some pain relief for you. Have you ever had diamorphine before?'

'No. Just give me something to make this pain go away. Just anything, it's doing my head in!' he begged. His friends were getting distressed at seeing their friend in pain. They squirmed helplessly.

Nick left the patient and went back to the A & E office. He made a few brief notes on the casualty sheet, which was on a clipboard. The Casualty officer had written a brief history and had ordered the relevant x-rays so that they were ready by the time Nick got down. He wrote beneath the Casualty officer's notes:

Thank you. Fractured left tib and fib, distal $^1/_3$ displaced. Poor foot pulses. Will need an open reduction. No current medical problems. No known allergies.

Plan – Theatre ASAP.

10mg Diamorphine IV stat.

50mg Cyclizine IV stat.

Signed,

Nick Forbes, SpR, Orthopaedics

Diamorphine was nature's best painkiller and it was made from the poppy plant which grew abundantly in countries such as Afghanistan and Myanmar (Burma). It was also better known as heroin or smack amongst drug abusers. There was nothing better for acute pain relief, but it could also caused nausea and sickness so cyclizine was normally given along with it for this purpose. Given intravenously, diamorphine worked very quickly. The Casualty officer had already inserted a venflon, a small flexible plastic tube, into a vein at the back of the hand to administer intravenous medicines or fluids.

Nick approached Meg in the office.

'It looks nasty. We will need to get him into theatre quite soon. I don't know if the general surgeons have got any cases lined up. The chap had something to eat only three hours ago so I'll see if the anaesthetist is happy to do him in the next couple of hours or sooner.'

'Okay, Nick. What are you giving him for the pain?'

'I've written him up for ten milligrams of diamorph and fifty milligrams of cyclizine.'

'I'll get one of the nurses to draw them up for you.' She smiled.

Nick would have to discuss the case with his boss first before making some phone calls to arrange the operation, so he was glad to get a little help. Once they had agreed on what was to be done for the patient, Nick then had to liaise with the operating theatre for a suitable operating time because it was likely that either the general surgeons or the gynaecologists may have an urgent case to do also. There was only one operating theatre in use during the weekend and sometimes Nick needed to negotiate with the other surgeons before booking a time. Ultimately, it would depend on which case was the most urgent. A life-threatening situation would always get priority.

One of the staff nurses was asked to draw up the drugs as prescribed by Nick. Drugs such as diamorphine were 'controlled' and were always kept in a locked cupboard, known as the DDA. A logbook was kept so the remaining stock of any controlled drug was always known precisely. Any person removing a drug from the DDA cupboard had to sign the logbook and enter the number of stock that was left. It was customary for two nurses to check a drug. Staff nurse Brenda Hawkins removed a vial of diamorphine from the box. There were six left. The number tallied with the logbook. She asked a colleague to check.

'Hi, Judy. Can you check this? Diamorphine, okay? There's six left in the box.' She had quickly showed her colleague the vial, clearly marked 'Diamorphine'. There were also six vials left, just as the logbook confirmed. They were locked back in the DDA cupboard.

She then drew up the sterile water into a ten-millilitre syringe. The diamorphine ampoule was easily broken at its neck. About two millilitres of water from the syringe were used to dissolve the drug before it was sucked back into the syringe, giving a total volume of just over ten millilitres. The cyclizine was drawn up from a separate ampoule into a two-millilitre syringe. It was already in a solution form and didn't need to be dissolved. Diamorphine was more stable in powder form and therefore had to be dissolved in water before it could be used.

Staff nurse Brenda Hawkins handed the two syringes to Nick. Doctors and nurses working together in a busy A & E department had to trust each other; there was no reason not to.

'I've got the diamorph and cyclizine that you asked for. It was checked by Judy.'

'Thanks, Brenda. I'll go and give it to the patient. Seeing his leg has put me off football for life!' Nick said with a mock concern. He went back to bay four.

'Hi. It's me again. I'm going to give you some diamorphine and another drug to stop you feeling sick. This will ease the pain and you will soon feel a lot better. Okay, here goes.' He said that with confidence, knowing the powerful drug would have an immediate impact on the patient.

Nick had deliberately been cavalier about his job. Often this gave the impression that the situation was less serious than that perceived by the patient. It was a tactic designed to offer some comfort to both the patient and the relatives. Sometimes it could be thought of as being flippant and some people may be offended by this approach, thinking the doctor was not taking the matter seriously. The art of medicine was complex and bedside manner was something a doctor either had or not. Nick did.

He pulled the small plastic cap off on the venflon and attached the two-millilitre syringe into the port. The syringe plunger was slowly pushed in, delivering the cyclizine. The ten-millilitre syringe was then place in the venflon and the diamorphine was slowly injected into the patient's vein, a little at a time to monitor for any reaction to the drug. The nauseating effect of the drug should be counteracted by the cyclizine.

The patient felt the liquid entering his arm before a misty tranquillity descended on him. The pain in his leg started to go away, in fact he felt rather good. He looked at his mates and smiled. Nick removed the syringe from the venflon after he had administered the diamorphine and pressed the cap back on. The patient seemed to be quite well.

'Okay. That should sort the pain out. We'll get that leg of yours fixed in just a little while. The porters will shortly come for you and take you up to the ward before you go to the operating theatre. I shall see you later.'

'Thanks, doc. That stuff is great; it's working already. Do a good job, yeah?'

Nick gave him a reassuring smile.

Nick went along to the operating theatre to speak to the charge nurse and also to the anaesthetist. They could do the case after 2 p.m. The anaesthetist would take a risk that the patient's stomach wouldn't be entirely empty, although it would be about six hours since the patient's last meal. It was crucial that the stomach contents didn't come up when the patient was being intubated for the general anaesthetic, a technique involving the insertion of a laryngeal tube into the windpipe. If any of the acidic stomach contents entered the lung, it would cause a serious aspiration pneumonia which could be a major problem for the patient. Nick had just arrived back at the ward when his pager went off again.

It was A & E. He picked up the phone, thinking this was going to be a busy day with yet another case waiting for him.

'Hi. Nick Forbes.' He said calmly.

Meg was on the line.

'Nick, you better get down here. The chap with the broken tib and fib. He's dead.'

'I'll be down straight away.'

He was wrong: it wasn't about another patient; it was still the same one. It had been a bad day out for him.

3

Sudden Death

Nick walked down the main corridor, situated in the older part of the hospital. It connected the surgical wards, operating theatres, x-ray department, and the Accident and Emergency department. The steady but measured pace of his footsteps echoed behind him on the solid floor. The sound did not register in his mind; it was in a deep, murky world despite the bright sunshine flooding through the windows. This was totally unexpected news. Damn and blast. There could have been any number of reasons why the patient had died so suddenly. The questions remained to be asked, if only to establish what had happened when he left the patient. He wanted to run all the way but there was no point. People died in hospitals all the time. Death itself was inevitable because everybody only passed through history. Doctors don't actually save lives, they only prolong them. Unexplained deaths, however, were not acceptable. Young people should not die like that. Right now, Nick was not interested in the meaning of life, only the meaning of this death.

The A & E department was just off to the right of the corridor where the old kitchen used to be. This part of the hospital had been rebuilt and modernised only recently. It was now a bright and well-planned Casualty area. Before, it had been the main kitchen with a tile-lined corridor running outside. The corridor had also been the main route to the changing rooms behind the operating theatres. Feral cats had roamed the ground between the kitchen and the operating theatres. Food trolleys had been lined up in rows, holding uncovered containers of food as people walk by. Cockroaches roamed at night, frequently emerging from beneath the floorboards to enter the operating theatre itself from the dark labyrinth of the old hospital foundations. They scurried beneath the operating tables, feeding on the small scraps of flesh which had lodged there during the day. The operating theatres were scrubbed down each day with disinfectant, but cleaning beneath the operating tables was more difficult. Despite being mounted on castors, they could not be turned over very easily to have the underside cleaned.

Rubbish from the operating theatres was dumped outside the sluice area, situated next to the kitchen block. Any infected material went into orange bags, with ordinary rubbish going into black ones. They were taken away by the night operating theatre orderly to the dump site in a creaky trolley which always woke the patients in the surgical block. Nobody thought about oiling the wheels. The post-operative infection rate was also unacceptable but it took an inquisitive university student working there one summer to point out that the window ledges above the operating theatres were covered in dust. He cleaned the whole lot using stepladders. By the time Nick arrived at the hospital, everything had changed. Even the cats had gone but MRSA was all the rage.

Death was an unavoidable aspect of any hospital. The drawn curtains and hushed silence in the ward would signify the passing of another soul. The porters would then remove the bodies to the mortuary, which was situated in the remotest corner of the hospital. This forbidding area was surrounded by trees and bushes, casting dark shadows even during the day. The mortuary was accessed through a heavy set of sliding doors, opened by a large key kept in the general porter's lodge, located across the road from the old kitchen. The mortuary itself contained a number of refrigerated spaces for dead bodies, in stacks of three along one wall. At night-time, there would only be one theatre orderly working. Taking a body to the mortuary alone was always a nerve-racking experience. A heavy trolley was used, which was difficult for one person alone to manage. The general porters always went in twos, but it was not part of their job to help the theatre orderlies because of an unspoken rivalry. Unlocking the heavy doors made the hair-bristle in the dark, as the area was only lit by a single bulb hanging above the door. Sometimes, even that didn't work. The logbook on the wooden table just inside the mortuary normally recorded the used fridge spaces. Anything blank would indicate an empty space in which to put the body in, but the logbook was not always correct. The theatre orderly could open the fridge door only to find a dead face staring at him. Sometimes the general porters played a joke but just so long as nobody pushed and closed the door of the big fridge.

The A & E department had become very busy all of a sudden. Only one incident was needed for all hell to break loose. As Nick walked into A & E, he could see the unusual level of activity compared to before. Bay four was now empty, but people were milling around the resuscitation room. This was just across the bays and consisted of essentially one large room which contained all the modern lifesaving equipment that could be needed. Several trolleys could be squeezed in at the same time if necessary. The individual bays were used for the more minor conditions.

On entering the resuscitation room, it was obvious the resuscitation team had decided to stop working on the man. Cardiopulmonary resuscitation had been attempted for nearly twenty minutes with no success and it was the team leader's job to make the decision to stop. Experience told them that any further effort was pointless. The rest of the team usually agreed. Nick surveyed the scene which must have been pandemonium just a few minutes ago. He caught Meg's eye. He had to speak to her but the anaesthetist got to him first. Mike Jones was the anaesthetic registrar on the resuscitation team that day.

'Nick, how was this guy when you left him?' he asked in a neutral tone.

'He was absolutely fine. What happened?' Nick replied.

'I don't really know. Sorry to ask a stupid question but how much diamorphine did you give him?'

'I gave him exactly ten milligrams of diamorphine and fifty milligrams of cyclizine. He said he wasn't allergic to anything as far as he knew. I left him with his mates with the curtains wide open so that the nurses could keep an eye on him. I then received a call from Meg to say he was dead. I have no idea what happened. What's your opinion?' Nick asked, looking worried.

'We worked on him for just over twenty minutes but couldn't get him back. He was given a shot of narcan to reverse the effect of the diamorphine, just in case that was the problem. He was already dead when we arrived, so right now I can't say if he went into respiratory failure or whether there was some other reason for his death. I'm afraid this is going to the coroner for a post-mortem. Sorry, Nick.' Mike Jones said.

'Thanks. I'm sure you've done everything possible. We were just about to operate on him but I'll need to go and speak to James Townell. How the hell did he just die like that?' Nick asked, without expecting an answer. The anaesthetist just looked blankly at him.

Nick left the anaesthetist and walked over to Meg. She was tidying up the bomb site. It always looked like that after a resuscitation attempt.

'Meg, what happened?' Nick asked, needing some information.

'We found him dead on the trolley,' she replied with little emotion, but deep inside she was disturbed, even for an experienced Casualty sister. She tried not to show it.

'Who found him? Where were his mates, the other two footballers that were there with him?' Nick asked desperately.

'Brenda Hawkins found him behind closed curtains. His friends had gone outside for some fresh air and left him alone for a while. They said he looked relaxed after the injection and was no longer in pain, so they let him rest.'

'Did your nurses not keep an eye on him?'

'Are you saying it was our fault, Nick?' Meg replied with a flash of anger.

'No. I am not saying it is anybody's fault until I know exactly what happened here. He was alive when I left him,' Nick responded with a terse reply.

'Look, I was called to bay four when Brenda sounded the alarm. She said she looked behind the curtain because it seemed too quiet. She spoke to him and then shook him but there was no response. He wasn't breathing. After sounding the alarm, she pushed the trolley into the resuscitation room and we started CPR. The crash team arrived almost straight away and took over. He was dead, Nick, when Brenda found him. That's all I know.'

She could see that Nick was upset himself; his voice was strained and he wasn't his usual breezy self. Nobody in the medical profession enjoyed losing a human life, especially a young one. People died from cancer or old age all the time, but seeing a young person die was just that bit harder to accept. Doctors swore on the Hippocratic oath to heal the sick and to save lives whenever possible. Occasionally, things did not work out as planned but that was part of life. Doctors could not allow themselves to be overwhelmed with grief because they had to get on with the business of looking after the other patients. Nick had to swallow his emotions and think logically before paging his boss from the A & E office to tell him the news.

'Hi, it's Nick. I'm down in Casualty and there has been a development. The chap with the fractured tib and fib has just died.' He spoke calmly.

'I see. Was there some other injury apart from his broken leg?' James replied.

'We don't know at this stage. We think he may have reacted to the diamorphine and suffered from a respiratory arrest. It was me who administered the drug.'

'Have the relatives been notified?' James Townell asked.

'I don't know. I'll ask the sister in charge but I will speak to them myself.'

'Okay, Nick. I don't envy you the job. Keep me informed. We've finished the ward round and the house officers will tidy up. There's not much else to do in the ward. I'll be at home if you need me. Is there anything else coming in?' James Townell asked. Hospital consultants didn't have to hang around unless they were needed.

'No, nothing just now. I'll cancel theatre,' Nick replied.

'Just for the record, I think you should speak to the medical director tomorrow and fill him in. We'll talk about it again in the morning. Don't be too upset with yourself. These things happen. Okay?' He tried to be reassuring.

'Yes, thanks. I'll phone you at home if anything else crops up.' Nick hung up. Somehow, he felt quite alone and vulnerable, but there was still the day to get through. Most people would have gone off with stress or some other excuse.

Meg walked into the office which made Nick looked up. The office was quite busy with various doctors writing up their notes and nurses going about their business. Mike Jones was sitting across from him writing up his report. He carefully documented all the drugs that were used. Medical negligence was caused by undue care and attention but in this case, Nick had done everything by the book. He had asked all the right questions and followed the procedure but the demons wouldn't leave him alone. The questions came thick and fast. Had he killed the patient with diamorphine? Was there another injury which remained undiagnosed? Did the patient have a severed artery and bled to death? His thoughts were disturbed by Meg, who was still annoyed by his earlier comment. She did not like his insinuation that the nursing staff had not done their job properly by leaving the patient unattended.

'The parents are here now. They are in the visitors' room. Are you going to speak to them or do you want me to do that for you?' Meg said, in a matter of fact way.

She had lost her friendly tone and the hard-nosed Casualty sister had taken over. He noted the sarcasm in her voice but knew it was his job to speak to the relatives. Medical school was never very good at teaching communication skills and this was perhaps the hardest part of the job. There was never an easy way of doing it.

'No, I'll speak to them.' Nick answered.

He could sense Meg's ongoing anger, but what had he said to her to make her so angry? He had only asked an obvious question about whether the nurses had kept an eye on the patient. Perhaps it was his primitive male psyche which had failed to understand the subtleties of the female brain. Meg's pride, as a dedicated nurse, had been dented by his professional challenge even if he had not actually said the nurses were sloppy in their job. To Meg, he had implied it. It was the battle of the sexes.

There was no option for Nick. He was the duty orthopaedic surgeon who had taken over the care of the patient and it now fell on him to speak to the parents. Telling a parent that their child had died was the toughest, most gut wrenching thing anybody could do, just as their world was falling apart too. Everybody reacted differently to bad news. Some kept their composure but others totally lost it. Nick dreaded speaking to them but the moment had arrived and he just had to get on with it. Meg could sense his discomfort and now realised how bitchy she had been just a short while ago. Maybe she was just upset, but knew Nick had not actually accused her staff of anything.

'Do you want me to come along?' she asked.

'Yes, if you want. I just don't know what to say. What do you think?'

'Just the truth. You can't go wrong that way. Are you okay?' she wanted to know.

'Not really, but let's get on with it,' Nick replied, with no enthusiasm whatsoever.

They set off for the visitors' room. It was a small room used for private consultations, usually with the patient's relatives. Sometimes it was to break bad news, just like on this occasion. It was furnished with simple but cosy armchairs and a small wooden coffee table. Cheap but cheerful pictures also hung on the walls to soften the mood. The NHS had obviously not gone to any great expense but the thought was there. Nick hesitated before opening the door, but felt a gentle prod in the back from Meg. He opened the door and they went in quietly. The middle-aged couple looked up from where they were sitting and stood up as Meg introduced Nick. She had already met them. The mother gave a small nervous smile but the father looked apprehensively at Nick with a worrying expression. Nick shook hands with them as Meg started the conversation.

'Hello again. This is Mr Nick Forbes, one of our orthopaedic registrars. He has some news to tell you,' she said.

She addressed him as 'Mr', a small quirk of the surgical profession. Historically, the Royal College of Physicians had refused to admit surgeons into their ranks, deeming them to be less learned and qualified to enter their noble profession. When the surgeons subsequently formed their own Royal College, they refused to call themselves 'Dr' and would be known as 'Mr'. Tit for tat.

'Hello, as Sister Wallis said, I am one of the orthopaedic registrars here at the hospital. Perhaps we should all sit down. I'm afraid I have some bad news for you.' Nick used the standard phrase.

He let the words sink in for a few seconds as they sat down. This was his preferred opening gambit, to let people's imaginations do the ground work for what was to come. The smile suddenly evaporated from the woman's face. Her husband remained quiet, bracing himself for the 'bad news' bit.

'What do you mean, doctor?' she replied.

'Your son died a few moments ago. I'm very sorry to have to tell you that. The resuscitation team tried their best to save him, but he didn't come through.' Nick said quietly, trying to sound as sympathetic as possible.

He could feel the sweat building up on him as he waited for the response. His heart rate had also risen and he just felt uncomfortable. He desperately wanted to get up and walk away, but that was not an option. Waiting for their response was excruciating, as the seconds ticked away.

The deep, heart-wrenching wail duly came in a crescendo, like a big wave sweeping all before it. The mother had just grasped the enormity of what she had heard. The father remained transfixed, still trying to comprehend the information, unable to utter any words or offer his wife any comfort as the penny refused to drop. He spoke to clarify the situation.

'Hang on a minute, we were told my son had a broken leg. Now you're saying he is dead. There is no mistake about this?' He sounded confused.

'I don't really know what to say. Yes, your son had a broken leg. He needed to have an operation as the fracture was badly displaced. He was in a lot of pain so I gave him a painkilling injection of diamorphine. I asked about his medical history but he said he had no known allergies to any medicines. He settled down very well after the injection and he was waiting to go up to the ward before going to the operating theatre later this afternoon. We don't really know what happened after that,' Nick tried to explain.

'I'm sorry, I don't understand. Are you saying that you gave him an injection and then had no idea what happened after that? I want to know who was looking after my son and how he was being treated.' The man's voice had risen by an octave.

Nick thought about his words but Meg stepped in before he could reply.

'I know this is going to be very hard for you to accept or understand. Your son was waiting to go to the orthopaedic ward and his friends were with him for quite a while. I think they were a little distressed to see how much pain he was in and decided to go outside for some fresh air. We can only presume they had pulled the curtains closed when they left the treatment bay. When one of our nurses checked up on your son she found him to be unresponsive and we tried to resuscitate him straight away.' Meg said.

'I can't believe I'm hearing this. Are you now saying that the lads were keeping an eye on him rather than one of the nurses and that it was their fault for pulling the bloody curtain across so that none of you could keep your eye on him? Is that it? What kind of a hospital is this? Shouldn't there have been a nurse with him all the time?' The man was now getting visibly angry with words coming out uncontrollably.

Meg knew she had stood on a minefield by mentioning the pulled curtains but she wanted to be honest. Sometimes it was better to keep it zipped up, but people will eventually dig up things which are hidden anyway. The fact remained that the cause of death was still not known. She just wanted to put all the facts on the table and hoped they would see it that way. It was going to be difficult.

'Your son was quite relaxed after receiving his injection and there were no signs of anything wrong. His pulse and blood pressure remained quite normal and this was checked several times over. We don't know exactly when his friends left him but they said that your son was quite well then. His condition must have deteriorated rapidly after that. This is a very unusual thing to have happened. Please believe me.' Meg was being sincere.

'Who ordered the morphine injection?' the father wanted to know.

'I did. I prescribed it and gave your son ten milligrams of diamorphine, the standard dose. This would not have caused a problem for a fit eighteen-year-old, unless he was sensitive to the drug or had a significant amount of the drug in him already. Do you know if he had any drug habits?' Nick asked.

'Are you now saying my son is a drug addict? What sort of doctor are you? No, he is not a bloody junkie!' The man was clearly exasperated.

Something in Nick's head then snapped. This was all going badly. He had done nothing wrong and he wasn't about to be questioned about his competence by a layman, no matter how upset the man was. He now spoke slowly and deliberately, looking directly into the man's eyes, trying to bring him to his senses whilst empathising with his grief. It was a difficult task and it needed all the tact he could muster.

'We are all as concerned as you are as to the cause of your son's death, and there will be a post-mortem to establish the cause of this. As sorry as I am about this awful tragedy, I am not prepared for you or anybody else to point the finger of blame at me or anybody else when we don't have all the facts. When I see a patient who is in a tremendous pain, it is my job to relieve that pain. I gave your son the most effective painkiller we have at our disposal. Your son assured me that he had no known allergies. He also denied having any other medical problems. I gave him the injection myself and had titrated the dose of the diamorphine first, which meant giving a small test dose first before giving the rest. He showed no signs of any reaction to the drug. At this moment in time, whilst I share in your grief, I cannot give you the answers you want. You will be given a copy of the post-mortem report which will be conducted on the orders of the coroner. I am telling you now that neither I nor anybody else in the Casualty department has done anything wrong.'

Nick felt genuinely remorseful and was hoping the man would accept the situation. He sensed that the couple were now pondering the matter as the man put his arms around his wife. The atmosphere in the small room remained tense and unbearable.

Meg tried to clear the air by offering to make them a cup of tea. That usually did the trick. They nodded their reply, seemingly unable to speak. It was a cue to leave the room. Right now, Nick needed out badly. He would have enough on his plate later on when the police took a statement from him. All sudden deaths in a hospital were referred to the coroner unless there was a clear-cut cause of death. The coroner would not normally request a post-mortem, such as when a person with well-known heart disease died from a heart attack. This case was different. He felt there was nothing more he could say to these people. Hopefully they would at least appreciate his honesty. He was about to leave the room with Meg when the father had a last word.

'Dr or Mr Forbes, I am going to look further into this matter. You can take it from me that I am going to speak to my lawyer.' There was venom in the voice.

'Fine.' It was all Nick could say.

The brown stuff was going to hit the fan and there was nothing he could do about it. There was no point in trying to dissuade the man from taking this course of action. Life was a bitch and some people simply wanted justice the way they saw it, no matter how ill conceived the notion was. The lawyer would always make something from it and there was never a shortage of them.

Hierarchy

Nick did not sleep well that night. He felt tired and was cruising on autopilot. As usual, the ward round started just before 8 a.m. It had that Monday morning feeling; the start of another week. The junior house officers were scurrying around, making sure all the medical notes and x-rays were available. Pregnant pauses were best avoided because they were too embarrassing in front of the patient. James Townell liked his firm to be switched on during a ward round. It minimised delay and fewer mistakes were made that way. The junior house officers had to make a good impression as a good reference could be the vital key to a decent career. The medical profession was just as critical as any other. Sloppy work usually meant a sloppy doctor and that could mean they made more mistakes. A bad shopkeeper who allowed his shop to run out of baked beans may cause some inconvenience to his customers but it didn't kill anybody.

The entourage included the specialist registrar, a senior house officer, two junior house officers, a ward sister or staff nurse and usually a couple of medical students from the Royal Free medical school. Medical students sometimes did not bother getting out their of beds but it was all noted down. JHOs rarely got into their beds. James Townell's team had been the on-call team that weekend and it was their job to review all the acute admissions since Friday, plus the post-operative patients from the previous week. Those fit enough could be discharged that day, making beds available for the new admissions. The bed managers were always keen for that. Despite patient complaints going up, the bed managers only concerned themselves with bed occupancy rates. It was their job, after all.

Ward rounds were normally conducted in a light-hearted but serious manner, but this depended on the consultant and the rest of the team. People differed, as did their personalities. Some were larger-than-life characters and joked a lot. Some were like little Hitlers, whose dictatorial manner just made life harder for everybody else. What determined a personality was harder to define. It had something to do with the limbic system in the brain. Sometimes a persistent problem with haemorrhoids made a person grumpy. The confident, competent doctor epitomised the profession. Those with a hang-up were a pain in the arse.

The new admissions that weekend included a couple of elderly ladies with broken hips, a man with multiple fractures from a motorbike accident, a middle-aged woman with a torn Achilles tendon from doing step aerobics and an elderly man with a broken upper arm after falling in the toilet in the middle of the night. Nick could usually deal with the more minor problems, such as fractured wrists or shoulder dislocations, without admitting these people to the ward. Overall it had been a relatively quiet weekend, which gave him some breathing space.

The tragedy involving the young footballer was on everybody's mind but nobody had said anything. The atmosphere was more subdued than normal, without the usual light-hearted banter. Everybody was aware of Nick's feelings. In fact, he really wanted the banter, if only to ease his thoughts. His brain refused to switch off, mulling over the event again and again. After the ward round, James Townell pulled him aside for a quiet word. He could see that Nick's usual aplomb just wasn't there.

'Nick, how are you today?' he asked.

'I'm okay. Had a little run in with the parents. I think they are going to take this matter to the lawyers. I just gave them the facts but they want to take it further even before the PM result,' Nick answered.

'As I said yesterday, I would advise you to speak to Bob McLean, the medical director. He needs to know about this. I trust A & E will be submitting their own report?'

'Yes, Meg Wallis will do that. I spoke to the police and gave them a statement. I have given diamorphine many times before and there has never been a problem. Presumably he reacted to the drug or else there was some other reason which we didn't know about,' Nick said.

'There's no point speculating on what happened. We will just have to wait for the PM report. In the meantime, it won't do any harm to speak to the Medical Defence Union also. Just put them in the picture. I'm sure the cause of death will turn out to be an unexpected event, so I really don't think you have anything to worry about,' James reassured him.

'I'll try and get hold of Bob McLean this morning after I've tidied up the ward round. Could you perhaps see a couple of the patients for me at the outpatient clinic before I get there?' Nick asked.

'Yes, sure,' James Townell replied.

He regarded James as almost his equal, being nearly a consultant himself. James was the down-to-earth rugby playing type who didn't stand to ceremony. He just didn't like incompetence or failure. Being a winner was all that mattered. He also cared about patients. The clinic usually started just after 9.15, depending on whether the ward round had finished on time or not. The outpatient clinic was a marathon on most days when Nick and his boss could see over twenty patients or more each. The senior house officer also saw patients with more minor problems, usually for post-operative reviews. Orthopaedic surgery in the NHS had enormous waiting lists which had something to do with too few surgeons in the country. The UK had spent less money on healthcare compared to the other major European countries for years and it showed. There were also fewer doctors per head of population, although each successive government had promised more.

Overwork and demoralisation went together in the NHS, but rich little old ladies were only too glad to pay for their hip replacements in the private sector. Despite the obvious problem in the NHS, every new health minister vowed to improve the health service by introducing more reforms. It was the last thing the highly bureaucratic organisation needed but reforms needed more managers to manage the reforms.

After writing up the patient notes and overseeing the various tasks of the day, Nick went into the small doctors' office at the end of the ward to use the phone. He found the telephone extension for the medical director in the hospital directory and called the number. Surprisingly, it was answered immediately.

'Hello, Bob McLean.,' the medical director said.

The unruffled voice at the other end of the phone sounded like Mr Kipling, the maker of exceedingly good cakes. Nick had seen him around the hospital many times before, but he didn't know him personally. Hospital politics was not one of Nick's interests.

'Hi, I am Nick Forbes, James Townell's registrar. I wonder if I could speak to you about a potentially serious matter,' Nick said without ceremony.

'Yes sure, Nick. How can I help you?' he replied in a friendly manner.

'I don't know if you have heard about the young man who died in A & E yesterday. He came in with a fractured leg but he died before we could get him to the operating theatre. I gave him diamorphine and it is possible he may have reacted fatally to it. James Townell suggested I should speak to you.'

'No, I have not heard about it as yet. Why don't you come up to my office now if you have a few minutes to spare? I have a meeting at 9.30 so you've got about fifteen minutes. Is that okay?' he replied.

He sounded slightly concerned. Unexpected deaths occurring in a hospital usually meant an 'inquiry' and that took up a lot of everybody's time. The NHS had had its fair share of scandals and bad press lately. He certainly did not want any bad news to come from this hospital.

'Yes, sure. I've got an outpatient clinic to do but I'll see you in about two minutes,' Nick said.

It would probably take five minutes to get to the medical director's office from where he was.

Nick quickly made his way from the ward and walked down the main corridor past the doctors' mess. He walked out of the building and headed towards the administrative block a short distance away. This was in the old nurses' home, where the top floor was said to be haunted after a nurse had killed herself in 1929. Bob McLean's office was on the first floor. It was the part of the hospital Nick didn't know too well. He had had his job interview in the boardroom on the ground floor. A signpost guided him to the medical director's office.

He climbed up the wooden stairs and went into the administration office where he introduced himself. The female receptionist phoned through to Bob McLean's office and spoke briefly to him. Nick was told to pop along two doors down the corridor. He knocked before entering.

'Hi, Nick Forbes.' He said with as much confidence as he could.

'Hello, Nick. Come in and grab a chair,' Bob said.

The medical director did not rise from his chair. He just beckoned with his hand for Nick to pull a chair and sit down. He was being informal. The room could only be described as functional. Besides the standard desk and chairs, there was a grey filing cabinet and a floor-standing bookshelf. A picture of a woman, presumably his wife, sat in a gilded frame on his desk. Two framed prints of sailing ships hung on the wall.

Bob McLean was a much respected consultant physician, but he was now doing an administrative job as the medical director. His role in the hospital was to run and oversee the clinical aspects of the hospital services. He had to make sure there were adequate numbers of doctors working in the various specialties to do the job. For that, he needed the budget for medical staffing. Frequently, the limited financial resources meant that it was a juggling act between employing doctors to do the job, or buying expensive new equipment, such as an MRI machine. Doctors are not much use without their equipment and the hospital needed them both. He had to work very closely with the chief executive, who had to justify any financial outlay, either for staff or equipment. They were the two big bosses within the hospital hierarchy. The chief executive answered to the health minister, but the doctors had to answer to the medical director. He had the power to potentially remove a doctor from their job.

'Now, what were you going to tell me?' Bob asked with a benevolent smile.

Nick gave an account of the preceding day's events. He also explained about his encounter with the patient's parents and thought that lawyers would be involved. It had already taken over fifteen minutes to explain the matter and Bob was acutely aware he had a meeting to go to. He would like to give Nick more of his time, but they both had to get on with their main jobs.

'Thanks for filling me in with the details, Nick. I want you to give me a written report. Just jot down what you have told me. I would also suggest that you don't discuss this matter with anybody else until we have the PM results and after you have spoken to me again. I'm quite sure it will come to nothing and no blame will rest on you. It's an awful thing, but deaths do occur in a hospital. It remains to be seen if these people will lodge a complaint. If they do, we will obviously have to look into the matter in more detail and I will give them a suitable report. Hopefully they will accept the PM report and we will hear nothing more. Try and not look so worried, Nick. It will be fine. I am sorry, but I will have to go to my meeting now. Speak to me again in a few days time,' Bob said.

With that, he rose from his chair and gave Nick an encouraging pat on the arm. Nick took his cue and started to walk out of the room. Just as he was about to do so, the phone on the desk rang. Bob picked it up. His secretary informed him that somebody wanted to speak. The call was transferred across.

Nick had raised his hand to gesture goodbye and had started to walk out when Bob waved him back in. He was now speaking to the person on the phone.

'Ah huh, yes, you are speaking to the medical director,' Bob said.

He was listening with great intensity. His face remained unperturbed but his colour had turned slightly red before he carried on.

'I have just heard about the sad news. Could we perhaps arrange a meeting to discuss this? I can assure you that there will be a full investigation into this matter.' Bob replied.

He had to hold the phone a few centimetres away from his ear to protect his eardrum. He was listening to the speaker but also thought about his meeting.

'All I can say is how very sorry I am for what has happened, but until we have conducted a full investigation, I really cannot say much more about this matter. I would be happy to meet with you and your wife at any time of your choosing. Can we arrange a meeting?'

The booming voice continued unabated. Bob McLean was now very late for his meeting and so was Nick for his outpatient clinic. He tried to end the conversation by passing the call onto his secretary.

'I would prefer to discuss this with you personally. If you will let me, I'll pass you over to my secretary to arrange a suitable time for us to meet. We shall discuss this matter again. Goodbye for now.' He put the call on hold, before transferring it to his secretary, giving instructions to be fairly flexible with the appointment time. He didn't want to inflame the situation any further.

'It seems that these people are going to sue the hospital and they are going to mention your name to the press. I'm sorry, Nick. I'll need to take this matter to the chief executive and get her advice. I just hope that we can sort something out before it all gets out of hand. I would suggest that you took a few days off until this settles down,' Bob said genuinely.

'I think you're probably right. The ward round this morning was a little frosty. People are thinking the worst but I know I did nothing wrong,' Nick replied.

'I understand, Nick. Take a couple of days off. Hopefully it will be sorted by then. When is the PM?' Bob asked.

'I don't know. Haven't heard any more from the police, but thanks for your help. I really appreciate it,' Nick said.

'Don't mention it. I will be around if you need me. It may be a good idea if you gave my secretary your contact details, including your mobile number, just in case we need to get hold of you.'

'Yes, I'll do that. I'll speak to James Townell about getting a locum in. I'll have to do the clinic this morning plus this afternoon,' Nick said.

'I really need to go for my meeting. Try and let this go over your head. I'm sure the whole thing will just fizzle out. Don't worry, Nick, you'll be fine. Goodbye for now.' Bob ended the meeting.

When Nick had gone to see the medical director, he had imagined it would somehow be a straightforward matter of giving his account of the incident. He now faced a full investigation by the hospital authorities, something he had half expected. Even the police had initially approached him as if he was another Harold Shipman, the family doctor who killed hundreds of his elderly patients with large doses of diamorphine for his own perverted pleasure. After taking his statement, the police appeared more relaxed about the situation and seemed satisfied that foul play had not been committed. Nick had explained that it was a staff nurse who had drawn up the diamorphine and that it had been checked by another fully qualified staff nurse. The dose prescribed had been correct. What happened after he left the patient was a matter for the A & E department to investigate.

5

Grief

An appointment was arranged to see Bob McLean the next morning. Bob knew this was going to be a difficult meeting and he had to look the part. The best suit came out of the cupboard along with a crisp white shirt and a smart tie. His personal secretary was going to be there also, to take down the details, but he really needed her there for backup. A careful record of the meeting was crucial. The couple were dressed in smart but casual clothes as befitted their status. They weren't there to impress, only to sound off. They were ordinary Londoners grieving for their son. The four people sat facing each other. The chairs had been arranged in an informal circle but the atmosphere was tense, even hostile. Bob started off the meeting.

'Hello, I'm Bob McLean, the medical director. We spoke briefly on the telephone yesterday. First of all, I would like to convey my condolences on behalf of all the medical and nursing staff who were involved in looking after your son. This has been a terrible tragedy and we are all immensely saddened by what has happened,' he said.

The man sat quietly and gently nodded his head to acknowledge what was said. He was looking intently at Bob, obviously simmering away like a latent volcano. Bob had to be careful with his words. The man did not introduce himself. There was no need. The pressure was on for Bob to speak again.

'As we briefly discussed yesterday, this matter will be fully investigated and there will be a post-mortem report to verify just how your son died,' Bob spoke.

He deliberately paused to let the couple speak. They must say something. Silence.

'Is there anything you would like to ask me?' Bob spoke again.

At last, the man joined in the conversation. He had been psyched up since Sunday. The vitriol was about to spill out.

'Let me get this straight. Our son broke his leg playing football and he was brought to this hospital to get it fixed. He was then seen by this young orthopaedic surgeon who gave him a morphine injection and then he just died. Just how in hell did this happen to a young lad of eighteen who has never been ill in his life apart from catching a cold? Are you now telling us that there was no way of finding out whether morphine was dangerous for him? Somebody didn't do their job and I want to know who is going to take the blame for this! At the moment, I am holding that surgeon responsible until somebody tells us otherwise.' He spoke with a North London accent.

'For the record, your son was given diamorphine, and not morphine. There is no way of predicting whether someone will take an adverse reaction to this medication unless they have reacted to it before or had been given too much. We still don't know the cause of your son's death and it may not be due to the diamorphine. We do know that he was given the standard dose, so an overdose is not an issue here,' Bob replied.

'I don't give a monkey's whether it's morphine or that other stuff. That surgeon bloke, Nick Forbes or whatever his name is, should have made sure our son was alright after he gave the injection. I am telling you now that we are going to speak to the lawyers and the press about this. The NHS has gone to the dogs as far as we are concerned. We had none of this nonsense years ago,' he said.

The London vernacular was coming straight out. His body language showed an offensive posture, sitting forwards in his chair as if trying to place his face in front of Bob's. His wife nodded in sympathy, tears welling in her eyes.

'I can see that you are very angry. Please understand that the people who work in the NHS are all highly trained and very dedicated to their jobs. We are not in the business of deliberately harming our patients. Occasionally mistakes do occur, but I want to point out from the outset that as far as I can see, Mr Forbes has done nothing wrong. He was giving your son pain relief with an extremely effective painkiller. The very nasty leg fracture would have given a lot of pain. I have also obtained a report today from the sister in charge of the A & E department to say that your son's football friends who had been with him that day did not report any concerns after he received his injection. If fact, they said he looked quite relieved as the pain had settled down very quickly. I can only urge you to consider all the facts first and to refrain from contacting a solicitor or speaking to the press until we have conducted a full investigation. The cause of death remains unknown until we have the post-mortem report to hand.' Bob spoke the truth.

'You people will always cover up for yourselves. We expect a full investigation alright but I want a lawyer involved from the start and I am going to tell the press what a crap hospital this is. You are not going to hide any facts from us and I am telling you that right now! The lawyer is going to press for compensation.'

The man was now sneering at Bob. His wife now suddenly decided to speak for the first time that morning.

'Just so you understand, we don't want the money but somebody has got to pay for killing our son. Nothing is going to bring him back.' She sobbed quietly.

It was a fair statement. Bob realised he was not going to win them over, much as Nick had already realised. His secretary was staring at the floor and had deliberately avoided any eye contact with them. She was feeling very uncomfortable herself. People never wanted the money but they always took it, despite the fact the NHS was already on its knees due to the lack of funding. Bob felt obliged to speak again.

'I am sorry you have decided to go down his line of action. There is probably nothing more I can say that will change your minds. If that is the case, we will be hearing from your solicitors. I am going to instruct a full investigation and we will stand by our findings. If any mistake has been made, the appropriate disciplinary action will be taken. I would like to just say that the press will print anything that makes for good reading. What is good for the press may not necessarily be good for the NHS or the members of the public. I would strongly urge you to reserve your judgement until a full investigation has been conducted,' Bob said.

'I don't care what is good for you or not. This hospital killed my son and that is all there is to say about it. We will see you and that surgeon in court.' The man spoke for the last time.

Having made his final statement, he stood up and waited for his wife to follow. They walked out without saying goodbye. Bob and his secretary were left sitting on their chairs feeling rather bruised from the encounter. Bob could see that she was shell-shocked but he felt just as bad. There was a sense of trouble ahead. The executive committee would need to meet and discuss this matter. It would take up the whole agenda. What a waste of time, Bob thought to himself.

'They seemed pretty upset. I am going to talk to the chief executive, but as far as I see it, we cannot release a statement until the investigation has been completed. Can you arrange a meeting, say this afternoon?' Bob asked.

'I'll see,' she replied.

The secretary said very little but she knew this spelt trouble. She had been involved with many complaint procedures before but this was somehow different. Complaints fell into two main categories. People either complained about a doctor's attitude or about their actual medical treatment. The lack of bedside manner was unfortunate but negligent medical care was more serious. On the face of it, this case was neither. She felt sorry for Nick. He seemed a decent type but she also knew of others who were less scrupulous. She had a vast knowledge of what went on in a large hospital, particularly amongst the hierarchy. What would the press give to know what she knew?

6

Torment

Nick had been off work for several days now. He found himself in a state of limbo after meeting up with the medical director. Sitting idly by and watching the seconds tick away like a praying mantis in contemplation was not his idea of life. He should be operating today, the best part of the job. As a competent surgeon, he was not only good with his hands but he had a brilliant clinical brain. He could imagine the body in a three-dimensional layout, much as a computer would. This helped him to understand how the human body has been put together and how to fix it when it went wrong. Getting the correct orientation was absolutely essential. Sometimes everything looked a messy tangle of flesh and blood. Each human body is unique, an intricate mass of living tissue where no two parts were identical. Even replacing body parts with a donated organ encountered rejection problems. The immune system was highly complex and unique to each individual. It doesn't like other people's bits inside its own body. His job was less complex. Replacing hips and knees only used bits of metal and plastic. He was becoming a master of his art.

It took a minimum of eleven years to fully train a surgeon from the first day at medical school to being in a smart suit as a consultant. It was a long, difficult journey littered with hundreds of ulcer-inducing examinations, each one designed to blow a career apart if it wasn't bypassed correctly. Thousands of hours were spent cramming what seemed like a million facts into the cranial vault. At each stage of the medical course a student could be kicked out for failing an exam, after being given a chance or two. Life was on a knife edge, either way it was looked at. Many students dropped out because they couldn't cope with the pressure; some just knew they had made the wrong choice. The selection process has to be tough to weed out the poor candidates. Only the brightest got through, but sometimes the odd psychopath or pervert conned their way in and gave the profession a bad name. Despite all the adverse press, doctors still remained the most trusted of all the professions. The public said so. Doctors were there to heal the sick but true miracles did not happen. The modern world had developed an unrealistic expectation of what the medical profession could do. Even the first hospital in the ancient world, set in Turkey, had told a lie. It had promised to cure everybody who went in it but there was a small catch. Those who were deemed to be incurable did not get in. Today, a clever surgeon with a one hundred per cent survival rate would only operate on those who would survive the procedure. Those with a fifty per cent track record were probably the better surgeons who took on the no-hopers and gave them a chance of life. The press may see this differently. The track record was obvious for all to see. Percentages were meaningless without context.

Nick felt depressed and did not know what to do about it. He turned on his old portable colour TV which was nearly black and white as the colour had evaporated from the tubes. Daytime television was a revelation to him. It was full of adverts for financial loans and personal injury claims by the ambulance-chasing lawyers. This was definitely something he didn't want to know about.

He turned the TV off and put the radio on instead, before turning that off also. He just couldn't settle down and the day went by very slowly. Nobody phoned, not even the medical director. Having heard nothing, he did not know when to return to work. He thought of giving his girlfriend, Emma, a phone, but she would still be at work. Emma was a gynae SpR working at the same hospital. They had met each other again when Nick came to London, having been to the same medical school in Dundee. They had been in the same year at medical school but mixed in different social circles. There had been no mutual attraction then, in fact they had hardly spoken. People usually got to know their peers with the same letter of the alphabet for the surname. Emma was a McPherson, a little way down from Forbes. Medical students stayed in groups of around eight, especially when learning anatomy. They usually bonded after the first day with the group. For most people, it was the first time they saw a dead body, lying on the dissection table during anatomy class. Some retched. The situation was now different; they shared a different bond by working in the same hospital far away from home. At medical school, Nick had seen the pretty girl who giggled a lot, but had felt nothing in common with her. He did not try to speak to her and it had cut both ways. Emma had now matured into a confident young professional, no longer the shy and impressionable thing she once was. Her looks had also changed. She was stunning, with legs which went a long way up.

Just like Nick, Emma was Scottish, but came from Glasgow, albeit Bearsden, the posh part. Her father was the senior partner of an architects' firm and therefore had done rather well. He had bought her a flat right from the very first year of university. She had rented out two of the rooms to her friends, also medical students, and had always pleaded poverty despite using the money to fund her relatively lavish lifestyle, for a student. People with money somehow seemed to do that, but not everybody was fooled by it. Perhaps it was their way of saying that they understood the privations in the world and they wanted to empathise with them. Slumming was definitely not on the agenda for Emma.

Her university life had been totally different to Nick's. Daddy had also bought her a sports car, a Peugoet 205` GTI. She had been part of the smart set, one of the Max Factor girls who always looked good and thought it was a privilege for anybody to speak to them.

Like many other students, Nick had to slum it and had stayed in a flat with two other non medics which just had a lavatory, not even a bathroom. The kitchen sink had also doubled up as the wash basin, but Nick and his flatmates used the showers at the university or the squash courts. It had been an incentive to play squash and at least the rent had been cheap. Life was not all bad.

Coming from Edinburgh, he had once lived in Liberton, a middle class suburb on the south side of the city. His father had been an officer in the merchant navy who frequently stayed away at sea for months at a time. He never knew his father but just had the faintest memory of him. There was a big commotion one day when his father had left the house with several large bags. His mother, seemingly reluctant to let him go, had been pleading hysterically. The man he had recognised as his father had sat him on his knee for the last time and told him to be brave soldier. Nick had then seen him for the last time, driving away in the estate car. He had waved to him cheerfully, with the emotional detachment of a three-year-old, holding onto his Donald Duck in the other hand. For many weeks after that, his mother hadn't stopped crying. The woman from next door had come round and looked after him quite often. She had been nice, but hadn't known how to wipe his bottom properly. His mother had been beyond caring at times, just sitting in a chair and sobbing her heart out. Nobody was able to tell him what was wrong, although he must have asked a thousand times. He had just been told that daddy wasn't coming back. The story had been that daddy had died in a car crash. He hadn't really understood what death was; it meant nothing to him, except that good people went to heaven and bad people went to hell. He had told everybody his daddy was having a good time in heaven, even laughing about it. It had been a fun thing to say. Everybody had made a big fuss and given him lots of sweets.

His mother had been a changed woman. She had done what she could to bring him up but, after a few years, she had just stopped caring, as the alcohol, valiums and cigarettes took over. She could not keep up with the mortgage payments on the house and had sold up, making a small profit which paid for the gin and fags. She had applied for a council flat and ended up in one of the better schemes in Oxgangs, just a few miles from Liberton.

Although they had lived in a tower block, the wonderful view of the Pentland Hills made up for it. As locations went, it wasn't bad. It could so easily have been in one of the rougher estates. The flat had been a far cry from the comfortable house in Liberton, but it wasn't in some crime-ridden fleapit where life could be sheer hell. Nick had to learn and adapt to living on a council estate but he was never accepted by the local children. He had made the mistake of telling them where he had lived before. There was the usual name-calling and bullying until the fights had started. The only advice he had got from his mother was to ignore them. She had hardly set foot outside the flat. Nick had fetched all the shopping and tended to all the financial matters. He had even registered himself at the local school. His mother had never once gone to a parents' evening. Even getting mugged meant a telling off for being too stupid to avoid it. Respect had to be got the hard way. He had fought back. The bullying suddenly petered out and he had been left to get on with his life. By the age of twelve, he had earned enough money from doing the paper and milk rounds to feed himself. He had lied about his age by saying he was thirteen, the legal requirement for earning money at that time. Getting through life on the estate had been tough, but his mother's daily drunken abuse had bothered him most. It was a daily barrage of personal insults. He had been told many times that he was a complete burden and was totally useless. In fact, it was his mother who was the psychological wreck. Even Christmas had been a non event. There were no presents or turkey. Nick was a high achiever, a survivor but nobody had told him that.

The vision of becoming a surgeon had been his driving force. His grandfather had been a doctor and he knew from a young age what he wanted to do. It would just be that bit harder to achieve without the love and support from either a father or mother. But even his grandparents had died when he was very young. There would never be the day when somebody would proudly announce their son or grandson had got into medical school. It was just like playing football for the school team using a pair of borrowed boots from a friend. Nobody had been there to see him play. He had walked home alone in the rain when the other boys had gone home in Daddy's car. He had also walked home after being run down by a car when out on an errand. Each step had been a searing pain in his hip and he just wanted to lie down and suffer quietly. There had been no point in telling his mother because she would not have cared, except he still got told off for not bringing the shopping home. Even the headmaster had laughed when he had said he wanted to be a surgeon. That was for the kids in public school, not the comprehensives. At least the headmaster had said he had aplomb. He had had to look it up in the dictionary. The decision to do medicine had been easy. Getting in had been harder, but luck had been on his side. He had received one offer from Dundee after personally going to the Faculty Office and speaking to the admissions officer. Nick was able to persuade him why he should be considered for a place at medical school. The average public school pupil would receive several offers and then had a major dilemma about which one to choose.

He decided to phone Emma. He desperately needed to talk to somebody and hoped she could come round tonight. His mind was going through a mixture of anxiety and boredom. The switchboard at the hospital quickly had Emma on the phone and he managed to speak to her for a short while before she had to rush off. She agreed to come over after work. At least this would give him some focus to his day, something to look forward to. He wandered into the kitchen to see what he could come up with for dinner. There were some chicken breasts in the fridge. This could go with some pasta in a tomato based sauce. The cooker clock only said 3 p.m. He was desperate to start cooking, just for the sake of doing something. It was ridiculously early to start cooking so instead he just made another cup of coffee. It was his fourth of the day. The caffeine was making him feel even more anxious and slightly tremulous. He paced around the flat like a demented tiger stuck in his cage. The flat had started to become claustrophobic, but he did not want to venture outside either. The incident was playing on his mind and he knew it. Simply not knowing what was going on at the hospital had made it all the harder to take. He just wanted that phone call to say it was all over, all was done and dusted. He was not at fault. The phone remained silent.

The flat had been built in the fifties and was solidly constructed from brick and mortar. It was situated on the main road in Palmers Green heading towards Enfield. There were three adjacent blocks, each containing six flats. A communal front door on the ground floor opened into a tarmacked courtyard at the front, separated from the main road by a low wall, a few small trees and the pavement. It was possible to drive on the courtyard but this was just for dropping off as the car park was at the back. The flat could also be accessed from the car park via the concrete fire escape stairs at the back of the building, which were actually more convenient to use as they led directly into the kitchen.

During the warm weather, it was nice to leave the back door open and let the breeze waft in. He often sat on the back step and admired the views of the London rooftops, stretching far away into the distance. Sometime ago London had been just a big swamp. Now it was a mass of concrete. Nick decided to sit there for a spot of contemplation. The autumn afternoon was still warm and he could see the hospital in the distance. In the middle of the hospital was an eight-storey tower block containing the gynaecology department and labour wards where Emma worked. He wondered what she was doing right now. Perhaps she was doing a caesarean section. He really missed not being in the operating theatre today. His gaze wandered upwards and he could see a plane flying high above, making contrails in the blue sky, and wondered where it was going. He would love to simply get away and forget about things for a while. He needed a reality check.

Normally he enjoyed cooking, but there would be no pleasure in it today; it would be purely routine, something to do. Cooking had become second nature to him out of necessity. His mother had never cooked for him. There was only so much spam a child could eat. At least when he had earned his own money, he had been able to afford a piece of steak now and again. From an early age he had taught himself to cook, learning the art of using herbs and spices to add flavour whilst his mother lived on tinned food and Indian takeaways.

He decided to pour himself a whisky first before starting the meal. He preferred malts to the blends. Malt whisky was different because the grains of barley had been steeped in water to start the germinating process. The starch within the grain became converted to fermentable sugars before the germinating process was stopped by drying the malted barley over a source of heat. Sometimes a peat fire was used which gave an intensely peaty character to the whiskies such as those from Islay. Whisky was also known as the water of life, or *uisge beatha* in Gaelic. A dram always helped to ease the pain, both emotionally and physically.

He made a tomato-based sauce with onions, garlic, chopped tomatoes, sun-dried tomatoes, oregano, balsamic vinegar, salt and pepper. The diced chicken breast was added before the mixture was allowed to simmer away slowly. He would wait until Emma arrived before cooking the pasta. The bottle of Chianti was already uncorked to let it breathe. The radio was back on again. At least it was some distraction. It wasn't long before Emma walked in from the back door. The door was still open.

'Hello, Nick. Still skiving off? What have you been up to when I have been slaving away? I wish I was off like some person I know!' Emma asked.

He gave her a kiss on the lips. He was pleased to see her.

'You know, a little bit of this and that. So, what's the news at the hospital?' Nick was desperate to know.

'I don't know. There's nothing being said very much. Then again, we gynaecologists are far too busy for gossip! I have had one horrendous day. Are you still worried about this thing of yours?' Emma asked.

'I have not heard from the medical director yet. Never mind. Hope you're hungry.'

'Smells good. What are cooking?' she asked.

'Chicken and pasta. Some wine?'

'Yes pleaseee. You've not asked me why I've had such a crap day,' she implored.

'I'm sure you're going to tell me anyway,' Nick replied.

'The clinic went on and on with all these moaning women. The baby I delivered the other night is doing badly and the mother was giving me a hard time about it. She should have been grateful I got the baby out in time. This other woman just demanded to have a c-section just because she doesn't want to go through labour. I mean, do I do pizza deliveries or what? People are getting so demanding. It's not as if they are paying for their treatment. I'm getting fed up with their attitude. Also the boiler in the flat packed up today so I couldn't get a shower. I'll have to take one here later.'

Nick handed her a glass of wine, which stopped her talking about her day as she slurped the Chianti, seemingly unsure about it.

'Wine okay?' Nick asked.

'Where did you get this? It tastes a bit rough but I suppose it will do. Now, what have you been up to?' She made a face, sniffing the wine again.

'Not very much. Still waiting to hear from the hospital. I presume these people have already talked to the press. So, what are people saying there?' Nick asked.

'Nothing at all actually. I'm sure it will all blow over soon. Is dinner ready? I'm starving!'

'Yes, it's ready. Pass me the plates. The Chianti tastes okay,' Nick said.

'No, it doesn't. The ones I have are much nicer.'

They would be.

Nick wanted to discuss his problem, having mulled about it all day. Emma just seemed too wrapped up in her own little world as usual.

Perhaps the situation at work was just a flash in the pan, as she said, and he was worrying too much. He needed to relax and put things into perspective. At least cooking the meal had kept him occupied. Emma had gone through into the sitting room and was watching the TV. She always moaned about his little portable TV. In fact she moaned a lot about everything but until now Nick had managed to ignore most of it. He brought the pasta to her, including his own. The meal tasted fine but he had lost his appetite. Perhaps it was the first sign of depression. They watched the six o'clock news and ate the meal in silence. He desperately wanted to give her a hug but Emma had sprawled out on the sofa with her shoes off. She then suddenly piped up.

'You don't mind if I have a shower, Nick? I feel grimy. Do you know anything about boilers?' she asked.

He had looked forward to seeing her so much today because he just needed some support. It was quite clear he was not going to get it. He picked up the empty dinner plates and walked through to the kitchen as Emma got off the sofa for her shower.

'I don't know. Why don't you look in the Yellow Pages,' he suggested.

He had no interest whatsoever in her boiler.

He cleaned the dishes whilst she had her shower. The regional news was now on but it was much the same as usual; somebody had been assaulted and the council tax was going up. Emma came out of the shower wearing one of his t-shirts. She looked rather good. Perhaps she might unwind a little and stay the night.

'Nick, I've borrowed one of your t-shirts. My clothes are a little stale. I'll return it to you this week. Do you mind if I didn't stay tonight? I need to get home because I don't have any clean clothes for tomorrow. Also, you're not the best company just now.' She didn't mince her words.

'Yeah, that's okay. Sorry if I have been a little grumpy. Won't you stay a little longer?' He tried not to sound desperate.

'I'm really tired, Nick, and I've got another busy day tomorrow. Maybe I'll see you at the weekend. You can let me know what's happening then, okay? Give me a big kiss.'

Somehow, her attitude felt patronising. His problem did not seem to matter and she wasn't bothered. He could feel the sense of hopelessness creeping in.

She gave Nick a lingering kiss but he knew she was desperate to get home. It was a fair drive to Hampstead where she had a swanky flat. He saw her off at the kitchen door and watched as she drove away in her BMW. Just then, he felt very lonely, more so than before. Perhaps it was his life that was wrong. Other people envied what he had: a successful career, his boyish good looks, and his fancy girlfriend. If only they knew the truth. He didn't have any love or support, the two things he needed most of all. You could buy a nice house or a car, but not that. He desperately wanted something which Emma could not give him. Even some understanding would do. Some of his ex-girlfriends had loved him, but he had been too insecure to accept it then. Things were different now, but he had a girlfriend who was too absorbed in herself and her own career to care much about him. She always bragged about her wonderful flat and her wonderful friends. If only she could feel proud of what he had achieved against all the odds. That was something she would never understand. Her life had been too cosy in the cosseting environment of her caring parents. Nick had just started to wonder if this was the right relationship for him.

7

Inner Strength

The letterbox rattled as the mail dropped onto the floor. Nick had now been off work for nearly two weeks and October was fast approaching. During that time he had spoken to the medical director only once, who had still suggested he remained off work. He was not officially suspended but the medical director had sensibly reasoned that he should stay off whilst the investigation was still going on at the hospital. Nick didn't even know about the post-mortem result, which was now available, because nobody had told him. Despite having nothing to wake for, he simply could not lie in bed just for the sake of it. His normal routine involved getting up just before 7 a.m, a quick shower before drinking a quick cup of coffee and rushing out to work. He was lucky in being able to get there in around ten minutes, living just three miles from the hospital. Other Londoners spend hours a day just travelling, either sitting in traffic or absorbing other people's DNA in the stuffy tube trains. The population of greater London alone was over twice that for the whole of Scotland. It was just possible to avoid another human being in the Scottish hills, but not in London, where it seemed that every other person was a Johnny foreigner. It was great for the café culture and kebab eaters. Nick loved London because it was so cosmopolitan. Edinburgh was a little staid by comparison.

He was awake anyway and quickly got out of bed on hearing the sound of the letterbox, despite the stiff whisky last night. At least a letter was some reason to get out of bed for. He padded to the front door in his bare feet. The rented flat was quite well furnished and the carpets were still in a reasonable condition, although they were not fashionable at all. They were heavily patterned and each room had its own. The pattered wallpaper also differed in each room. It was very much down to the individual taste; none at all in this case. The old couple living here before had passed away and left it to their daughter. Nick was happy enough to rent for now as the property prices were beyond his income. He would look for somewhere permanent to stay once he got his consultant's post.

He picked up the mail. It was the usual rubbish. Everybody wanted to offer a credit card. The medical journal would get read sometime, but the white envelope looked very formal. It had GMC on it. He went into the kitchen to make himself a cup of coffee first. It was instant. Somehow, most instant coffees never tasted very good except for one brand. Eight out of ten people probably preferred it to other brands. How did they know? Filter coffee was too much hassle.

He took a sip of coffee before looking at the white envelope again. GMC stood for the General Medical Council. It was the medical profession's governing body. The GMC had the power to strike a doctor off the medical register, effectively ending a doctor's career and livelihood. Nick felt his stomach tighten instantly. A wave of nausea washed over him as he looked at the envelope again. With trembling hands he slowly opened the thick envelope and eventually managed to get the letter out. It was good quality paper. GMC registration was mandatory for all doctors working in the UK. You couldn't work without it and the fee ran into hundreds of pounds every year. Quite clearly the GMC didn't believe in saving money when it came to quality stationery.

The letter inside simply said that they had been notified of an incident and the matter was under investigation. Nick was suspended and must not work in his capacity as a doctor until the GMC had decided otherwise. This bit of news hit him like a hammer blow and his mind started to race again. Somebody must have reported the matter to the GMC and he needed to speak to Bob McLean urgently. Without finishing his coffee, he phoned the hospital, despite it being just after 8 a.m. He asked for the medical director who, thankfully, was in his office.

'Hello, Bob. It's Nick. I need to speak to you.' Nick wanted to get to the crux of the matter.

'Nick! How are you?' He sounded his usual genial self.

'I'm not feeling too good to be honest. I have just received a letter from the GMC saying that I have been suspended. Do you know anything about this?'

'Yes, I am sorry, Nick. We had a general meeting with the chief executive and the other hospital administrators following the post-mortem report and it was decided to refer this matter to the GMC.'

'Why was I not told about it? What did the post-mortem say?' Nick asked.

'Oh, I thought a letter had been sent to you. Have you not received it? The autopsy report showed that your patient was killed by a large amount of diamorphine. It concluded that he must have been given at least thirty milligrams, not ten milligrams as stated in your report. I think the police will be in touch with you again,' Bob replied.

'But, Bob, you can see on the medical notes that I had quite clearly written ten milligrams on the casualty sheet.'

'Yes, but did you check the dosage yourself?' Bob asked.

'No, it was checked by two staff nurses. I don't understand how it could have happened.'

'From our initial inquiries, it seems that the Casualty sister had checked the box of diamorphine and there were six vials left as recorded in the DDA book. We cannot account for how the patient received the larger dose. You were the last member of staff to see him alive, apart from his friends,' Bob said.

'Bob, are you saying I deliberately gave him thirty milligrams of diamorphine?'

There was a short pause from the medical director, which probably said more than words could.

'Listen, Nick. I have no doubts whatsoever about your clinical skills. The fact remains that the public are acutely aware of the Harold Shipman business, which is still very topical. The public are right to be scared when doctors give diamorphine and people suddenly start to die. We have carried out our investigations as much as we can and we are drawing a blank. The fact remains it was you who gave him the diamorphine. It is now in the hands of the police and the GMC and I can't help you because I have nothing else to go on, unless there is something else you want to add.'

'No, there is nothing more I can say and you know that,' Nick replied.

He knew he was beaten and felt totally crushed by this new development. He was up against a wall with nowhere else to turn. The news had really shaken him.

'I am truly sorry for you but we will be in touch if anything more develops. Take care of yourself. Bye, Nick,' Bob said curtly.

The phone suddenly went dead as if Bob was desperate to stop talking to him, like he was some kind of a pariah. If he had been miserable yesterday, he felt much worse today. Everything had gone wrong for no good reason and nobody seemed to care. The hospital authorities had not even bothered to write to him to tell him about the post-mortem result or the fact that they had referred him to the GMC. It was an appalling way to treat anybody, let alone a dedicated young surgeon who had given so much to the profession. His emotions were running riot and that sinking feeling just got deeper. He had to pull out all the reserves now. Everything he had been through in his life had just been compounded by this awful situation. He knew that truth was on his side. It was a question of how to find it. Giving up would be easy, just taking the rap and hoping the GMC would give his licence back at some time after a period of retraining. That was something he could not do. People could achieve the seemingly impossible if they put their mind to it. Those who gave up were losers. Nick was determined to win, just like in every other situation he had been in. He was emotionally intelligent without knowing it. He could control his emotions and channel his thoughts into positive action when all else would lose their heads. He had to turn this feeling of absolute despair into something positive. He had to fight this.

He had almost been accused of deliberate negligence. The police may even be looking into a murder charge. His career was now in question and he was staring into the abyss. All the years of hard work and sacrifice would come to nothing. Out of desperation, he phoned the hospital to speak to Emma again. He knew she was doing an outpatient clinic that morning. All he needed was a few minutes. She came on the phone.

'Emma, I need to speak to you. It's very important,' he blurted out.

'Nick! I'm in my clinic just now. Can this wait? Can I phone you later?' She sounded busy.

'Could you come round tonight? I need to see you.'

'It's a little bit difficult as I am going out for a drink with the gynae people. How about tomorrow night? Do you want to come over to my place then?' she asked.

'I don't know. I have just been suspended by the GMC. I'm feeling a little rough just now. No, you go out with your friends tonight but come around later if you want,' Nick said.

He didn't want to be a burden but secretly hoped Emma would change her mind about going out. He needed her now and it was time she gave him something.

'I am really sorry to hear that, Nick, but I'm sure they will get this nonsense sorted out. You'll be back at work in no time. Why don't you go and have a few pints with some of the orthopaedic people? It will do you good to get out. It's just that I have promised and I don't want to let them down. We'll be out in town so it will be difficult for me to come round later,' Emma said.

Emma had made up her mind. Nick was screaming in his head. He desperately wanted to tell her that he needed her tonight more than at any other time, but he could not bring himself to sound that pathetic. It was quite clear that she was totally oblivious to his anguish. Emma was just being her normal self and it was unlikely she would change her ways. Being logical, Nick realised there was really not much point in carrying on with their relationship. He was asking for something he would never get. Her lack of understanding and patronising attitude had always annoyed him but right now it was unbearable. As far as Nick was concerned, she was living on another planet. Her career would always come first and Nick knew he deserved better. Plenty of fishes in the sea came to his mind just then.

He just put the phone down without saying another word.

His relationship with Emma had never been very strong but at least it was something. He now felt totally numb and detached from reality. One piece of bad news after another had simply destroyed his mind. It was like being in a state of fugue where the brain just switched off from all the nastiness. The shrinks would call it psychomotor retardation but essentially, he was mentally depressed. He barely registered the phone when it rung. It was Emma again.

'Nick, you put the phone down on me. What's the matter?'

'Sorry, I can't explain it. I think it is best if we ended our relationship.'

'Tell me what's wrong! Are you seeing somebody else? Is that it?'

'No, I just can't cope with your attitude or your whinging any more.'

'Nick, don't be silly. You are depressed with this GMC nonsense. Look, I have to go out tonight but why don't you let me buy you a plasma TV or something tomorrow and cheer you up? You can't keep watching that awful TV of yours. It's nonsense to say I have an attitude problem. You're just not making any sense.'

'Emma, I can buy my own plasma TV if I want to. You really don't understand. Look, it's over. Accept it,' Nick said.

'Nick, you don't know what you're saying. Nobody dumps me! Damn you!'

'Sorry, but I just have.'

This time he hung up but left the phone off the hook. A slight feeling of relief came over him, however bizarre it felt. Emma could never understand that he would have loved her even more if only she had even bothered to even make him something as simple as a bacon sandwich. He knew she couldn't cook to save her life but at least she could have made the effort. She hadn't, and Nick was no longer prepared to run after her. She had been emotionally cold, totally lacking in any feminine skills. Nick's love could not be bought even with a Porsche, if she had offered. It was time somebody got the message across and her ego would probably go mad. Too bad.

8

Paparazzi

The Glampic photo agency had its offices in the King's Cross area of London. It was sandwiched between Pentonville and Caledonian Road in a wedged-shaped mews-like development. The location was ideal, as it was easily accessible to all the major areas in London where the celebrities lived. Hampstead was to the north and Notting Hill to the south-west, not to mention other desirable residential areas such as South Kensington and Primrose Hill. London was the home of cool Britannia and the economy was doing very well. It was the place to live. King's Cross, however, lacked the glam but had the sleaze. It was full of run-down hotels where a certain type of business went on. Punters cruised in their cars or came off the train and got laid. Many of the young working girls themselves came on the train with a day return ticket. It was nice to go home after a busy day at the office. Some didn't have a home to go to; they lived under the shadow of low-life pimps who frequently used violence to intimidate. Drug habits cost money, lots of it. It was a bad way to live but it was all they knew; to be used and abused. They were beaten up by the pimps or clients for refusing to 'extras', usually servicing two men at once. Some came from broken homes or had been sexually abused by their by their fathers and uncles. Others came from nice families but they had developed a drug habit, particularly crack cocaine. Crack was just too addictive. When the money ran out, sleeping with dealers got them a piece of rock. Moral principals had been thrown out of the window. This was the ugly side of humanity; abusing and degrading another human being was a way of life. The young victims had not learnt the tricks of self-preservation, unlike the seasoned pro. They exposed themselves to unsafe sexual practices where the spectre of HIV lurked with every contact. Anal sex without a condom earned them a few pounds more.

The whole of King's Cross was ripe for development but money was being poured into major projects, such as the St. Pancras railway station. The showpiece terminal for Eurostar now said Britain was part of Europe. The back streets, however, remained undeveloped, providing the sex industry with a place to carry on. Perhaps it served the needs of the capital, reducing the frustration of men for whom a DIY hand-job was not enough. Confucius noted that it took a man nine months to come out of a woman but he then spent the rest of his life trying to get back in. Some men preferred them both, men and boys. It was illegal to cottage in dirty toilets but even pop stars did it. Sex was a basic need, except for monks perhaps. For some, it was the thrill of the unknown, of rough and unrequited sex. The innate pleasure of paying for a service with no emotional comebacks proved too addictive, even for judges and politicians. Prostitution remained the oldest profession in the world and would always thrive. Some people couldn't get laid otherwise.

Many of the former slum areas in the capital had been transformed into desirable places to live, such as the Docklands area. It took great vision and an enormous financial undertaking from major institutions. King's Cross may yet have its day, but for now it was the pimp's paradise. Drug dealers dominated the area and it was here that Glampic had its headquarters. The rent was cheap and the property had ample parking spaces, a winning combination in London. Sleaze was thrown in free of charge. A legalised sex industry would undoubtedly be safer for the sex workers and the chancellor of the exchequer could even slap on tax and VAT. It was a service industry after all, but sanitising the business would have lessened the appeal of something which was naturally sordid. Sex was a basic need, the dirtier the better.

Ricky Davis was a short, fat and brash Londoner who had been brought up in Hackney, not a stone's throw away. He had dyed blond hair which was always gelled up, unless he had just woken up with a hangover. He was permanently suntanned and dripped with gold rings, heavy neck chains and bracelets. His fingernails were well manicured at the end of his podgy fingers, but his right index and middle fingers were stained with tobacco. He spoke with a fast London accent and couldn't give a toss about anything, loving life for what it was. As far as he was concerned, everything had to be bigger and better. Anybody who got in his way was met with a string of expletives. His profanity was just an extension of his character and it meant nothing. Swearing was just a series of words. Telling somebody to go and fuck themselves was theoretically impossible, but it was one of his favourites.

Ricky was the founder and sole proprietor of Glampic, a photographic agency which mainly took pictures of celebrities and sold them on to the highest bidder. The British tabloids were good customers. He had left school without a single O level, but had done some odd jobs before deciding to go on a photography course. It had been at the council-run night school where he had developed his natural flair for photography. Luck had stayed with him and he had got a job as an assistant photographer with the local journal. He had shadowed the pro until he got the hang of the job. Then it had been photographing local charitable events and school activities until he had got bored with it. Being a typical street wise Londoner, he had got on well with the other photographers and had heard about a vacancy at a larger newspaper. They had taken him on. He was good at the job and had quickly established a reputation for getting the all-important pictures. His bulldog approach and knowledge of the London streets got him to the right locations at the right time, all the time. It had occurred to him one day that instead of being on somebody's payroll earning an average income, he could freelance and sell off his 'exclusives' to the highest bidder. It had been a gamble which paid off handsomely. His battered Ford Sierra had become the office; the mobile phone and camera equipment the tools of the trade. Business had quickly picked up and it had become too much to handle alone. Being out on location and taking calls was not a good thing. It only took a second to miss the vital shot. Often he had a hunch that a certain celebrity would be in the area and he was often right. It was always better to loiter somewhere quietly and discreetly. Noisy mobile phones just tended to give the game away. He had needed somebody to take the calls and to make sure the money was coming in.

Initially, he had cajoled his girlfriend to give up her job as a part-time hairdresser and set up the business for him. They had used their small flat in Dalston, where the living room soon became a mass of computers, faxes, printers, and filing cabinets. The phones had rung incessantly. Ricky had frequently been away on photo shoots and had rarely come home until late at night. He kept in touch by mobile phone but it wasn't enough. After spending all day in the flat by herself, she had got fed up. She could put up with Ricky's attitude and heavy smoking, but it was the smell of other woman which had been the final straw. Ricky was a bad boy but he just loved women, lots of them. He preferred the young and bubbly type, the ones who were impressed with money. Being short didn't lessen his sex appeal. He had an animal attraction driven by testosterone; the sex was usually entertaining and stimulating, bordering on the bizarre. His girlfriend had not been able to handle the situation, and had left. Ricky's immediate reaction had been to find somebody else to manage his business. He had had no romantic notions about losing her. Men like him drank Australian lager.

He had put the word out about finding a place and a manager. One of the paparazzi had said they knew of a property in Pentonville Road for rent. After making a quick call, he had secured the small office. It was within a larger office complex which suited his needs. Again through word of mouth, he had heard somebody was looking for a job. She was, apparently, bright, motivated, and had a great sense of humour, but hated her current job at another photographic agency. It had sounded ideal. She had been easily talked into resigning.

Cath Malone was in her early thirties. Being a workaholic, she could not bear to stay at home and do nothing. At eighteen she had gone to the local polytechnic in Tottenham and done a secretarial course. She had then drifted from one company to another, struggling to find her own niche. She had hated the secretarial hierarchy and petty squabbling. The longest serving member of the secretarial pool often considered themselves to be the Queen Bee, but some of the younger girls were better at the job. This had often led to trouble and Cath wanted none of that. Being of London Irish stock, life for her was not all about stress. It was bad enough that by the grace of God she did not have any children, despite trying hard with her husband for many years. A strong marriage was important but jobs could come and go. London was awash with temping agencies and getting a job was never a problem. Her husband was a big docile man who worshipped the ground she stood on. He did not want his wife to work but, without children, he knew she would not be happy just staying at home. It was a challenge, being the manager of a new company, albeit with just one staff member, her.

Ricky had not had to work too hard to get Cath to do things his way, but instinct had told him to back off and just let her run with it. She had had the whole small office to herself, a single room measuring forty square metres which had been totally empty when they first got there. Now all she had had to do was set up the company, get the phone lines installed and order all the necessary equipment, the coffee percolator being the most important. Ricky had mouthed off in his usual fashion when he saw the bills, but had known he had to cough up the money as a business outlay. Somehow Cath didn't take offence at his language but often remonstrated with him in her demure London Irish twang. He actually enjoyed being told off like a naughty schoolboy. She, on the other hand, liked his forthright manner and hands-off approach in running the business. Her canny ability to pander to his quirks without being dominated was a healthy recipe for success. They formed a good team and Ricky knew he had a very special woman under him, not in a sexual connotation, although she did have huge breasts.

As the business had taken off, they had needed more staff, more equipment and more space. By the miracle of good fortune, the tenancy for the whole mews complex had become available when the other 'fly by night' company had vacated the premises. The luck of the devil had favoured the fortunate; it was a gamble Ricky took by deciding to rent the whole complex despite money still being tight. He now had several paparazzi and office girls working there. Cath handled the employment contracts and wages, effectively becoming the 'de facto' manager of the company. The agency now sold pictures to various newspapers and magazines on a regular basis. The price per picture had risen to several thousand pounds each, on average. In the space of six months, money was coming in steadily and Ricky was getting richer by the minute. He rarely bothered to leave the office to go on photo shoots any more and simply left it to the boys to hang around in the rain. His main role was to get to know the key players in the business, particularly the newspaper editors who were now on first name terms with him.

He drove his photographers hard with a philosophy of no photo, no money, and that was the way he did his business. Requests of money to cover expenses were usually met with a tirade of 'f' words which would have made the shrinking violets of the world wither and die. The hardened paparazzi knew that Ricky was more mouth than menace and just accepted his manner of speaking. They often answered back, and the worst that could happen was to be told to 'fuck off and don't come back'. Jobs were easy to come by so it was no big deal.

Ricky usually sat at his big desk, surrounded by whitewashed walls covered in photographs which were either taken by himself or somebody else at the agency. They hung there like trophies, which made him feel quite smug with himself as they had all fetched a good price. His desk was cluttered with more photographs, an ashtray, cigarettes, a lighter and a bundle of fresh newspapers. He would chuckle if he saw one of his photographs in a newspaper, especially if it made the front page. However, he was also scanning for any big stories or scandals which needed the right sort of photograph to go with it. The best photos to have were the ones which nobody else had. Exclusives brought in a lot of money; they were his speciality. It also had something to do with vanity, providing something nobody else had.

Photos did not come any bigger than that of Princess Diana and Dodi al Fayed seen on a boat. Photograph like that could fetch hundreds of thousands of pounds, possible more, and the stakes were high. To get such a photograph cost a lot of money in the first place. The agency had to get several photographers on location and plus hire a high speedboat to get close enough. The photographic equipment also had to be state-of-the-art, with extremely long lenses costing thousand of pounds each. They were also prone to damage, usually by irate celebrities. Modern cameras used a digital format which enabled the photographer to download the images onto a laptop computer before emailing them around the world in seconds. The agency could receive a photograph almost in real time from anywhere around the world within minutes. Selling to the highest bidder was the difficult part because it was almost guaranteed that somebody else would have the same shot. The trick was to do the deal as quick as possible. Newspapers wanted it hot off the press.

Ricky slurped his coffee noisily from a mug which said 'Boss' on it. Small things like that amused him and he would go berserk if anybody else used it. He scanned the newspapers for any suitable news item and caught sight of a front page photo of a sad-looking couple with the headline 'The hospital killed my son'. He quickly read the article and circled it with a marker pen. He moved on to the other newspapers but found nothing else of any interest. After finishing his coffee, he returned to the circled article. It described how a young man had died after breaking his leg playing football. Some young orthopaedic surgeon was involved. The saga of doctors killing their patients brought Harold Shipman to his mind and he needed photographs of this surgeon. It should fetch a few thousand pounds, as the papers were bound to run more articles on it. The story itself wasn't his problem, that was for the newspaper hacks to write about it, but he wanted to be the first to supply them with some photographs. Putting a face to a name always sold more copies. His job was to provide that face.

Ricky's personal office was just off the main office itself. The original room he had rented was now a storeroom, being too small for their expanding operation. He could look out through the glass window partition into the main office area and see it all happening. Cath had her own desk and was clearly in charge, buzzing around the girls and making sure everything was done correctly. She was not the bossy type but had adopted her own style of management in a quietly authoritative way. The girls knew exactly what was expected of them. If somebody had failed to email or fax an important photograph to a buyer on time, she would inform them that the business had just lost several thousand pounds. Ricky would give them a bollocking. Cath knew the form when it came to recruiting new girls. They just had to be young, pretty, hardworking and have some brains in their heads. Being tough and not breaking down into tears when they were shouted at was also another essential quality. Once they met the criteria, they had a good job with an above average salary. For all his verbosity, Ricky had grown up in poor house. He knew all about hard work and hated whingers who were not prepared to graft for a living. He was very generous to people who worked hard and stayed loyal. He shouted across to Cath to come over.

'Cath, find out who this guy is. Get someone to the hospital and take his picture,' he ordered.

She read the article and noted the name. Getting a photographer to the hospital was the easy part. Getting a picture of the right person was more difficult. There would be a lot of doctors in white coats walking about. Judging by his name, they could at least exclude any non-Caucasian doctors, but many West Indians also had westernised names. It may be an idea to find out where he lived first of all, so the telephone directory would be the obvious place to look. Most doctors were ex-directory for obvious reasons, but this one might just be in there.

She looked up the telephone directory under Forbes, N. Being a Scottish name, there were only a few in the book, but such an entry did exist. It may be the wrong person but Cath had struck gold without knowing it as yet. When Nick had first moved into the flat, his mind had been preoccupied with the new job in London. Remembering to go ex-directory was not top of the list. He had now been traced by the paparazzi in a matter of seconds. Cath asked one of the photographers to stake out Nick's flat. Paul Lewis was given the job. He drove out to Palmers Green, taking the road to Tufnell Park, then onto Archway, East Finchley and the North Circular Road, before turning left up Green Lanes towards Palmers Green. He easily located the flat and parked on the main road within a good view of the flat, but it was unlikely that his man would be in at this time of the day. He could see that the three blocks of flats had six apartments each. The target could be in any one of the apartments in the block furthest to the left.

He would do a quick reconnoitre of the building. It was always useful to know the lie of the land. People always tried various ways of avoiding the paparazzi when they knew they were about. Some buildings had more than one exit to escape from, and it was just too easy to miss the crucial shot by covering the wrong doorway. That mistake could cost somebody a lot of money.

When on the 'recce', any encounter with the target would probably be at short range. Paul snapped on the 80 mm lens onto the SLR camera body which would allow him to take a photo from a relative short distance away. The camera was also easier to conceal with a shorter lens. He would use a 300 mm lens if he was going to take a shot from his car, but for long distance work, a 1,000 mm lens was needed. This had to be mounted on a tripod due to the weight. He had taken photographs up to a mile away and the person would not know anything about it. Satellite cameras were even more formidable and could take pictures from a thousand miles away with absolute clarity. Such was the state of modern technology.

Paul Lewis stepped out of his VW Golf and crossed the road, after waiting for the number twenty-nine bus to go by. The Golf was a fairly ubiquitous car which did not attract any attention. A Ferrari would have been totally wrong for this job. He checked out the building and could see that there was a main door leading into the flats. There was no way of knowing where the right man was, but it would be easy enough to find out which flat belonged to Forbes. It would say so at the door. He quickly walked up the side road and could see that there was a car park to the rear of the building. A concrete stairway at the back also led to the flats above, serving as a fire escape or a second entrance. He didn't want to walk around the back in case some nosy neighbour saw him. Rather than going back to the car, he made a snap decision to enter the building. The building didn't have an entry buzzer, being of an older generation. The name he was looking for was on the on the door of the top right flat.

Nick had not bothered to get a name plate because he was only renting the property, but had stuck a piece of paper with his name on with blu-tack. Paul made no attempt to knock on the door and went downstairs quietly. He met one of the neighbours as she came in the front door. It was an opportunity to find out some information.

'Hello. I'm looking for an old university friend called Nick Forbes. Do you know if he lives here? I knocked on the door with his name on it but there was no answer. I'm not sure it is the right person because I only got the name from the phone book.' He spoke with a broad smile.

'Yes, Nick lives upstairs. Are you a doctor too?' she asked politely.

Paul instantly knew he had his man.

'No, I was never that clever! I did something else. I'll go and leave a note in his door so that he can phone me later. Thanks for your help,' Paul said.

He smiled again sweetly; lying had become easy. It was all in a day's work. He climbed the stairs again and waited until the lady had entered her flat before quickly leaving the building to return to his car. It was a little too obvious being on the main road so he drove into the side street from where he could see both the front and back of the building. It was now a waiting game; the most boring part of the job. All hell would break loose when a prey was spotted, like a cheetah setting off in a sprint. He ripped the paper wrapper of the Mars bar and slowly nibbled away. It was nearly 5 p.m. so hopefully Nick would be home soon. As he had no idea what he looked like, he would have to take pictures of any man entering the building and then make a phone call to the flat with some excuse to see if it was the same person. A great clue would be when the lights came on in the top right flat. Paul waited several fruitless hours and did not see anybody enter the building who remotely looked liked a young surgeon. He did see the lights go on. How the hell had that happened unless Nick was already in the flat? Even the most ardent paparazzi knew when it was time to go home.

9

Hassle

It was just after 9 a.m. the next day when the telephone rang in Nick's living room. He had a slight whisky head this time. Feeling a little bit sorry for himself, he knew he had to answer the thing. What a bloody nuisance. However, it could be the medical director phoning to say everything was now back to normal. Some hope.

'Hello, can I speak to Dr Forbes please?' There was an unfamiliar male voice on the phone.

'Speaking. Who's calling?' Nick replied unenthusiastically.

'I am Sergeant Baillie from the Enfield Police. Is it alright to have a quick word with you just now?'

'Yes sure, what is it about?' Alarm bells started to ring in Nick's head.

'I don't want you to worry, sir, but we were given a report from the hospital a few days ago with some new information about the incident. We just want to take another statement from you in light of the post-mortem findings. I phoned the hospital to speak to you but the switchboard put me through to the chief executive's office. I believe you are on leave just now.' He said that very tactfully.

'Yes, I'm off for a short while. I have already given the police a statement,' Nick said.

'Yes, I know, sir, but we need a new statement. I could send one of my officers to your address if you wish, but, alternatively, you could come down to the station. Some people would prefer to do that,' the sergeant said.

The police no longer knocked on people's doors just to say 'hello' any more. Getting a visit either meant you were a victim or criminal. Either way, the neighbours would talk.

'No, that's okay, I'll come down to the station. When would you like me to come?' Nick asked.

'You could come at any time today, but preferably this morning if it is convenient. Just ask for the duty sergeant, which will be myself this morning.'

'I should be there in an hour.'

'Okay, sir, I'll see you then. Goodbye.' He hung up.

Nick was depressed. The whisky last night didn't help. He was already feeling low but this was all he needed. As far as he was concerned, there was nothing new to say. He had already given a statement, but it would be a bad idea to antagonise the police. There was no choice; he had to go. The police might even tell him a little more about what was going on. The medical director certainly wasn't doing that. Despite having nothing to do all day, it would seem a bit keen to go straight away. He badly needed a hot shower and a coffee to clear his head first. On the way there, he might as well pick up a few essentials at the supermarket. Shopping early in the morning was always much nicer as it was quieter. He hated pushy people getting in the way with their trolleys. The smell of freshly baked bread from the bakery made him feel good about life. The whisky head was soon sorted with a glass of water and a couple of paracetamols. The shave and shower made him human again.

The weather was still warm enough not to need a jacket. Nick grabbed his keys and walked out of the back door, locking it behind him. He sprinted down the stairs in his usual manner. The Audi TT unlocked itself with a small click as he pressed the fob. He got in the car and closed the door with a satisfying thump. It was his little baby. He didn't see the photographer sitting in the parked car on the side road.

Paul Lewis was just aware of somebody coming down the back stairs in a quick athletic sprint. He just had time to grab his camera before Nick entered the Audi in one swift move. There no chance of getting a good shot. He watched him drive off and decided to follow. From the brief glimpse he got, the man he saw was in casual clothes and, if this was the man he was after, he must be off work today. It was just as well he hadn't hung about the hospital.

Nick waited for a gap in the traffic on the main road before turning right towards Enfield. Paul quickly started his car and did a smart three-point turn before following behind. By the time he got onto the main road, Nick was well ahead, but it was easy enough to follow the blue Audi through Enfield. Nick drove into the supermarket car park and parked just a little further away from the building. The chance of getting hit by somebody's car door was reduced that way, particularly by the big Chelsea tractors. They always seemed to swamp the space. Why would anybody need a gas-guzzling 4 × 4 in the city?

Paul Lewis parked his car at a discrete distance away with a good view of the TT. He could get a good shot from the driver's window without getting out of the car. With some luck he should not be spotted unless Nick was really vigilant. The weather was good so the window could stay down, giving him clear space in front of the camera. It was now the usual waiting game. There was no time for a Mars bar, just in case Nick was a quick shopper.

He waited for about twenty minutes before Nick appeared. He could follow him on the digital camera screen as he approached the TT with his shopping bags. Paul pressed the shutter button. Click, click, click. He got several shots in. With one gigabyte of memory on the flashcard, he could reel off hundreds. He usually carried several spares in his pocket, just in case. The memory cards could be changed in a couple of seconds, unlike the old SLR cameras which used rolls of film.

As Nick got nearer to his car, he could sense that somebody was watching him from a parked VW. A camera was now pointing at him. A cold feeling of dread crept into him. Irrationally, he thought the police might be watching him and suddenly felt self-conscious. He looked at the VW again after putting his shopping away. The camera was still on him. Curiosity now got the better of him. There were rights in a free society and he wanted to know if he was under surveillance. The man was now brazenly taking more photographs of him even as he walked up to the VW. Nick was now visibly annoyed that his privacy had been invaded. He strode up to the photographer and could see he was a man of about his age, clean shaven with a stylish haircut.

'What are you doing?' Nick asked.

'Are you Nick Forbes?' Paul replied with a question.

'Who are you and why are you asking?'

'I work for a photographic agency and we wanted some photos of you,' Paul said.

He was being brutally honest, knowing that the freedom of the press was on his side, except he wasn't strictly the press. Nick was caught by surprise by this unexpected development. He was partly relieved it wasn't the police, but felt annoyed by this paparazzi intrusion. He needed this like a flea on a dog's back. Somehow it just felt very wrong that his privacy could be invaded like this. He should have asked first. Nick was going to demand that his pictures were erased from the camera when Paul accidentally pressed the camera button again. The camera clicked away just a short distance from Nick which seemed to be the catalyst which ignited the fuse in his brain. He immediately lost control and grabbed the camera through the car window. With one mighty swing, he hurled the camera across the car park and smashed it. Cameras don't like that sort of treatment. Nick did not consider what the owner might do and Paul had not seen it coming, being too slow to react as Nick had taken the camera from him. All he could do was to yell loudly, telling Nick not to do what he thought he was going to do. The camera belonged to Ricky Davis and had cost several thousand pounds. He saw it fly through the air before it became a piece of junk. It was now his turn to be angry. He flung the door open and flew at Nick. Despite raining blows on each other, neither got hurt badly, but they became exhausted very quickly.

A congregation of shoppers had stopped to watch the fight from a safe distance but the police had been called. Two patrol cars with blue lights flashing drove into the car park. Four policemen separated the two men. They were cautioned and arrested for breach of the peace before each was taken away in separate cars to the police station. Nick was heading there anyway.

They gave their statements but neither wanted to press charges. They were free to go after the usual warning about causing affray in a public place. Hot heads had cooled down and there was a slight mutual respect between them. Nick also gave another statement about the hospital incident. It was exactly the same as before and he wasn't about to be arrested for suspicion of murder just yet. By now, all the recent events plus the fight had totally drained him, both emotionally and physically. Nick looked awful and the duty sergeant actually felt sorry for him. He ordered one of the patrol cars take him back to the supermarket to pick up his car. Paul Lewis was not so lucky. He took a taxi but was gone by the time Nick arrived.

10

Balls

Yesterday had been the worst day in his life. There was still no word from the medical director and now he had been charged with breech of the peace by the police. Nick was still suspended by the GMC and the possibility of facing a murder charge remained. He was facing another uncertain and boring day, not knowing what ill omen was in store. It was good to talk, according to the psychologists. British Telecom said so too. When he had lived in the leafy suburbs of Edinburgh, the neighbours had always seemed happy to help out. When they had moved into a tower block, people had seemed hostile and unfriendly. Everybody there had looked depressed.

Tower blocks were the architects' idea of communal living. Suddenly, people found themselves unable to talk to each other over the garden wall any more. They stayed within their concrete shells and became depressed. The Gorbals in Glasgow was a typical example. It had once been a tough working-class area with tenement blocks where everybody had been poor and but seemed happy. There had been a sense of community. Areas like the Gorbals had been knocked down by the well-meaning but short-sighted town planners, who had replaced them with high-rise tower blocks. The architects who had designed them would never live there themselves. It was a solution to cattle class accommodation. Hong Kong would have won the prize for sardine packing with 12,000 people per square kilometre in some areas. They weren't happy either.

Nick just wanted to talk to somebody. Right now he desperately wished he had a father to give him the emotional support he so badly needed. He didn't want to burden his friends with his problem; they probably had their own. Even his medical colleagues had all suddenly disappeared from the face of the earth. They either felt awkward or simply did not want to get involved. Emma should have been there for him but she was too wrapped up in herself to care. He had thought he could rely on one of the friendly hospital pharmacist for some advice, but even he had kept his distance. He didn't need fair-weathered friends. The doorbell rang.

It was Saturday today and he desperately hoped it would be Emma, coming to apologise for being such a self-centred bitch. He would forgive her if she just said sorry for being so thoughtless. He opened the door expecting to see her, but instead stood facing Paul Lewis. This time his brain went totally blank. He tried to comprehend what was going on.

'Hey, Nick. Can we be cool about this?' Paul said.

'What the hell are you doing here?' Nick answered.

'I was just passing. Look no photos, okay.'

He held up his hands to show he did not have a camera on him. He also held up four tins of lager as a peace offering.

'You'd better come in and tell me what all this is about. I am not in the mood for any nonsense today,' Nick said.

Paul Lewis read the body language and he went into the flat cautiously, noticing that it was a little untidy. Newspapers and magazines lay on the floor and chairs but at least they were in some sort of pile rather than being strewn about. The front room had cloth-covered settees which had seen better days, but they were just so hopelessly old fashioned. They would certainly not pass modern fire safety standards. Nick didn't smoke, except cigars on special occasions.

'Do you want a lager, mate? I just wanted to say sorry for getting you so pissed off yesterday. That happens a lot in my business but I've never seen anybody get so mad before. You're in a lot of trouble, right?' Paul said.

Nick thoughtfully accepted a lager just to break the ice, but wondered what the deal was. He felt compelled to say something.

'I'm sorry about your camera but I wasn't expecting to get photographed by the press. I hope you're not here to ask me about the hospital incident because I cannot discuss the matter,' Nick said.

'It's alright, mate. I'm not the press. I just take photos.' Paul grinned.

'Yes, but you sell the photos to the press, don't you?' Nick answered.

'Yeah, I know what you're saying. A lot of people think we're scum. I'm not here to argue the toss but I just want you to know what the game is. I know there are some journos and paparazzi hanging about the hospital looking for you. The word is you killed some bloke with diamorphine. Your photo on the front page will sell loads of copies, you know what I mean? I reckon that if I can't get a shot then I don't want some other bugger to get the exclusive,' Paul said.

'Is that what you have come to tell me?' Nick was starting to get a little annoyed with his uninvited visitor.

'No, hear me out. I'm just saying that if you go to the hospital, there will be a bunch of guys there who will hassle you. If you start fighting with someone, it will be an even greater photo opportunity. So all I'm saying is watch what you do.'

'I don't even know your name,' Nick said.

'It's Paul Lewis.' He stretched his hand out. Nick paused for a few seconds before shaking it.

'Look, Nick, I know you can't tell me anything official, but is there anything I can help you with? This will be off the record,' Paul asked.

Nick desperately wanted to talk, but certainly not to a photographer he had been in a fight with yesterday. He was sceptical of his uninvited guest.

'I just can't talk about this. Do you paparazzi guys ever give up?' Nick asked in desperation.

'No, but I want to help you, mate. The story says that you gave the diamorphine after some nurse had drawn it up in the syringe,' Paul said.

Nick remained silent. He felt he was now being baited for information but he would let the man talk and say what he knew.

'Some of the nurses were talking about it in a pub to a couple of guys. They were journalists, trying to get the inside angle. They started talking to these nurses after buying them a few drinks and their tongues got a bit loose. It happens, no matter how professional people are supposed to be. The question is, if this guy died from an overdose and you didn't do it, Nick, then someone must have put it in the syringe, am I right? I can see you're not going to tell me much. Some of the guys reckon that you have got a killer in the A & E department. Maybe somebody set you up. You thought about that, Nick?' Paul said again.

'I honestly cannot think why anybody would want to set me up. I have done nothing to upset anybody,' Nick replied.

'Envy, mate. It's the strongest reason in the world. Some bastard will always want what you've got and they'll shaft you for it.'

'Listen, Paul, thanks for your concern but I can't discuss this case with you, I really can't. Just accept that whatever is printed about me in the newspapers will be untrue. I am not going to oblige you with a photograph either just in case you're asking,' Nick said.

'Wasn't asking for one, mate. I'm surprised the other paparazzi are not at your doorstep already. Don't worry, I'm not going to tell them where you are because I don't want them to get the photo either. But if you turn up at the hospital, it will be a free-for-all. If I'm there, I'll have to do my job. My boss, Ricky, was pretty pissed off about the camera by the way.'

'It must be one of the hazards of your job. Surely it's insured?' Nick asked.

'Yeah, that's his problem. You're some mean fighter, mate. Look, I'll give you my card. Just call me if you want my help,' Paul offered.

He stood up to leave, draining the last of his lager from the can before leaving it on the table. He passed a business card to Nick at the same time. Nick felt obliged to shake his extended his hand again but he had a burning question to ask his visitor.

'Tell me, Paul, why do you guys do it, I mean take pictures of people going about their business and then publishing them without their consent?' He could see that Paul was a little irritated by this outburst.

'In this world, Nick, you don't get something for nothing. I had the balls to come here and apologise for the bust up yesterday. You broke my camera which cost over two thousand quid and I'm not asking you to pay for that. On the other hand, some people get a lot out of our photos because they get all the exposure they want and then they become famous because of it and make lots of money. You've got your job and I've got mine and we can't all be surgeons and neither do I want to be. Do yourself a favour and just ask yourself how that diamorphine got in that syringe. If you knew who did it and I got the photograph of that person, I'd make some money out of it but that person would also be history. Even if they weren't locked up in prison, the publicity would make sure that nobody employed them again in that line of job. It's up to you what you want to do. I'm just giving you some options. If you want to give me her name, I'll make sure her face gets plastered all over the country, but I want the exclusive on that one and nobody will ever know how we got onto it. That nurse is trying to stuff your career because she is trying to save hers so don't be a mug and let it happen, mate.' Paul spoke his mind.

Nick felt chastised by the long speech. He felt uncomfortable with that idea, but he could see Paul's point of view. Paul was a brash but likeable guy in his easygoing cockney manner. He seemed honest enough about his job and Nick could not fault him for trying to earn some money. It was just a reflection on modern society that the paparazzi would always be around doing their business, peddling in somebody's misery. Something Paul said made sense. He was right about the possibility of a set-up. Nick owed it to himself to find out how and why the large dose of diamorphine had got into the syringe. His whole career depended on getting the answer. It had certainly been a very strange afternoon and Paul was the last person he had expected to see but what he said made a lot of sense. Why would somebody deliberately try to implicate him in a suspicious death unless it was for a purpose?

'Listen, Paul, thanks for your offer but like I said, this matter is confidential and there is an investigation going on. If somebody is found to be at fault, they will be dealt with appropriately. I'll see you out,' Nick said.

'Okay, Nick. You take care of yourself, mate. Give me a call if you change your mind,' Paul said as he left the flat.

After seeing Paul off at the door, an idea crossed his mind. Nick phoned the hospital. He asked to be put through to the A & E department and kept his fingers crossed, hoping Meg would be there. A staff nurse answered the phone; thankfully it wasn't Brenda Hawkins. Meg was on duty but was not in the office, so he held on until she could come to the phone.

'Hello, Meg speaking,' she said in her professional tone.

'Hi, Meg. It's Nick Forbes. How are you?' he asked.

'Nick! It's great to hear from you. I'm okay, how are you, more to the point?' She sounded genuinely happy to hear from him.

'I'm okay. Can you do me a very big favour? Just listen for a couple of minutes. The post-mortem on the chap showed he died from a diamorphine overdose. I gave him what was in the syringe and as you know it was made up by Brenda Hawkins and then checked by another nurse, or so she said. I believe the number of ten-milligram vials left matched the number recorded in the DDA book.' He was interrupted by Meg.

'Yes, Nick. Also, during the hospital investigation they took away all the ten-milligram vials and had them examined in a pharmaceutical laboratory. The diamorphine contained no impurities and they were all exactly ten milligrams,' she said quickly.

'Meg, can I ask you, do you keep thirty-milligram vials in A & E?' Nick asked seriously.

'Yes, we do,' she replied.

'Could you check them?'

'What are you thinking of, Nick?'

'I just wonder if Brenda drew up thirty-milligram instead of ten-milligram by mistake. It could be murder if she did that deliberately,' Nick said.

'Oh Christ! Are you serious? If she had drawn up thirty milligrams then why did it show that a ten-milligram vial had been used as recorded in the DDA book, which corresponded to the numbers of vials left in the box?' Meg asked.

'I don't know, Meg. Could you go and check the thirty-milligram vials? Were they taken away for examination?' Nick asked.

'No, I don't think so. We hardly ever use thirty milligrams of diamorphine in A & E. This is the dose we may use in a heroin addict where thirty milligrams is nothing to them. I'll go and check and will call you back in a few minutes. What number are you on?' Meg wanted to know.

Nick gave her his home number and then waited anxiously for her to call him back. He desperately needed to see if his idea was correct. The phone duly rang and he snatched it up with trembling hands.

'Nick, I've checked the thirty-milligram vials and something is definitely odd. There are seven vials in the box which corresponded to the number in the DDA book. Now both the ten and thirty-milligram vials were almost identical in appearance except for the numerical figures. They both have diamorphine written on them in black against a white label. Just as I was putting them away, I noticed that one of the vials had been turned around. That was the strange thing, it said ten milligrams,' Meg said.

Nick's mind was now racing, trying to compute all the facts. Why was there a ten-milligram vial in the thirty-milligram box? An idea suddenly hit him.

'I think I know what could have happened. Brenda must have drawn up thirty milligrams by mistake and had not realised it at the time. She thought she had drawn up a ten-milligram vial and had entered it in the DDA book correctly. There must have been seven ten-milligram vials and seven thirty-milligram vials to start with, but she took a thirty-milligram vial thinking it was ten-milligram. This left six thirty-milligram vials, but it was wrongly recorded as being six ten-milligram vials when there was actually seven left in the box. After the patient died, she must have gone back to the DDA cupboard to check she had not made a mistake. Presumably, she realised she had used the wrong vial and had taken one of the ten-milligram vials and put it in the thirty-milligram box, hoping nobody would notice this. The numbers of ten-milligram vials now corresponded with the DDA book, which was six, as did the numbers of thirty-milligram vials which was seven, except that one of the vials contained only ten milligrams. As far as I know, the stocks of diamorpmine are frequently changed because they go out of date quite quickly. If you say that the thirty-milligrams were hardly ever used, then there was a good chance they would have been disposed of when they go out of date without anybody noticing the presence of the ten-milligram vial amongst the other thirty-milligrams, unless each vial was checked individually,' Nick concluded.

'That is almost too hard to believe, but I guess there can be no other explanation. I would presume that when the diamorphine was checked by the second nurse, she had either failed to check the dose or had assumed that thirty-milligrams was the correct dose that was to be given. I think I will have to speak to the senior nursing officer about this and we will have to make some major changes regarding how intravenous drugs are drawn up. Look, do you want to meet up for a drink later to discuss this? I finish at 7.30 p.m.,' Meg asked.

It was the best offer he had all day, in fact for quite a while. Having spent two of the most miserable weeks of his life being stuck alone in his flat, this sounded not only good but it was just the tonic to restore his battered psyche. Life had a strange way of sorting itself out and this was so unexpected. Paul Lewis had been both his stalker and saviour and right now, he was just too confused to know whether he liked or loathed the paparazzi.

'Yes, I would like that,' Nick said without hesitation.

'Okay, tell me where you want to meet up,' Meg replied.

Nick felt a wave of emotion wash over him, sweeping away the unbearable tension which had enveloped his life over the past few weeks. It was like being released from prison, to be able to walk in freedom and take his rightful place in society again. Meg had restored his confidence in a very short space of time and he was going to come out with all guns blazing. The most difficult thing now was to decide where to go this evening. He had not been out socialising for a while and the thought of having good food and a couple of drinks was almost too much to contemplate.

'Why don't you meet me in Wood Green. There's a good curry place just around the corner from the tube station,' Nick said.

'Yes, I know the place. Say about 8 p.m.?' Meg replied.

'Okay. See you then.'

'Bye,' Meg said, and put the phone down.

11

Feelgood

Meg finished her shift at 7.30 p.m. It would only take her fifteen minutes to get to Wood Green by car. There were no tube stations near the hospital so getting the Piccadilly Line would have been a waste of time anyway. She changed from her theatre blues into a pair of jeans and a casual top, the clothes she came to work in. If only she had known she was going out tonight, but it was just for a curry, she said to herself. Nick had briefly explained about his encounter with Paul Lewis, the paparazzo. The discovery of the drug vial in the wrong box was also too sinister to let go without discussing it further. Nick obviously did not want to be anywhere near to the hospital in case other paparazzi were hanging about, even at that time of the evening.

He arrived at the tandoori restaurant first and asked for a table for two. Being a Saturday night, the restaurant was nearly full, but with so many places to eat, especially further down the road in Turnpike Lane, he had not thought it was necessary to book ahead. He ordered an Indian Cobra beer, which somehow always tasted good with a curry. Regardless of which country it was, the local drink usually went perfectly well with the cuisine on offer. It was a symbiotic fusion of food and drink, just like Scottish haggis and whisky. Haggis actually tasted very good even if most tourists thought they were little furry animals with short legs. Just then, Meg walked in. She looked around the restaurant and beamed when she saw Nick. One of the waiters acknowledged her as she came in with a warm welcome.

'Hello, Nick. Hope you didn't have to wait too long.' Her scent was delicious.

She had simply wafted in and easily negotiated herself through the tightly packed tables of happy eaters. The restaurant had the usual subdued lighting and ubiquitous red wallpaper found in many curry houses, better to hide the curry stains with. This only served to add to the soporific effect of the large meal which Nick knew he was going to subject himself to. Getting back home afterwards and digesting the meal in comfort was preferable to pouring more beer into his full stomach. He had done that many times after the rugby at Murrayfield, and had even thrown up once in Rose Street in Edinburgh. He never did manage to do the eighteen watering holes there.

'No, you're okay. Just got here myself. You look great,' Nick said.

He stood up to greet her and meant every word of it. She looked stunning, even in a pair of jeans. They were not chummy enough to give each other a friendly peck on the cheeks yet, he thought. They sat down.

'You have obviously been to charm school. If I had known I was going out, I would have put something decent on. Never mind, I'm here now, so let's eat!' Meg said.

She exuded a certain confidence about her and it was quite clear she had a relaxed attitude to life, except where her work was concerned. That was something she took seriously most of the time, but she did her job with great humour as befitted a competent professional. However, she was refreshingly low maintenance and couldn't care less if she was having a bad hair day, unlike some prima donnas who made a song and dance about nothing.

'So, what are you having?' she asked, looking at the extensive menu.

'I'm going to have a king prawn puri followed by an aloo ghosh. I just love the combination of lamb and potatoes.' He was referring to the main dish.

'The jalfrezi looks good, but I'll start with some pokoras. What's that you're drinking?' Meg asked.

'It's a Cobra beer. Try one.' He didn't have to persuade her.

They ordered their food and a Cobra for Meg. Nick had a lot on his mind and was keen to find out what had been going on at the hospital since he was last there.

'So, what's happening at the hospital and how did you get on this afternoon?' he asked quickly.

'Well, I phoned the senior nursing officer and told her about what we discovered. She said she would have to take the matter further and would get back to me. Later on in the afternoon, I was a little surprised to see her with the chief executive down in A & E. They wanted to speak to me so we went to the visitors' room. I told them the whole thing and could see they were concerned because chief executives rarely come in on a Saturday unless there is a flap on,' Meg said.

A waiter arrived with her beer and poured it into a glass. She took a small sip before carrying on.

'They had made the decision that no further stocks of thirty-milligram diamorphine vials would be kept in the department and we just had to use multiples of tens if a bigger dose was needed. It was a totally sensible decision. The hospital pharmacist has been told to remove the thirty-milligram vials and, during our conversation, one of the staff nurses popped in to ask me for the DDA keys, saying that the pharmacist was there to do that. I later checked the DDA cupboard and the thirty-milligram vials had been removed and signed for by the pharmacist.'

'And then what happened?' Nick asked.

'After that, I was told to keep this matter confidential and I assured them that I would. I have not discussed this with any of the staff nurses but I think somebody is going to take the rap for this. So now, Mr Nick, you can relax and eat your food,' Meg said cheerfully.

Nick felt totally relieved as the heavy burden of blame had been lifted from his shoulders. He was really hungry now. Right then, he thought Meg was the most beautiful person in the world. The first course arrived which took his thoughts away. He could see the juicy king prawns tucked up in the Indian fried bread which was smothered in a tangy hot sauce and freshly chopped coriander. Meg didn't wait to stick her fork into one her pokoras before lifting it to her mouth, delicately nibbling the spicy savoury treat before carrying on with the conversation.

'The past two weeks have been a complete nightmare. First of all, the press came around asking a lot of questions about you. Of course nobody said anything and the official line was that you were on holiday. The hospital security people tried to keep them away but they kept popping up all over the place before they eventually lost interest. We even got a hard time from some of the patients telling us to make sure they didn't get killed, which I'm sure was meant as a joke but it felt awful, as if we were all murderers. All the while, I had to keep everybody's spirits up whilst Brenda was making my life difficult." Then, suddenly realising she had been talking too much about herself, she changed direction. "You've not said much, Nick! So tell me your story. How have you coped with all this?' Meg asked.

She seemed genuinely concerned about him, looking him straight in the eye, which made him feel very self-conscious. He squirmed a little at the undivided attention, but it was a good thing.

'I've done nothing except get into a fight with a paparazzi chap called Paul, and got charged by the police for doing so. I saw him taking pictures of me in a car park and I just lost my temper. I then broke his camera and then we had a little sorting out to do. I then couldn't believe he came round to the flat to talk about it afterwards. I'm glad he did because it made me realise that things were not as straightforward as they seemed. I know I asked for ten milligrams of diamorphine and the only person who could have screwed up was Brenda. If we hadn't figured this out, I'd still be in deep trouble. So thanks for digging around this afternoon. Thank God the pharmacists didn't remove the thirty-milligram vials when they analysed the ten-milligram samples or we would never have got to the bottom of this,' Nick said.

He broke out in a small sweat, either from the king prawn puri, which was decidedly spicy tonight, or from the thought that he may have been shafted by somebody and not been able to prove it.

'Do you mind if I ask you about Emma, Nick? Are you still together?' Meg asked.

Nick was totally unprepared for this. He carried on eating for a few seconds, thinking about what to say.

'Er, no,' he replied.

'It's okay if you don't want to talk about it,' she said, trying to sound reassuring and non-threatening.

'No, that's alright. There's not much to say. We decided to split up, or rather I did.'

'Oh, I didn't know that. Sorry! How long have you been together?' She was looking at him again.

'On and off for over a year. It really wasn't much of a relationship. We were both wrapped up in our jobs, exams, trying not to screw up, you know how it is,' Nick said.

'Did you love her?' she asked.

'Wow, you don't hang about! No, I don't think I did and I guess it was the same for her,' he replied.

Somehow, Nick didn't mind Meg asking him about Emma because he really needed to talk about it with somebody. He was still confused about ending the relationship at a time when he was at his lowest ebb, but Emma's patronising attitude had been unbearable. It was a question of cutting his losses, just like a shareholder selling out when the shares were sliding down in price. Dumping her was a regrettable necessity. She had been one of the Max Factor girls at university after all, all made up with nothing beneath the veneer.

'You sound as if you didn't mind too much about breaking up,' Meg said.

'I never thought Emma was the right person for me but she was somebody I knew from medical school. She was always more concerned about being seen to be doing all the right things, to end up with a nice job at some top hospital just to show everybody how brilliant she was. That was all she ever cared for.'

'Not everybody is like that, Nick. What about happiness? Didn't she want that?'

'I could never figure out what really made her happy other than talking about houses or holidays. She also whinged a lot about her job and I think she was quite stressed by it. She kept reminding me that my job couldn't possibly be any worse than hers,' Nick said.

'She sounds like a real bitch or a bad listener,' Meg added.

'I don't know, it was probably a lack of insight into life. She was a fantasist living in her own world, but who could blame her? Don't we all want the good things in life?' Nick asked.

'Yes, but these people are superficial and have no substance. Emma didn't strike me as being that type. She was very clinical about her job and I'm sure she is a good gynaecologist but I wouldn't say she was desperate for recognition. I think you're still being Mr Angry, Nick. My career is important, but I wouldn't put it before a good relationship,' Meg said.

'Perhaps you misunderstood me. No, I don't think Emma wanted to be some famous gynaecologist but all I'm trying to say is that she was very focused on herself. If something didn't figure in her life in any way, she didn't want to know. I needed to speak to her, to tell her what I was going through, but she just ignored me. Do you know what it was like to be suspended by the GMC?' Nick said.

'No, Nick. Please tell me because I can see how upset you are. Couldn't you have talked to your parents about it?' She saw Nick looking down at his plate, overwhelmed by sudden sadness.

'No, my father died when I was young and my mother was psychologically destroyed by that. She never got over his death and gave up on life years ago. She just made my life difficult, more than she should have done,' Nick said.

'I'm sorry to hear that.' For once that evening Meg left at a loss as to what to say. She had touched on something raw. Thankfully the waiter returned to remove the plates from the first course and brought over a hotplate containing two burning candles inside. 'I didn't know about your father.'

'That's okay. I never knew him so it doesn't really matter,' Nick said.

'I think it does by the way you are eaten up. You know you can always talk to me, don't you, Nick? Don't let your past eat you up,' Meg said with honesty.

'Yes, I know it shouldn't but it isn't so easy to let go,' he replied. The main dish arrived, interrupting their conversation before the waiter left the table.

'How did your father die?' Meg asked. Nick could see she was wanting to know more about him and it wasn't a flippant question.

'My mother said he died in a car crash. The earliest memory I had of anything in my life was on the day he left. I was about two years old and he had found some beetle in the garden. He put it in a matchbox and let me play with it. My mother was really upset and even got hysterical at one stage, not about the beetle but because he was leaving. He then left with a lot of bags and I never saw him again. He was an officer in the navy and was going back to join his ship. I played with the beetle for a little while longer before tipping it into the garden.'

'Was there anything in the house which belonged to your father?' Meg asked.

'No, I don't think there was. He left a scrapbook with some photographs of when he was a boy. That is the only thing I have of his.'

'Don't you think that was strange?' Meg asked.

'What do you mean?'

'I mean, if he was going back to sea, there would be all the things he wouldn't be taking with him, like his clothes, shoes, that sort of thing,' Meg said.

'I suppose you're right. I have never though of that.'

'Have you ever asked your mother what really happened?' Meg asked.

'No, I just presumed he had been killed,' Nick said.

'Could it be possible that he left your mother?' Meg suggested.

'I don't know. I didn't think of that,' Nick replied.

'Think, Nick. Think why your mother has been so upset all these years. Surely she must have loved you even more when there was nobody else in her life,' Meg reasoned.

'That was just it. She gave me nothing, not even so much as a pair of football boots or a football shirt. I was the only kid in the school who didn't even have that. There were plenty of kids with families on social security but she was too proud to sign on. We lived on practically nothing but she still had the money to spend on alcohol and cigarettes,' Nick said.

'I find that hard to believe. How on earth did you end up in medical school? Other kids with a lot more end up on the scrapheap, doing drugs or crime. You're not lying to me are you, Nick?' Meg asked.

'I wouldn't. The few friends I had knew what I went through. The boys on the estate picked on me but I fought back. They left me alone, enough to let me get through my exams and into medical school. I worked the rest of the time to earn money to live on and met some great people. They made me realise that anybody could achieve anything they wanted to. One of the guys I worked for said I would become a doctor but despite all that, I cannot help the feeling that my life has been a failure. We never had a happy Christmas because my mother would get so drunk and set fire to what few presents there were. She was desperately unhappy and I only know that now, but at the time it was hard to accept. It was a relief just to get to medical school. At least it felt like I was moving on from a very miserable life.' For the first time in his life, he had opened up his life story to somebody. It came as a big relief.

'Nick, I don't blame you for wanting to be angry. You are the best surgeon I have ever met but don't let all that anger spoil the person you are. Don't ever become a cynical consultant and don't let Emma get to you. She wasn't right for you and you deserve so much better. Okay?' Meg asked.

'Yes,' he answered meekly.

That was the best he could come up with. He smiled and caught her eyes for a brief moment, connecting to her inner thoughts for what seemed like an eternity. She was truly a beautiful person, not just her body but her soul. A deep feeling of happiness crept into him, an experience he had never known before. There was a very special person sitting in front of him and this woman had understood his pain in a way Emma never could. Perhaps his father was still alive. That possibility had never entered his mind. In fact, a whole range of possibilities had suddenly opened up before him and he wanted the evening to go on but knew the magic couldn't last. There was no easy way to end the dinner except to pay the bill. She absolutely insisted on paying for half so there would be no pressure either way then. They went outside into the night.

'It's not so warm now.' Nick struggled to say something.

'It was really nice to see you tonight, Nick. I'm sorry I knew so little about you before, despite the fact we have been working together for so long. You really don't have to worry about this death any more. Everything will work out just fine and you'll be back at work soon enough wondering why you haven't taken more time off! I'm going home now to put my feet up after a really, really nice meal. I meant what I said about talking to me anytime you want to,' Meg said.

'Would you consider doing this again sometime?' he asked anxiously.

'Yes, sure. I would like that. Get in touch when you get back.' She smiled.

'Okay, I'll do that. Bye for now,' Nick muttered.

'Bye.' With a final smile she turned and walked away but she did turn around to wave.

Nick walked to his car with his feet barely touching the ground. He looked at the blue TT and fell in love again for a second time that night. Life suddenly felt good again.

12

9/11

Flashback: 11 September, 2001

Nineteen Arabic men checked into three different airports along the Eastern seaboard of America that morning. They were very discreet and attracted no attention, appearing to be just like any other passenger. After clearing security, they went to the departures lounge and waited for their flights to be called. Once on board their respective aircraft, they took their allotted seats and sat quietly amongst the other passengers before the flights took off. United Airlines flight UA175 left at 7.58 a.m. from Boston and headed for Los Angeles, as did American Airlines flight AA11. Flight UA93 left Newark Airport in New Jersey at 8.01 a.m. and headed for San Francisco, just before flight AA77 took off from Dulles International Airport in Washington at 8.10 a.m. to head for LA. Once the aircrafts had settled down into their individual flight paths, the men left their seats and positioned themselves strategically at various places within the aircraft before announcing their intentions. They brought out the smuggled box-cutters and threatened to use them on the cabin crew. The cockpit was the main focus of their attention, which offered no resistance in the absence of a security door. The men had been trained to fly aircraft in a rudimentary fashion and took over from the pilots. They altered the flight path. The four airliners had been hijacked and nobody, apart from the hijackers themselves, knew their intention. Fighter jets were not scrambled to shoot them down because the precedent for doing so had not yet been established in America. In the name of Allah, America, the great Satan, would reap his wrath for its crusade against the might of Islam. The martyrs had been taught well, not only in the *madrasas* or religious schools, but also in the training grounds of Afghanistan. The hatred for the infidels had been fomented by their tough physical and psychological training, and today was the day of deliverance; they were going to paradise where vestal virgins awaited them.

The Boeing of flight AA11 from Boston flew spectacularly into the north tower of the World Trade Centre at 8.46 a.m., followed by UA175, which smashed into the south tower at 9.03 a.m. Both towers erupted into gigantic fireballs as the aviation fuel ignited on the hot engines, sending shards of glass and metal down onto the ground below. The intense heat generated from the inferno melted the outer casing of the giant buildings, weakening the structure until they collapsed in a huge cloud of dust and rubble, taking nearly three thousands souls with them. Flight AA77 crashed into the Pentagon at 9.45 a.m., destroying one section of the building, but flight UA93 crashed in a wooded area in Pennsylvania, after the passengers fought back, probably saving hundreds of lives as the plane had clearly failed to reach its destination. They were real American heroes as were the men of the New York Fire Department.

Al-Qaeda had declared war on America and the message was quite clear: this was the beginning of a *jihad*, a Moslem war against the unbelievers. Al-Qaeda itself was a radical Islamic terror group set up by Osama bin Laden, whose sole purpose in life was to embark on a complete and total jihad against America and her allies. Bin Laden had been born in 1957 and belonged to a wealthy Saudi-Arabian family. Despite his privileged upbringing, he had decided to join a fundamentalist group at the age of sixteen. He had gained battle experience in Afghanistan by fighting the Soviets in 1979, before setting up Al-Qaeda in Sudan. He had also established other training bases in Somalia and Afghanistan, recruiting young men mainly from Chechnya, Pakistan, Egypt and other Arab states to fight his war.

His terror group had earlier attempted to blow up the World Trade Centre in 1993 with a huge car bomb which failed to destroy the building. The American embassies in Kenya and Tanzania were also bombed, as was the USS Cole, a US navy destroyer moored in Aden, the Yemeni port. More bombings would follow across the world, targeting westerners, none more brutal and mindless than the Bali bombing of the innocents, where young holidaymakers were blown apart simply for being in a disco bar. The message was very clear: nobody was safe and any good Muslim was capable of becoming a suicide bomber with the promise of martyrdom. The converts had reached the point in their lives where they no longer cared if they lived or died, as they had lost touch with their humanity. Christians valued the sanctity of life, not martyrdom, and this fundamental difference in ideology would lead to further bloodshed. The bombings had just begun.

The intelligent services in America had failed to stop the 9/11 attacks. In fact, the FBI had already detained the 'twentieth hijacker', Zacarias

Moussaoui, without knowing it. Moussaoui was a French-born Moroccan whose affiliation with al-Qaeda had begun when he moved to London and attended mosques which preached Islamic extremism. Moussaoui had come to the attention of the FBI in America after paying for flying lessons, but was only interested in knowing how to steer the plane. He hadn't asked how to land the thing. The American FBI and CIA had failed to stop al-Qaeda, and the British intelligence services such as M15 and M16 now had to work closely with the American agencies if there was any hope of fighting global terrorism. No single nation, regardless of its resources, could fight al-Qaeda alone. The tentacles of evil had spread too widely across the world, engulfing many countries including the USA and UK itself. They had shown their determination by destroying the civilised societies and were quite capable of using weapons of mass destruction. Even the dirty bomb, a non-nuclear device consisting of radioactive material, would contaminate a city for decades without actually causing much damage. The risk to the UK itself remained very high, not only from the foreign terrorist but also from British-born Muslims who bombed the transport network with impunity. The government had allowed the radical imams to preach their hatred without arresting them. Many aimless young and unemployed black men with criminal records had been forced to convert to Islam in the tough council estates of London and other British cities.

They had been given a shaky theology lesson on Christianity, citing that the Bible had been rewritten several times by men and not by God. The only true god was Allah, and Mohammed was his disciple. It was therefore better to follow God's army rather than dying through a bullet in the head for selling drugs in the street. As a member of God's army, it was their duty to carry bombs and blow up the infidels. Richard Reid, the British shoe bomber, tried to blow up an airliner with plastic explosives concealed in his shoes.

"The ruling to kill Americans and their allies – civilians and military – is an individual duty for every Muslim who can do it in any country in which it is possible to do it, in order to liberate the al-Aqsa mosque and the holy mosque of Mecca from their grip, and in order for their armies to move out of all the lands of Islam." Osama Bin Laden, February 1998.

13

Afghanistan

Afghanistan was a magical and beautiful country surrounded by Turkmenistan, Uzbekistan and Tajikistan to the north, Pakistan to the south and east, and Iran to the west. It was also impoverished and landlocked, with few natural resources. The south consisted mainly of the Pashto-speaking tribesmen who made up the ranks of the Taleban, an organisation of ultra fanatical Islamists. Their fundamental beliefs were at odds even with the Muslim faith, which preached peace and tolerance. Warped interpretation of Islamic law often led to bloodshed, where beheadings and amputations were carried out in football stadiums. Adultery usually meant death for the woman, whether proven or not, but homosexuality was tolerated, even considered normal practice. Bribery and corruption was a way of life; without it, the system came to a grinding halt. It was almost impossible to move around the country without paying a bribe to the local warlord. This part of the world had simply gone mad, fuelled by the heroin trade.

Against the Taleban stood the Northern Alliance, a loose organisation consisting of Tajiks, Uzbecs, Hazaras and other Dari-speaking minorities who collectively controlled about ten per cent of the country. Despite the alliance between the fierce and powerful northern warlords, they could not be expected to defeat the vastly superior Taleban, with al-Qaeda fighting next to them. The country was quickly falling into the clutches of the Taleban, a band of murderous zealots who raped and murdered their way through the land. Scores of buildings had already been destroyed, including schools and hospitals. Education, the cradle of any civilisation, was banned, as was the use of radio and television. Western music was totally taboo; taking photographs not allowed. Just like the killing fields of Cambodia, Afghanistan was rapidly spiralling out of control, driven on by the infectious insanity of a group of madmen. The black garb worn by the Taleban resembled the symbol of death itself. All that stood between the people and the Taleban was the Northern Alliance. Afghanistan had known how to fight and survive

81

foreign invasions before, but this time they were fighting their own people and the foreign Arabs fighting for al-Qaeda.

The British Imperial Army had failed to conquer the country more than a century before. The Russians had failed to do the same after ten years of bitter fighting. The country would not yield to brute force alone, no matter how powerful the invading army was. This was due to the toughness of the Mujahadeen warriors who had fought and died in the mountains. They had suffered terribly from the lack of basic provisions but the spirit to survive had been unbreakable. They were now the guerrillas fighting their own countrymen.

In any guerrilla war, the home side usually had the advantage by knowing the local topography better than the enemy, but the Taleban also knew the country. The British had learnt the art of guerrilla warfare in the Second World War, but had managed to fine-tune their tactics by fighting the Chinese communists in the jungles of Malaya in the 1950s. They turned the communist guerrilla tactics around by taking the fight to them in their own backyard. Elite troops led by the Special Air Service Regiment went into the jungle, searched and then destroyed them. They were able to do this by first winning over the hearts and minds of the local population. In doing so, they gathered useful information about the enemy and also managed to persuade the locals to deny the enemy any logistical support in the way of food and supplies. Some of the local Malays who helped the British paid the ultimate price for their co-operation. They were tortured and publicly executed in front of the whole village as a means of deterrence. Despite these acts of barbarity, the communist insurgency in Malaya was defeated when the enemy knew they couldn't fight a war without support, particularly from a population they had brutalised. The British were seen as the good guys, but the Royal Marines frequently brought communist heads out of the jungle, as it was easier to carry them than whole bodies for identification purposes.

The Taleban menace had made it essential for America and Britain to send in the American Green Berets and a smaller contingent of British SAS to help the Northern Alliance. The Americans wanted the chance to kick ass for 9/11, but the SAS thrived in this kind of warfare. The Green Berets had been formed as an elite fighting unit in the late 1950s along the same idea as the SAS. Once dropped behind enemy lines, they were expected to fight and survive for long periods of time without being re-supplied, unlike a conventional army. They were highly trained and could be infiltrated into enemy territory by a variety of means, including parachute, submarine, helicopter, boat, land-based vehicle or by foot. They could also fight in the desert or jungle, in urban areas or in the countryside. They were skilled in conventional, unconventional, hand-to-hand combat, clandestine and water-borne operations. In brief, they were an elite fighting force and were more than a match for the Taleban. For the relatively small numbers of soldiers deployed, they would kill a disproportionate number of the enemy. The SAS also roamed the countryside on search and destroy missions.

The Green Berets had been tasked with assisting the various warlords in the Northern Alliance, of which General Dostum was literally the biggest in terms of physical size and importance. He was an ethnic Uzbec with an intense hatred for the Taleban and al-Qaeda. Being both physically and militarily a powerful man, he was feared by both his own men and the enemy. In many ways, he was a brutal commander in a brutal country and if the end justified the means, he was the man to support. The Green Berets' main task was to provide him with close air support (CAS), which brought badly needed fire support from the coalition aircraft to his poorly equipped troops. Each CAS team usually consisted of four men operating within a twelve man unit and were allocated to the various warlords. They brought with them the expertise to direct an enormous amount of firepower onto the enemy, which would help to nullify the advantage held by the Taleban and al-Qaeda forces.

The key weapon was the Special Operation Forces Laser Marker (SOFLAM). This laser device directed laser-guided bombs to the target with pinpoint accuracy. Once a target had been identified, the operator made contact with an aircraft in the vicinity to assist in the operation. The SOFLAM was then used to fire a laser beam onto the target. The 'lased' or 'painted' target reflected the laser beam which would then guide the bomb in. Any circling fighter-bomber or strategic bomber, such as the B1 or B52, would release a guided bomb on picking up the reflected signal. From then onwards, the bomb simply had to follow the laser beam down onto the target until impact. The Northern Alliance needed any help they could get.

From a strategic point of view, it was vital to retake the important northern city of Mazar-e-Sharif, the gateway to northern Afghanistan. The city was essential from which to spring an attack on Kabul itself, the capital city. Without gaining control of Mazar-e-Sharif, it was only a matter of time before the Taleban took control of the whole country. Mounting a counter-attack then would have been impossible and the Northern Alliance would have been annihilated. If the war was lost, the whole country would have been at the mercy of the Taleban and a dark age would have descended on the entire population. Many more would have been butchered and mutilated unnecessarily. The world had already witnessed the destruction of the ancient Buddha carved from the ancient hills of Bamian, as a foretaste of what was to come. Civilisation itself was at stake.

The Green Berets and SAS were deployed in several areas of northern Afghanistan. One Green Beret unit was infiltrated into the Darye Balkh Valley, an area to the west of Mazar-e-Sharif, with the specific task of providing Close Air Support to destroy the enemy positions there. The Taleban controlled much of the surrounding areas around Mazar-e-Sharif, which had already fallen to them. The Special Forces needed to gather information very quickly about the enemy's strength, positions, combat readiness and morale in order to formulate a strategy for winning the war. They had to start an offensive campaign immediately to weaken the enemy whilst conducting a 'hearts and minds' operation at the same time by supporting the local people with gifts of food, medicine and clothing. It was a difficult task given the logistics but they had the training. Guns would also be provided to the Mujahadeen, but loyalties had a bad habit of changing quickly depending on the prevailing situation. Everybody was only too aware that Dostum himself had decided to fight for the Russians at one stage before changing sides again. The Mujahadeen on the whole seemed a safe bet, as they were intent on destroying the Taleban, having seen thousands of their own people slaughtered in many towns and villages. Death and torture had become a routine spectacle here and both sides were guilty of that. Most of the people here seemed desensitised to all the pain and suffering, but perhaps God had simply abandoned this country.

The twelve man CAS team on board the special operations MH 47 Chinook helicopter focused on the job ahead. Each man knew what he had to do and tried to enjoy the ride for as long as it lasted. Another Chinook followed behind, containing a quick reaction force (QRF). The QRF may be needed to extract them if things went pear-shaped. They may find themselves in a hot situation against overwhelming odds and may need immediate extraction. The Chinooks were flown by the best pilots who were highly experienced in these types of mission. Their job was to make sure everybody got to the landing zone in one piece.

They flew low over enemy territory to avoid radar detection, although it was unlikely that the Taleban had any in working order capable of tracking them. Russian-made radar-controlled anti-aircraft guns still dotted the ground, and shoulder-launched Stinger missiles were available. They had been supplied by the CIA in a different war, when the Afghans had fought the Russians over a decade ago. The pilots prayed the Stingers did not work any more, after spending years in the harsh, dusty climate. It would have been a tragedy to die from an American missile. The helicopters were fitted with missile detectors and counter measures for dealing with them, but a sustained missile attack would still get through. Chaff would be deployed to confuse the incoming missile, but the slow-flying helicopter was still very vulnerable. Vigilance with their Mk1 eyeball was still their best hope of staying alive. They had to stay alert.

The men in Chinook were deafened by the noise from the twin engines above them. The two contra-rotating rotor blades created opposite torques which stopped the aircraft from spinning, unlike a conventional helicopter which needed a tail rotor to overcome this problem. The rotor blades at the front were driven by a synchronised drive shaft to avoid hitting the rear blades. The helicopter was constantly jinking and flying in a wavy line to minimise the risk of getting hit. Even the handheld rocket-propelled grenade (RPG) had been known to take down a helicopter from a lucky hit, despite being relatively crude and inaccurate. They were abundant and ubiquitous in most theatres of war because of their cheapness and no self-respecting terror organisation could do without them. The Chinook was hardly a stealth machine, but it was a supreme troop carrier.

The Green Berets prepared themselves for action. They checked and rechecked their weapons as their lives depended on it. A malfunctioning weapon could mean an instant death warrant. They were using the M-4A1 assault rifles, which was a shorter version of the M-16, the weapon used extensively in Vietnam against the Vietcong's AK47. It had a collapsible stock and a heavier barrel. Each magazine held thirty bullets which could be used up in seconds on automatic mode. Telescopic scopes and night-vision devices could also be mounted on the body of the weapon, as could a 40 mm M203 grenade launcher. This was slung beneath the weapon and could hurl a grenade up to a distance of 400 metres, giving the men a formidable weapon system. Some carried Minimi machine guns instead of the M-4A1, which could spit out 5.56 mm bullets at a rate of 1,000 rounds per minute.

Their personal weaponry was still no match compared to the SOFLAM which could rein in 2,000 lb laser-guided bombs. They were all set to go and psyched themselves up mentally, except this time there was no rock and roll music. Rolling Stones was a Vietnam thing. The aircraft approached the designated landing area and the pilots carefully looked ahead for any signs of the enemy. They had to satisfy themselves first that the area was sterile, free of the enemy, before making their approach run. Although the mountainous area was almost barren, the enemy could easily camouflage themselves and be hard to spot from above. The load master at the back of the aircraft kept a sharp lookout from the rear door, ready to yell if they were getting incoming fire. The second aircraft, containing the QRF, provided a reassuring presence nearby in case they were needed. The machine gunners swung their Gattling guns out from the side opening, ready to pour lead from the six rotating barrels.

The large Chinook flared as it came to land with the rotor blades churning up clouds of dust. The visibility dropped to zero as the pilot was now flying blindly. The landing area had already been chosen and they all waited for the impact of hitting terra firma at any moment. The load master signalled to the troops to get ready. He saw them gripping their weapons, faces locked onto him as they waited for the signal to go. When it finally came, they stormed out of the aircraft into the swirling dust. An all-round defensive circle was formed to provide 360 degrees of cover, each man covering his own arc of fire. The backpacks were then hurled off the back of the helicopter before it quickly took off. The dust continued to swirl around them as they regrouped a short distance away from the landing area. The helicopters hung around long enough to ensure the men were not taking enemy fire before clattering off in the distance. They were now alone in hostile enemy territory with no immediate backup. It was the best way to be, free to roam and fight with simple rules of engagement. When they were sure the area was clear, they collected their equipment and waited for their escorts to appear. They had been deliberately dropped off some distance away from the friendly village in order to avoid drawing any unwanted attention. The Taleban would butcher anybody who had any contact with the American or British troops. The Mujahadeen or Afghan freedom fighters would meet and take them away to the little village which was being used as a base. These tough men had fought and survived in the inhospitable mountains with precious little in the way of food or equipment. They relied on locally-made weapons such as the Kalashnikov AK47. It had the advantage of firing a heavier 7.62 mm bullet with a higher penetrating power than the lighter 5.56 mm ammunition used by the M-4A1. The bullets could easily go through a rock and kill the man behind it.

The overall plan very much involved the Mujahadeen doing the bulk of the fighting in their country. The Americans would provide the aerial fire power and logistical support. Committing large numbers of American ground troops at this stage would be politically unsound, as the sight of hundreds or thousands of body bags would not be tolerated. Despite 9/11, the country which had lost 57,000 people in the Vietnam War did not want to lose thousands more. It was time somebody other than America took the fight to the bad guys, although in Vietnam the people had just wanted their own country back from the colonialists. Al-Qaeda and the Taleban were different.

The Mujahadeen had no knowledge of laser-guided bombs or daisy cutters, which were huge non-atomic bombs capable of neutralising vast areas. The handful of soldiers sent to help them at first seemed like a token gesture and they wondered why America and Great Britain had not sent thousands of troops. The escorting party of Mujahadeen had no problems meeting up with the Green Berets and noticed these men did not look like the standard GI Joe, strapped from head to foot in equipment. The soldiers had deliberately dressed down and wore semi-Afghan clothing in order to make them blend in with the Mujahadeen. They and their equipment had been transported to the village on horseback through the barren but beautiful landscape. It had been a pleasant trip in the warm sunshine, but looks could be deceptive. The mountainous terrain was deadly, being freezing cold at night with little in the way of food, water or shelter. It would also be a very different situation if the Taleban were on their tails. Their hosts spoke no English and communication was through sign language. The local men wore local clothing and the typical Massoud hat, so named after the beloved General Ahmed Shah Massoud. He had been a charismatic and respected leader amongst the Northern Alliance but had been assassinated by the Taleban. It was obvious the Mujahadeen were in desperate need of equipment and supplies. Their hosts welcomed them with a traditional cup of tea. They would repay the compliment with a stack of supplies.

The village itself consisted of nothing more than a few mud brick buildings scattered about with no great thought or planning. They had no running water or electricity and just contained some rickety furniture. Chickens and goats roamed freely, the main supply of eggs and meat. Two of the houses were given over to the soldiers for their use. Space was limited, but it meant sleeping under a roof and keeping warm. The nights were bitterly cold and the reputed hospitality of the Afghans did not extend to sharing their wives, unlike in Tibet.

After arriving at the village, they unpacked the satellite phone and sent a situation report (SITREP) back to the command centre at K2, in Uzbekistan. The messages were automatically encrypted so they could speak in clear language. Failure to follow this standard operating procedure (SOP) could mean they were in trouble or had suffered equipment failure. The base commander would not know if the men had been killed or captured. Communication was therefore absolutely essential. Bravo Two Zero, the SAS unit in Iraq during the first Gulf

War, had not been able to contact their command base to ask for extraction and had had to fight it out until they were nearly all killed or captured. Only one man from the squad of eight had got away. The Green Berets were now on the ground, in bandit country, and the show was about to start.

It was decided that two four-man CAS teams would accompany the Mujahadeen the next day to seek and destroy. They set off on horseback with their personal weapons, laser designators and communications equipment. After a lengthy journey, they entered Taleban territory. There was no demarcation zone and the soldiers had to rely on the local knowledge of the Mujahadeen. Territories frequently change hands and it would be a bad idea to blow up friendly forces.

The Mujahadeen had a very clear idea of where the enemy were. After dismounting from their horses, the CAS teams decided that one should go forward with the Mujahadeen to engage the target whilst the other acted as backup. Invisible to the naked eye was a camouflaged bunker. The forward CAS team crept towards the target without being seen, using the rocks and boulders for cover. Once in position, they set up the spotting telescope to survey the target. The SOFLAM was made ready and communications established with the circulating aircraft up above. They were in luck as two navy F18 Hornets were in the area. They had flown a long way in from their aircraft carrier in the Indian Ocean, and could only loiter around briefly. The pilots were only too glad to be of assistance. Returning with bombs intact was not good.

The laser designator 'painted' the bunker. The men inside did not have a clue that martyrdom was coming, courtesy of a 1,000 lb laser guided bomb. The soldier targeting the SOFLAM remained calm as he guided one of the F18s onto the target. The aircraft had picked up the reflected laser signal and it was time to release the bomb. Flying at 18,000 feet above, it would take about ninety seconds to hit the target, depending on the wind conditions.

The soldiers covered their ears and opened their mouths, to prevent their eardrums from bursting when the shock wave arrived. The Mujahadeen did they same, not knowing where the bomb was coming from. The fast-moving projectile was just a blur as it sailed straight down. The bunker suddenly erupted in a massive shower of earth and stone, throwing body parts into the air. The concussion effect from the explosion hit the men with a mighty punch and the air was scorched by the tremendous heat. War had now been declared on the Taleban and al-Qaeda. The occupants were vaporised but there were still a whole network of slit trenches. Many of the Taleban survived but they were disorientated, deafened and injured, and they were in no fit state to fight. The Mujahadeen whooped with joy and charged towards the enemy positions. It was clear the Taleban had been totally demoralised by the bomb strike and showed no signs of wanting to fight any more. They were rounded up but it would have been far easier to shoot them on the spot rather than keep them prisoner. Food was a scarce resource amongst the Mujahadeen and the prisoners had to be fed. The Americans played by a different set of rules and cold-blooded murder was not their way of doing things. Dropping a 1,000 lb bomb on an unsuspecting enemy was somehow different. The Green Berets were keen to get away before the massed ranks of the Taleban surrounded their position. They were there to hit and run, not fight a conventional war. The prisoners would be interrogated for information and it had been a successful mission. The Mujahadeen also knew that the Taleban would exact a terrible revenge for this action and taking them back to the village was a mistake. It would have been better to simply finish them off here but the Americans had won the day. They would soon learn that fanatics did not give up until they were martyred.

14

K2

Blowing up the bunker had been both exciting and an anticlimax. The Mujahadeen had now seen the power of the 'death ray' and were convinced this weapon would win the war for them. Somehow, it had all been too easy. The Taleban gave up without a fight; there was no fun in killing the enemy this way. The soldiers returned to the village with the prisoners tied up together in a line. They looked traumatised by the explosion and the long walk to the village had exhausted them. Their presence in the village caused a big commotion and a big argument flared up. The village would be targeted if they escaped and, also, their meagre food supply would be depleted in no time if they had to feed them. The Americans viewed the prisoners as a source of information and they could be flown out by helicopter if necessary. Logistical backup was just a satellite phone call away and food could be brought in if needed. The problem was not insurmountable as far as the soldiers were concerned. The Mujahadeen, on the other hand, had never seen a helicopter bringing in supplies. They lived in an alien world where MacDonald's did not feature in their eating habits. They also didn't want the Taleban to bring death and destruction to the village if the war was lost.

The soldiers were aware of the uneasy feeling within in the village and sent a SITREP to the command base informing their commanding officer about the destruction of the enemy bunker and the prisoner situation. They needed an interpreter to interrogate these people and get some urgent food supplies. Taking them out to K2 was not an option at present because it was in a different country and that would not be permissible. The Mujahadeen would be supplied with food, medicine and warm winter clothing, but they also needed heavier weapons. The Green Berets were tasked to bring in any supplies that were needed, if only to boost their morale. They had been fighting the better-equipped Taleban with little more than old rifles and couldn't stem the tide. The situation would soon change. They were informed that a Russian-built MI-8 helicopter would be on its way with the supplies and the interpreter.

These rickety flying machines were commonly seen in Afghanistan and would not attract too much attention for delivering supplies. They were also used for other covert operations.

The prisoners were caged together in a small compound towards the rear of the village with their hands and feet still tied together. Some of the Mujahadeen had wanted to slit their throats and be done with this matter. For the Green Berets, it meant they had another job to do, to keep these people alive. They badly needed intelligence before the assault on Mazar-e-Sharif itself. The first blow had been delivered, but many more bunkers had to be destroyed before the Mujahadeen had any hope of winning.

The campaign had to go into full swing and the other special ops units would soon be calling in air strikes. The men decided that only two CAS teams from this unit should operate at any one time, keeping one team behind to guard the prisoners and monitor the radio traffic. They could divide into three man units but decided not to. The hired MI-8 helicopter was currently being loaded at K2. They were to wait out for further instructions.

K2 was an old Soviet facility in Uzbekistan. It was the nearest airbase from which the Americans could conduct their operation in Afghanistan. The Uzbekistan government received a substantial payment for its use but it did not make the Russians very happy. This was once USSR territory and now the Americans had muscled in. Despite the thaw in US-Soviet relations, the military activities would be closely monitored. Russian Migs were stationed only a few hundred miles away.

The Russian crew loading the helicopter were keen to finish for the day and get a drink. They were civilian pilots prepared to take on the hazardous mission for hard currency. There was always money to be made in a war. The old helicopter was crammed with food, medicines and warm weather parkas for the Mujahadeen. There would also be a passenger who was to be dropped off at the village. They would ask no questions. Their job was simple, to fly in, drop the cargo and fly back. They would be a little richer with US dollars in their pockets.

By the very nature of their work, the special forces do not like any publicity. They also do not like to be photographed on special missions. Photographic images of war were first recorded during the Crimean War in 1855 by Roger Fenton, an Englishman who was one of the earliest people to see the potential of the camera. He helped to establish the Photographic Society and took pictures of British soldiers during the five months he spent in the Crimea. For the first time in history, the images of war had been captured for posterity. As photography became more mainstream, momentous events in history were recorded which often showed the banalities of war. People seem obsessed with destroying each other and photographers were there to record it. The photographers who got up close to the action themselves were either brave, mad or both. Some led a charmed life but others perished with the soldiers next to them. The Vietnam War was relayed into the living room on a daily basis, to be viewed from the comfort of an armchair. The people who made this happen risked their lives and were often in the thick of action. Some were adrenalin junkies and lived for the 'bang bang' factor, whilst others wanted to capture the realities of war, to show the world these indescribable horrors and man's cruelty to man, none more graphically illustrated than those of the Nazi concentration camps. A photograph could do what a thousand words could not. The image of the naked little Vietnamese girl seen running away from a napalm attack on her village had been indelibly etched in the mind of the viewer forever.

Jeff Richards was a freelance war photographer. He was a lean and wiry Brit who didn't look particularly tough but had remarkable physical and mental strengths. As a hardy, well-seasoned professional who had been around the world, he looked more like a presenter of some gardening programme, ready to get his hands dirty and loving the job. He had covered the troubles in Northern Ireland, Israel, the Falklands War, the first Gulf War, the student uprising in Beijing, the Balkans War, Chechnya and now Afghanistan. He was still single, in his late forties and had never wanted to settle down. Secretly, he was an adrenalin junkie. As a young man, he had done a humdrum job as a clerk of courts, but had soon got fed up of spending hours a day smelling other people's body odour on the tube trains in London. His large reserves of energy had been taken up with karate, but after getting the black belt, there just didn't seen much left in life to achieve. He had applied for law school but had failed to get in. There was no option. He had to quit the job and sell the flat before going on a world tour. Staying in London would have driven him around the bend at that stage of his life.

A year later, he had returned to London with no job or money and stayed with his parents for a short while. He had felt absolutely restless, taken up a photography course at the local polytechnic and had never looked back. He had started doing wedding photographs for a small company, and freelanced for a local newspaper at the same time. Even this was too mundane so he had decided to go to Northern Ireland and photograph the bombings there. At least that was real photography and he had to be on his toes and not tread on others, especially those belonging to the paramilitary people. He had recorded what was legitimate, usually the aftermath of an explosion. The IRA had welcomed that, as it was sending its message out, and Jeff was merely portraying their handy work. He was clever enough to know never to venture into territory where he was not welcomed, but had broken this rule only once. It had been risky, but he had wanted to do an IRA funeral and quickly learnt not to do this again after his camera equipment had been smashed. This was a dirty war and the next man in the pub could easily have killed him because of his English accent.

He had wanted to take pictures of a real war and not just of places which had been blown up. His chance came up with the Falklands War, when he applied to sail with the group of photographers. Apart from his camera equipment, he had learnt to travel light, constantly ready to move at a moment's notice. He always wore German army-issue moleskin combat trousers which were robust and grey in colour, rather than the British army's olive green offering, which was not as thick or as comfortable either. He also liked his dark blue thick cotton t-shirt and his safari waistcoat, containing numerous pockets for the various bits of equipment. A warm Berghaus fleece always stayed in his sixty-five litre dark green Karrimor rucksack, as did his Lafuma waterproofs. He preferred to use heavy-duty walking boots, rather than army-type boots, which were notoriously uncomfortable. Apart for a change of clothes and a blue shirt for wearing whilst shooting the breeze at the bar, he carried little else except for two seventy-five millilitre Sigg aluminium flasks kept in the side pockets of his rucksack, a medical kit and his toiletries.

The camera gear was stowed away in another well padded smaller rucksack, which was waterproofed against the elements. A passport and a small stash of US dollars were kept in a waterproof bag which went with him everywhere, even to the toilet. He could afford to lose his clothes and perhaps his cameras, but not his passport and money.

After flying into Uzbekistan, he found his way to K2, the US military base which saw an increasing amount of activity as the war in Afghanistan heated up. The big battle was going to take place in the north of the country and it was not possible to ship in supplies from the ships stationed out in the Indian Ocean. The patrolling fighter-bombers flying from the aircraft carriers just had enough fuel to get to the combat area and back out. Supplies going into Afghanistan had to come in from a friendly neighbouring country, although this was previously a Soviet territory, a potential diplomatic headache. Despite a fragile relationship between the two superpowers, the Russians fighter base nearby was a reminder that all was not well in this small world. The American presence was a strange new development in a country more used to seeing Russian troops, but since America was the only realistic superpower left in the world which could deal with the Taleban, their purpose was understood and presence just about tolerated.

Jeff hung around the K2 base until he became a familiar face. There were a few Russian pilots loitering around, who had very little to do apart from drink vodka when they were not flying. He ingratiated himself very quickly and it was relatively easy to buy his way onto a flight. He wanted to see Afghanistan at first hand, to get a feel for the country by setting foot on the ground. The Russians had offered to take him with them on their mission to deliver food and equipment to a Mujahadeen village. They could not guarantee his safety and he had to pay up front in US dollars as this was the standard trading currency. There would be one other passenger going to the village. The deal was concluded over more shots of vodkas. He would be flying with them tomorrow and there was a good chance the helicopter would not even make it. They could even be shot down, so why not live for today? He just needed to make sure that he didn't get blind drunk and suffer from a major headache. That would really spoil his ride. He could not wait to go into bandit country and be the first unofficial war photographer to get into Afghanistan. He wanted to take real photos, not the sanitised junk the authorities only allowed once the fighting was over. Tomorrow would just be an orienteering trip, to get a feel of the place. He would figure out how to get to the hot spots and shoot his war later on. For now, he was getting on famously with his newfound friends. He downed another glass of the fiery liquid and felt a course Russian hand slapping him in the back, a sign of being a real comrade.

15

Execution

Day two; time to kick more ass. The Taleban prisoners had been left out in the open overnight with very little food to eat. It was a deliberate policy to make then cold and hungry, to reduce their will to fight. The tactic was legitimate. Two CAS teams had already gone out earlier with the Mujahadeen to seek and destroy more targets, leaving the four soldiers behind to guard the village and the prisoners. None of the Mujahadeen could speak English. It was a bad situation and they desperately needed the interpreter. The big, tough-looking sergeant went to the prisoners' compound just to check up on things. Two of the Mujahadeen had been given the job of being the jailer, but they would rather execute the men. He could sense the seething hostility amongst the Taleban and knew they had murder on their mind. The sergeant had left his rifle behind, but carried a Glock 9 mm automatic pistol in a holster strapped to his right thigh. He needed to make sure they were still tied up nice and tight. These fanatics would kill everybody in the village if they had the chance. Many had the blood of women and children on their hands and they wanted more. The steady beat of a helicopter in the distance became louder, drawing the attention of the Taleban and Mujahadeen alike. It made a ponderous approach over the mountain tops but the sergeant kept his eye on the Taleban. He knew it was the supply helicopter so didn't bother to look up. His buddies would have briefed the village folk of its imminent arrival and they were ready to carry the supplies in.

Jeff Richards was sitting in the back of the noisy Russian helicopter, gently shaken by the vibration. His travelling companion appeared to be a man from these parts, an Afghani who spoke good English. His English was faintly American and Jeff just presumed he was working for them. It was too noisy to talk, although Jeff would have loved to get the inside information. He knew none would be forthcoming if this man worked for the CIA or some other secret agency. The man certainly looked at him with suspicion. They had taken off from the

Uzbekistani base and crossed into Afghanistan without any difficulty, flying through some incredibly beautiful countryside, across winding rivers and lush fields. The helicopter climbed slowly upwards as the mountains approached, struggling to clear the heights. The scenery changed dramatically when they were in the mountainous area and it wasn't long before Russian pilot indicated they were going to land. From the perspex window, Jeff could see them approaching a small village almost in the middle of nowhere, just a sparse piece of emptiness where no sensible tourist would choose to tread. To him, it looked like paradise. The pilot searched and found a suitable landing site just short of the village, in a slightly elevated position. The landing was straightforward and the helicopter touched down with a gentle bump. The engines eased off quickly before the rotor-blades came to a halt. There was no point in wasting precious fuel. Jeff's eardrums had taken a battering and the sudden lack of noise was a relief.

The pilot got off his seat and went into the back of the helicopter before sliding the side door open. There was a sweet smell of aviation fuel and exhaust fumes coming from the helicopter as the dust settled down. Jeff was in Afghanistan, the forbidden country. The interpreter jumped out and headed straight for the village to do his job. Jeff surveyed the scene slowly, taking in the rugged beauty of the place, before getting out of the helicopter. Already people were rushing up from the village to meet them, eager for the supplies. The pilots seemed only too keen to unload the cargo and started to throw out the packages onto the ground. This was no holiday sightseeing trip and they would hate to have the Taleban remove their testicles with a rusty knife. They knew what had happened to the Russian soldiers who were unfortunate enough to be caught in the last war here.

Jeff looked through the viewfinder of his digital SLR camera and focused on the village. He fired off a few shots of the village before panning the camera around. He saw the crowd of people and then a soldier in American-type fatigues with an assault rifle coming towards him. The rifle was being carried almost casually, but Jeff was sure this man knew how to use it. He took a few photos of the people and the soldier before scanning his camera again back to the village, this time concentrating on just one area. He could see a group of men tied up together. They were different from the other Mujahadeen as they were wearing black clothes. Another soldier in combat fatigues was with them, including two local Mujahadeen, judging by their Massoud hats. The soldier seemed to be doing something, perhaps checking the hands of the prisoners, whilst the two Mujahadeen were more interested in looking over to where he was. Jeff could see through his camera lens that the men in black had fierce murderous eyes, even from this distance. Some of the men looked agitated, as if they knew something was going to happen. He was mesmerised by the scene and had to keep his camera on these people. He then saw a brief scuffle before all hell broke loose. The camera kept clicking.

As the sergeant checked each Taleban in turn, one in particular was waiting for his chance to strike. He had managed to slip his hands free from the rope and stayed focused on exacting his revenge. The other men had read the situation and braced themselves for action, despite being bound up. As the sergeant approached, his attention was draw to another man calling from behind him. He lost eye contact for a split second but that was enough. The man saw his chance and made a grab for the sergeant's pistol, trying to remove the Glock from the holster. The sergeant reacted immediately. He punched the fanatical man on the forehead, but the black turban-like material absorbed the blow. The man came at him again; this time he was on his feet and tried to press his thumbs into the sergeant's eyes. The sergeant twisted his head away to stop his eyeballs from being popped out whilst reaching down for his gun with his right hand. The Glock had already been chambered, the round sitting snugly in the barrel. All he had to do was to flick the safety catch off and pull the trigger. He pushed the man off with his left hand as hard as he could whilst bringing up the automatic.

He only had a split second to aim his weapon and shoot before the crazed man came at him again. It was no problem. He put in a double tap into the forehead, freezing the heathen in his tracts. The man dropped dead as his eyes rolled up to his maker. The other Taleban had risen to their feet in anticipation even as their colleague was just seconds from death. They saw him reaching for the gun and prayed he would shoot the American and the two guards, but they were wrong. The Mujahadeen turned their attention on them and pointed their guns. Suddenly, the Glock went off, twice. It was a signal for them to open up. At close range, the 7.62 mm bullets tore into the bodies with sickening thuds, shredding the internal organs from the pressure waves created by the high-velocity bullets. Some came out the other side, creating bloody wounds which looked like raw mince. It was divine providence that they died immediately, but God hadn't been around when they'd taken their time to rape and kill without pity. The Mujahadeen just felt relieved and justified; they didn't have to waste their food on these people now.

Jeff saw the soldier shoot the man twice in the head before the rest were killed by automatic gun fire. From his position, it looked like a deliberate massacre, as the men in the compound were still tied up. The camera had clicked away, taking more than sixty frames of the incident over a space of eight seconds. He did not know who the soldiers were but presumed they were either American or British special forces. He would never be allowed to leave here with the photographs, but he knew he had to.

The soldier coming towards the helicopter had suddenly turned towards the sound of the gunfire. He cocked his weapon and rushed back down into the village with the gun pressing into his right shoulder, ready to fire. The shooting had only lasted for several seconds before it all became quiet again. Jeff saw his opportunity and quickly changed the memory card in the camera. With shaky hands, he popped open the compartment containing the memory card and inserted a fresh one, shoving the used one down into his underpants. He started to snap away again but the pictures he was now taking only showed the aftermath. Several soldiers had appeared and checked over the dead men, turning them over one by one. They all had glazed and unresponsive eyes. Although Jeff was not unduly disturbed to see dead bodies, he felt slightly nauseated at the thought of witnessing a massacre. Everything seemed to have happened very slowly, as if time had been suspended. The images had been captured on camera and they would be absolutely sensational. It was a real problem trying not to shake from the emotional drama. He desperately wanted to get back on the helicopter and take off with his pictures safely tucked away in his underpants.

The Mujahadeen around about him could see that he looked green and sweaty. They presumed he was shaken by the sight of men getting killed and smiled at him in mock sympathy. The soldier had now returned in double-quick time, but he was not smiling. He came straight up to Jeff and didn't play with his words.

'Who the fuck are you?' he asked in an American accent.

'And who are you, dear chap?' Jeff replied, in a quaint but mock-British accent.

'Don't fuck with me. I asked you, who are you?' He was angry.

'My name is Jeff Richards. I'm a British war photographer.'

'Did you get clearance to come out here?' he asked again.

'No, I'm freelance.' He could see the special forces soldier was not happy.

'I don't give a fuck about you arseholes. Is that the only camera you got on you?'

'No, I've got a compact as well in my pocket,' Jeff replied.

'Are they digital?'

'Yes.'

'Give me the memory sticks.' He simply demanded them.

Jeff didn't argue. He removed both the one-gigabyte compact flash cards from the cameras. He was going to lose a lot of shots but he was hoping the soldier would not search him.

'Look, I only used the big camera. Can I keep the memory from the compact camera? It has a lot of photos that has nothing to do with this place.' Jeff tried to argue, knowing very well that he did not mind losing both the flash cards so long as he had the important one.

'That's just tough. I am going to tell you this once. I don't like you people and I don't want to see your ass around here. What you saw back there was jack shit. Shoot your mouth off and I'll come for you, no matter where you are. You got that? Now give me the memory cards and fuck off,' he shouted.

The soldier was in a bad mood and Jeff just did as he was told. The Russian pilots didn't want to get involved with this situation and were only too glad to leave as soon as possible. Thankfully, he was not body searched, which came as a relief. The soldier had screwed up big time and if he was angry now, he was going to be mightily pissed off when these pictures make the front page news. Killing the enemy in combat was fine, but not when they were tied up.

Jeff was only too glad when the doors slammed shut and the helicopter engines burst into life once more. The Russian pilots gave him a 'thumbs up' sign and increased the power before the lumbering machine slowly lifted off the ground. Jeff had one last look through the window. He could still see the soldier glaring at him from the ground through the fine layer of dust. He quickly reinserted the compact flash card into the SLR camera and fired off a few hasty shots of the soldier. The helicopter turned around after gaining some height and headed north towards Uzbekistan. Jeff's heart was pounding furiously when he realised that he had just got the scoop of a lifetime. The memory would not leave him, especially of the murderous look on the soldier's face. He was probably a psycho killer.

16

Euphoria

They had made back it in one piece to the bleak Uzbekistani base. Jeff Richards was totally elated at having got away with the photographs; his nervous system had been nearly fried from the tension. The journey in the rickety helicopter had seemed to take for ever and he prayed hard the engine wouldn't conk out. His camera contained some hardcore shots of what had essentially been a massacre by the coalition forces. This was going to be extremely controversial and cause a huge political uproar when the world woke up to these images. The special forces were notorious for avoiding any publicity and this stuff could invite a lot of trouble. It was also worth a lot of money. The situation in Afghanistan was extremely dangerous and to go back there once these pictures had been published would be suicidal. Accidents had a habit of happening to those who didn't make friends; it would be his first and only trip there. The special forces could roam the countryside with impunity, but they had the backup of the biggest military machine in the world. Freelance photographers were at the mercy of anybody who wished them dead. It would be a while before the regular troops were on the ground and even then, most photographers were escorted to designated areas where the military wanted them to be. Jeff knew he had been lucky, but there was a time when luck would run out. The soldier meant his words and Jeff knew if was time to get the fuck out. He had already made the decision to get back to the UK and quit being a war photographer.

Once safely back in London, his job was to sell the photographs to the highest bidder by contacting all the major newspapers and current affairs magazines. It wasn't long before an offer came along. The buyer wanted to remain anonymous and Jeff was not about to ask questions. The sum was reasonable, but not as much as he had hoped for. The photos would not be published, that much he knew, but it was also an offer he should accept. The threat was not overt, but the message had been very clear. Not being able to see his pictures printed in the papers was a blow to his personal pride but common sense told him to take

100

the money and shut up. Even with £40,000 in the bank, he needed to work. Reaching fifty was proving to be a difficult age and he could not keep on doing this job for much longer. The stress of working in a war zone was starting to play havoc with his body. Already the odd bout of palpitations and chest pains had started, which he knew was the first sign of heart trouble. Even his blood pressure had not been checked for a while. It was time to settle down and get a less demanding job. To get a decent sleep without the fear of getting bombed would be a nice. His body badly needed some attention after eating all the crap they served in those godforsaken countries. War had a way of stripping the goodness from the land and while the politicians waged war, the people often starved.

He heard about Glampic on the grapevine. They had a vacancy for an experienced photographer with special skills. Initially, he wondered if this involved taking pornographic pictures, but the job actually required a professional who could snap celebrities without being seen. It required the art of camouflage and after crawling around in war zones, this would be a piece of cake. The risks were lower and there wouldn't be bullets flying around, unless he took some photos of some rap star who felt 'dissed'. Respect today had a different meaning and this usually meant the size of somebody's gun rather than grey matter. He needed to work and it did not matter what sort of photographs he took, even if it was of self-important hoods with oversized medallions.

He applied to Glampic, got the job, and got on famously with Ricky Deans. They bonded with a serious amount of champagne and good cognac. Stuff Afghanistan, this was much better; the only loud pop came from the champagne bottle. There was no point in working himself to death any more, he thought.

17

The Game

The phone rang twice before the man in the pin-striped suit reached out for the receiver.

'Hello,' he answered in the usual measured tone.

'There have been some developments. There will be a public inquiry about the incident after all,' the other voice said. It was equally polished and obviously public school.

'Damn it! Why can't they just leave it alone! The French have already stated the cause of the accident,' he replied.

'Somebody has collated all the eye witness reports onto a website. We have been monitoring it and numerous claims are being made. The most serious one involves a claim that the driver was seen being injected with something immediately after the accident.'

'Are there any photographs of this?' he asked.

'No. The French police confiscated them all.'

'Is this something we need to worry about?' he asked worriedly.

'Not unless there is some credible witness. It was rather dark in tunnel after all.'

'What about the paparazzi? Have they said anything?'

'They gave the usual statements to the police. Most were several hundred yards away when the crash happened, but at least one of them was in the tunnel at the time of the crash. The rest arrived shortly afterwards.'

'Was there a particular statement from this person?'

'We don't have any direct transcripts but our French sources have indicated what was in them. We should remember that the motorcycles were ridden by professional bikers, hired for the occasion and the paparazzi were on the back. Both the paparazzo and the rider stated that they saw another biker tending to the driver. They thought the person had injected something into the driver, perhaps in an attempt to save him.'

'Damn, can we get the Paris people to sort this out?'

'I'll speak to them but the paparazzo was British.'

'We have to do something about that. Could you see to it?'

'Yes, of course. By the way, something interesting has just turned up.'

'Go on.'

'Our contact at one of the newspapers has just informed us that somebody is trying to sell some photographs taken in Afghanistan. They show some kind of massacre going on.'

'Is that a problem for us if these people are butchering each other?'

'No, except when possibly the American special forces were involved. Several faces could be clearly identified from the photographs. One of them shot a man at point-blank range in the head. It looked like an execution and we have some of the photocopies.'

'Are we sure they are genuine rather than fakes?'

'I think they are genuine.'

'That was a little untidy. Do we know they were American for sure?'

'Yes, we think they were Green Berets. No SAS assets were in the area.'

'Who is the source?'

'It's a British war photographer. He is bona fide.'

'Hmmm, I think it would be wise not to upset our American friends just when the war has just started. What do you suggest?'

'I suggest we do them a favour and buy them.'

'How many photographs are there?'

'About twenty, I'm told.'

'Okay, buy them. Offer him a fair price on the condition that we have all the copies. Send them to the Americans with our compliments, but keep a copy. This material could cause an unholy stink if it went public.'

'Yes, I thought much the same. I'll speak to their people. I just hope the photographer isn't too greedy because it won't go down well with the finance people. Should we mention his name to the Americans?'

'Yes, do that.'

The conversation ended. It would be up to the Americans to do as they wanted with the photographs and they would no doubt investigate the matter, horrified lest it should go public. Atrocities went on in any war, especially after a battle when emotions were running high from the adrenalin rush and from seeing members of your own platoon or battalion getting killed in action. A well trained and disciplined army should not harm or kill their prisoners but it went on. Sometimes the situation got out of control and overwhelming desire to shoot everything which moved became too much to contain. It happened in Vietnam and it would happen again. The best way to keep quiet about a massacre was to dispose of any evidence, especially photographs and eye witnesses.

18

GMC

The General Medical Council was established under the Medical Act of 1858. It was essentially the governing body of the medical profession, with effective legal powers to strike a doctor off from the medical register. They were not there to protect bad doctors, but rather to protect members of the public from bad doctors. It was often a sceptical point of view, but the knowledge, skills and attitudes of poorly performing doctors were often scrutinised in microscopic detail, should they come to light. Doctors could be struck off for a variety of reasons, including medical negligence and sexual harassment. Intimate medical examinations were not usually necessary for chest infections, but a rectal examination could just pick up the undiagnosed bowel tumour. It was an ethical dilemma. Most people tolerated the rectal but abuse could be just a difference of opinion.

The council itself was made up of thirty-five members, comprising nineteen doctors, fourteen laymen and two academics, appointed by educational bodies such as the universities and medical royal colleges. They had the authority to decide on serious cases where harm had been caused by the incompetent or unethical actions of the doctor. Despite its powers, the GMC had no way of spotting the rogue medic until it was too late. Psychometric testing of potential medical students had been considered to weed out the undesirables, but to detect the potential mass murderer amongst them was a different issue. It was not an exact science. Killers masquerading as doctors have been noted in history.

The single-handed general practitioner knew his luck would run out at some time. It had to. After graduating from medical school, he worked at a district general hospital before becoming a GP. His addiction to the morphine-like drug pethidine was only discovered after his blackouts and forged prescriptions. Following his conviction at the Magistrate's Court, he was dismissed by the medical practice but sought help immediately by admitting himself to the local hospital. This undoubtedly saved his career, but he was barred from doing jobs which gave him access to drugs. Despite this restriction, he managed to work as a clinical medical officer in another hospital. Luck stayed with him and he was able to join a different medical practice. The lure of morphine was too strong and it was a need he couldn't run away from. The risk of being caught again was high and this would definitely destroy his career for good. There was no other option. He had to set up his own practice by taking as many patients with him as possible. That would not be a problem as the patients loved his bedside manner. Being his own boss meant nobody watched his prescribing methods. Morphine was easy to come by again, which fed his habit. Something, however, was gnawing away at his mind. He felt like a slave to the calling, something he had to obey as if drawn towards the edge of another darker world. Lucifer beckoned unto him, promising him the ultimate pleasure.

Suspicions of malpractice had started to come out of the woods. The local undertakers had noticed the high death rate was especially amongst the little old ladies who lived alone. It was bad to question things when business was good, but something was amiss. Even the doctors at the neighbouring surgery had also noticed the unusual death rate. They had been asked to countersign a steady stream of cremation forms for patients who had died suddenly despite having showed no signs of any recent illnesses. The dead patients had either been found by the doctor himself or by their relatives, shortly after he had seen them. The coroner had grown alarmed at the number of death certificates and cremation forms coming into the office. The police were informed of this, but couldn't act until some proof came to hand. It duly did.

An elderly widow had suddenly failed to turn up at a charity function where she normally volunteered to serve meals to the other old-aged pensioners. Following her death, a new and recent will was produced by the solicitor. The original was totally different in its content; the whole estate had now been left to the doctor. The will was challenged by the dead woman's daughter and the police now had sufficient grounds to intervene. Forensic evidence found traces of diamorphine in the woman's body, the probable cause of death. A typewriter had been found at the doctor's surgery, used to forge the will. Medical records had also been altered. The doctor was charged with murder. Greed had been his undoing but his addiction had not been confined to morphine alone; killing had become his bête noire. Lucifer had indeed been correct; the taking of a human life had become more addictive than anything else. He enjoyed the power of giving life or death, of playing God. Whilst providing excellent care to most of his patients, he also killed without any remorse or guilt, running into hundreds.

Enter the mind of the serial killer. The psychopathic brain, unhinged from the norms of reality, made killing a pleasure. The genetic make-up predisposed the psychopath to a journey of deviancy, triggered by the various adverse life events during the formative years of childhood. Everybody had the potential to kill; to some it just came more naturally. Some children enjoyed torturing and killing animals; they just moved on to people. Killing a patient with morphine was technically easy to do just as it was easy to justify using it; severe pain and distress were good indications. In suspicious situations, the coroner had to decide whether the use of morphine had contributed to the cause of death. It was a thin line between administering pain relief and killing, no matter if the person was riddled with cancer. The law was clear on this issue. The GMC had a more difficult decision to make. When is adequate pain relief ever enough and was the doctor competent to make that decision? True killers in the profession were rare and they were simply struck off the register when the courts were done.

Nick Forbes had lived in dread whilst the GMC deliberated its verdict. They could ultimately find no fault with his clinical decision so he was not negligent. There was also no proof that he had deliberately tried to harm the patient so no criminal proceeding could be pursued. There would be no disciplinary action taken against him, but several recommendations would be made to the hospital in order to ensure good clinical practice.

The white envelope duly dropped through his letterbox, which he opened with trepidation. He felt relieved after reading the contents and immediately phoned James Townell to say he had been cleared by the GMC. He was told to relax before getting back to work, not the next day, but the day after. It was generous of him. Nick didn't care as he was just glad to get the weight lifted from his shoulders. He was suddenly at a loss as to what to do, having been so emotionally distressed over many weeks. His nerves were frayed and he never wanted to be investigated by the GMC again. Despite the GMC's clear mandate, many in the UK still regarded the GMC as an organisation run by doctors for the doctors. The GMC, in reality, had a very tough job to do by maintaining the highest standards possible within the profession. Changes to the death certification procedures should prevent another psychopathic doctor from killing large numbers of patients without detection. It would make no business sense to kill off too many patients, in any case, as the average general practitioner made more money from a bigger list size. Nick wasn't paid by the number of patients he had, but killing them would be bad for his career. Despite his tough upbringing, he wasn't a psychopath.

19

Backstab

Nick got a message from the medical director via his secretary to say he wanted to see him to discuss a few issues. An appointment had been arranged for the next day, but he felt glad somebody had bothered to phone him. It was just a formality, he presumed. The press had long gone away after losing interest in the story and it was time to move on and put all this behind him.

He woke up bright and breezy and even made some filtered coffee before driving to the hospital. He parked in the staff car park across from the administration building and walked in confidently. He was shown to the medical director's room by the secretary, but he knew where it was anyway. She wasn't smiling today; perhaps it was her time of the month.

'Hello, Nick. Thanks for coming. Sit down,' Bob McLean said in a serious tone.

'Hello. I presume you've heard from James Townell that the GMC have dropped the case?' Nick said without much emotion, wondering why Bob was being a little unfriendly today.

'Yes, I did. We have discussed this whole business with the chief executive, the hospital administrators and the nursing authorities. They are a little less happy with things as they stand,' Bob said.

'Why, what do you mean?' Nick was confused.

'I believe that you and Sister Wallis had suggested that one of the staff nurses was to blame for this incident.' Bob let his words sink in deliberately.

Nick tried to figure out what the opening gambit was all about. Bob's body language gave some clue that this wasn't about a cosy chat. Nick had to consider his response and decided to go for the straight approach.

'Yes, we found a ten-milligram vial of diamorphine amongst the thirty-milligram vials. It was quite clear that somebody had switched them around. The pharmacist took them away at the request of the chief executive and senior nursing officer. Did you know about this?' Nick asked.

'I am aware of Sister Wallis's report, but the situation remains that the nurse in question has denied any knowledge of this. We also don't have any proof regarding the diamorphine vials. This has put us and the hospital in a very awkward position,' Bob replied.

'I don't understand. The pharmacist who took the thirty-milligram vials away must have noticed the ten-milligram vial,' Nick said.

'I have personally checked the DDA book and can see that the duty pharmacist had removed the thirty-milligram vials but there was no mention of anything else. I also checked with the chief pharmacist and all of the diamorphine vials have all been destroyed.'

'Sister Wallis and I saw the ten-milligram vial,' Nick said desperately.

'I would like to believe you but there is no proof of that. This situation has left a nasty feeling amongst the staff in the Casualty department and it is destroying morale. This matter must be settled quickly, which I'm sure you'll agree, but we basically have an unsolvable problem on our hands. The hospital will have to take the blame for this anyway and our lawyers may even suggest we settle out of court. I don't need to tell you that we are already in a poor financial position and a big claim could sink us. It would mean closing another ward or losing more staff,' Bob said coldly.

'So what are you really saying?' Nick asked.

'The chief executive has recommended that you resign from this hospital, but we will obviously support you in your application for another job. We appreciate that you have less than a year to go to complete your SpR training, but we can speak to some people and find you a slot somewhere else, even in London. People will soon forget about the press article,' Bob said.

'There is something funny going on and you know it. Brenda Hawkins drew up that diamorphine and it was she who made the mistake, not me. This matter is not over as far as I am concerned, so you can forget about my resignation,' Nick replied calmly.

The anger was welling up but there was no red mist this time. He just felt a calm detachment descend over him with a strange steely determination to get to the bottom of this diabolical situation. It was only too obvious some conspiracy was going on and Bob had somehow gone along with it. Nick had lost any respect he once had for the medical director. If this was medical politics, it stank, but he still had a lot to learn. Bob struggled to look at him straight in the eye. He should have been Nick's mentor but he was now nothing more than a backstabber, a person beneath contempt. The pain of betrayal speared through his chest as he listened to the medical director's words. He was to be the sacrificial lamb rather than the nurse, but he wasn't about to walk away without a fight. It was time to throw down the gauntlet and challenge the hierarchy, and somehow, it felt good. Bob tried one last throw of the dice to win him over, but to what purpose?

'Nick, you're a young man with a great career in front of you. Don't make things harder for yourself. It may prove to be difficult to get a consultant's post if you intend to be difficult. Nobody here wants to see that happen, but you must understand that your reputation will go before you, especially if you make it very obvious,' Bob said.

'I think you have said enough and I don't like to be threatened. You can take it from me that I will be returning to my post on Monday and you can pass that message on to the chief executive. There are no grounds for my dismissal and you know it. There has been incompetence and corruption somewhere along the line and I plan to find out. Believe me,' Nick said.

He walked out of the office after giving Bob a final look of disgust. For the first time in weeks, he felt mentally strong, enough to challenge wrongdoers, but the odds were against him; it was nothing new. The nurse had made the mistake and tried to cover her tracks. It added to the crime, but she wasn't taking the rap. So what was going on? He went down to A & E to look for Meg. The other staff members saw him walk in and just acknowledged his presence without trying to engage in a conversation. They still felt uneasy, but it was nothing personal. Meg looked subdued but she sparked up a little when she saw him. It was obvious that this was not the place to talk. She decided to take her break and suggested they went to the staff canteen. Tongues would wag but it was nothing new. They deliberately said very little until they got there.

'I've just been to see the medical director,' Nick suddenly announced.

'Oh yes? How did you get on?' Meg replied curiously.

'Basically, they said Brenda Hawkins had denied any wrongdoing and they wanted me to resign. She has obviously lied about everything and, by implication, blamed me instead. The thing I don't understand is why they should believe her rather than me? I have done absolutely nothing wrong to upset the management,' Nick said, trying to be rational.

'Yes, its odd, isn't it? They have also given me a hard time and suggested we made a mistake about the diamorphine vial. What do you think about that?' Meg said.

'I don't know but something is going on. Apparently, the ten-milligram vial was not noticed by the pharmacist who took it away,' Nick replied.

'What? They said that? Sorry, Nick. I was stupid enough not to have documented the vials in the presence of the pharmacist or another witness. I just presumed the pharmacist would do that automatically. Do you suppose they just conveniently buried the evidence, or did the pharmacist really not check the vials? The DDA key can be held by any number of people during the day, but it was usually the charge nurse of the shift who had it.' Meg was annoyed at her own carelessness.

'Why would they cover this up? Is there something we are missing? Why would somebody believe a nurse any more than they would me? What do you know about Brenda? Has she got any connections?' Nick suddenly saw Meg's eyes open a little wider as she nearly choked on her coffee.

'Oh my God, you had just hit the nail on the head. I think she is the chief executive's daughter! Why didn't I think of that? That would make total sense. It wasn't well known because Brenda never talked about it. At least she was quite professional that way,' Meg said.

'Are you sure about this?' Nick asked.

'Well, she has the same surname. I wasn't on the interview panel but I had seen all the CVs of the people who were applying for the staff nurse job. Her CV was as good as anybody else's and somebody had mentioned it as a joke that she could be related to the chief executive because of their surnames. It was actually the senior nursing officer who hinted that she might be, but none of the other sisters took it seriously. I have no idea if the decision went in her favour because of who her mother was, but I think she had interviewed well and got the job on her own merits. That was why I never gave the matter any thought and never associated her with the chief executive. What do you think we should do about this, Nick?' Meg looked worried.

'I don't know, but I have an idea,' Nick said.

Information was king and a devious thought had just crossed his mind. A self-knowing smile melted across his mouth. Maybe it was payback time, but Meg could sense he was in a fighting mood. Somehow, the gleam in his eye was different to the way he had looked recently; it didn't say loser any more. She felt the mood had mellowed enough to poke some fun. It made a nice change.

'Oh, Nick, you're so masterful!' She returned his gaze with a gentle smile.

'Cut the crap or I'll pull your wings off, Tinkerbell. I'm heading off now but why don't you phone me at home later. We need to talk about this,' Nick said.

'Yes, sir!'

'Go take a jump!'

He stood up and walked away with a wide grin on his face. She followed him with her eyes. She was falling in love with a younger man.

20

Payback

Nick went out to the car park and climbed into the Audi, minding to watch his head on the low frame. The door closed with the same satisfying thump. The 225 brake horsepower under his right foot was driven through four wheels, but before starting the engine he thought about the matter. Everything was so blatantly obvious. In an attempt to cover up for the chief executive's daughter, he would take the blame. The fallout would have reached all the way to the top if they couldn't find a scapegoat. The medical director was in cahoots with the chief executive, totally disregarding Nick's own career. He was in no doubt that a glowing reference would have eased his passage to another hospital, providing he had towed the line and cited personal reasons for wanting to relocate. The whole matter would then have been put to bed with an out of court settlement. Nick would have resumed his career at another hospital and everybody would have been happy ever after. Wrong; he had other ideas. He whipped out his wallet from the back pocket and found the card. Paul Lewis had several numbers but the mobile was the best bet; it was now an indispensable tool of modern life. Paul answered immediately.

'Hello, who's this?' he asked with his London accent.

'It's Nick Forbes,' Nick replied in his soft Edinburgh accent.

Paul was surprised to hear the voice. Nick was one person he could not forget; he didn't fight with just with anybody.

'Nick! How are you, mate? It's a surprise to hear from you. What's up, doc?' he said, to mimic the well-known cartoon character.

'Listen, Paul, can I pick your brains about something?' Nick asked.

'You can try but there's not much of it,' Paul replied

'I'm having some problems at work and I wanted to know if you can help me in some way. Is there somewhere we could meet up later?' Nick asked.

'I'm out on a job just now so I don't know how long it will take. But there's nothing happening right now so why don't you tell me about it on the mobile?' Paul suggested.

'Well, basically I wondered if you knew of any journalist who could dig some up some information for me,' Nick wanted to know.

'Ermm, I only know some dodgy hacks which I would not recommend. But I do know a man who might be able to help you. It's my boss, Ricky. He knows everybody to know in the business. Do you want me to speak to him?' Paul asked.

'Well, I need a journalist to find out something which is in the public interest. Could you ask if he will see me? I'm free all day today,' Nick said.

'I'll phone you right back.' Nick's number had been logged in the SIM card. It rang two minutes later.

'Nick, yeah, it's cool. Ricky will see you at the office. If you're coming from Palmers Green or from the hospital, head for Turnpike Lane, then straight down to Finsbury Park, down into Caledonian Road into King's Cross. Swing a left into Pentonville Road. The office is in a mews courtyard about a hundred yards up. Don't go too fast or you'll miss it. The company is called Glampic. You got that okay?' Paul asked to make sure.

'Thanks, Paul, I'll catch up with you later,' Nick said.

'By the way, Ricky knows it was you who smashed up his camera. Just ignore his language. He's a fat bastard.' It was his term of endearment. Paul rang off.

Nick smiled as he started the car and drove out of the hospital gates. He liked Paul's way of putting things, succinct and to the point. He turned left and then right at the crossroad before heading down the road which joined the A10 just a little further down from the large junction. The Audi TT powered down the road with ease, although the turbo charged engine wasn't the smoothest in the world. It needed a V6 and Audi knew that. He kept an eye out for the speed cameras; three points on his licence was enough. Despite the traffic, he made it down to King's Cross in good time as he managed to weave in and out of the traffic. London driving was getting easier and he found the place quite easily. Several parking places were still available in the courtyard. A lurid sign hung above the entrance. The designer must have been inspired by dodgy chemicals or perhaps he was a genius. It captured the essence of the company. The sign was not discreet but big and brash.

Nick strode towards the main door and went in. Inside, the foyer was lined with worn linoleum and smelt musty. Beyond the foyer was an office area which was visible through the upper glass partition, the bottom half was made up of blue painted wood. It was definitely 70s kitsch but nobody seemed bothered. Nick had to go through another door to get into the office inside. The office was essentially open-plan with various desks scattered about. Several people looked up when he walked in and one of the young girls spoke to him.

'Hello, what can I do for you?' she asked.

'Hi, I'm looking for Ricky. My name is Nick. He is expecting me,' Nick replied.

'Rick, somebody for you!' she shouted.

'Well, show him in then!' he bellowed back.

Ricky was in the inner office, which was essentially an office within an office. Nick was shown in and beckoned to sit down as he was on the phone. The room was filled with a mixture of cigarette smoke and expensive aftershave.

'Just give me a good price; it's a fantastic photo taken by my best snapper. I can get a lot more for that so don't insult me. She's got a nice pair, believe me. Speak to me later.' He put the phone down before standing up, and offered his hand to Nick, which had a heavy gold chain dangling from the wrist.

'Hi, you must be Nick,' Ricky said.

Nick saw in front of him a larger-than-life character. This type of man could ruin your holiday on the Costa del Sol. He was loud in every sense of the word: vocally, mannerism, dress-sense and attitude, in equal measures. Nick felt a little lost about what to say or think. First impressions were important and this just blew him away. This man looked like a lager lout who drank champagne. He was the epitome of a nightmare rather than the discreet and professional journalist. There was no way he would discuss anything confidential with this man, but being polite cost nothing. He struggled to speak but somehow got the words out.

'Hi. Paul said you may know of somebody who could possibly help me. I'm really looking for a journalist,' Nick said.

'Well, I'm not a journalist but I know a few. What is it you want to discuss?' Rick now gave his full attention and his demeanour had already changed from lager lout to an attentive priest. Nick felt compelled to confess.

'It's a difficult matter and I can't say too much because of confidentiality issues,' he muttered.

'Yeah, I know about your problem. I sent Paul to take your picture because it was a juicy story. Some guy died after you gave him morphine. That's old news now so your picture won't fetch much money. Relax, there's nothing in it for me but it's up to you if you want to give me your angle on it. If it makes things any easier, we also heard that it was some nurse who made up the morphine injection so you have nothing to worry about. You can tell us who it is and I'll make sure she gets in the news. Is that what you want from me?' Ricky came to the point quickly.

Nick had to be very careful with his words. Obviously the word had leaked out about the nurse's involvement. It would be very easy to land her in the brown stuff but he wanted the whole truth to come out. He had to tell Ricky something without breaching any patient confidentiality.

'All I can really say on the matter is that it wasn't me who made the mistake but there has been a cover-up. You have already heard about the nurse's involvement, but some people within the hospital hierarchy are still trying to put the blame on me. I think the nurse in question is the chief executive's daughter. A lot of questions would be asked if that was true. It seems I am expendable, but I would still feel a little guilty if I gave you the nurse's name. I'm sure you know already,' Nick said.

'Alright, Nick, I'll see what I can do. It sounds like you've been shafted, mate. These people are outrageous!' He said that with mock concern, knowing full well that his line of business was not only outrageous but downright obnoxious most of the time. He continued. 'Oh, here's Jeff, he's one of the new guys. Jeff! Come in here for a minute.' Jeff heard his name being called and saw Ricky gesturing for him to come into office, in a similar way the mountain came to Mohammed. 'This is Nick. He's a surgeon so be nice to him because you might need a new hip someday after all those bombs you've been dodging!' He laughed at his own joke.

'Hello, Nick. We don't often get surgeons in here. Is Ricky asking for a beer belly reduction?' He was laughing also. There was a refreshing friendly atmosphere about the place.

'Jeff, Nick is the guy who's involved with the bloke who died at the hospital but he didn't do it, right! I want you to get some pictures of the chief executive from the hospital, preferably at her house. Find out where she lives. I'm going to speak to one of the press boys so I'll need the pictures quick to get the story out. Nick is being a real gentleman, he won't tell us the name of the nurse who did it but she could be the chief executive's daughter so get her mug shot as well. I think her name is Brenda Hawkins. And you never saw Nick, okay?' Ricky said.

Ricky knew it was the best thing to keep Nick out of this business. Nick had already given them enough information for them to piece the whole thing together. At the end of the day, Nick had not actually revealed the nurse's name. It remained to be seen if the paparazzi could keep their source of information quiet. If Nick was unsure about coming here in the first place, he was definitely worried now. This whole thing could go out of control very quickly and the story could blow up in his face, especially if he was seen taking to the paparazzi. Ricky could see Nick was worried. People generally had a problem in trusting him, but a man in a smart suit was no more trustworthy. This story had some mileage; it just smacked of skulduggery. Besides, it was in the public interest to expose the incompetent and duplicitous bureaucrats in the NHS. Ricky felt obliged to say something to Nick.

'Listen, Nick. There are two kinds of people in this world. They are the winners and the losers. From what I can see, these people don't want you to win simply because they have a lot to lose themselves. If somebody tried to do that to me, I would hit them hard first with whatever I've got. You're doing the right thing, mate,' he said.

'I'm a little bit concerned about this whole thing, for obvious reasons,' Nick said.

'You're doing the right thing by standing up for yourself. I respect that in a man. We'll nail them for what they are and they won't know what's hit them. Just sit tight. It will be okay,' Ricky said.

Ricky was in control. He already knew how the printed article would read. With his pictures, it was going to be a bloody good story. Nick was less sure. He could envisage this whole thing going horribly wrong and be dragged into the quagmire of litigation. It all felt very wrong somehow and perhaps he should not have approached the paparazzi, but it had seemed like a good idea at the time. Ricky seemed to be a decent guy, despite his outward appearance. He didn't once mention about the broken camera and he wasn't really a 'fat bastard' as Paul had called him. He was a little overweight but it suited his image as a man who enjoyed enjoying himself. Nick went back to his car and drove home in the rush-hour traffic, feeling somewhat indifferent. He had taken the initiative and fired a shot back at his tormentors. As Ricky said, there were winners and losers. It was a sad reflection that the world had come to this but the order of nature dictated that the weak did not inherit the earth.

Fuck you, Nick thought. He was beginning to think like Ricky Deans.

21

Gotcha

It was easy enough to find the chief executive's house, although it was ex-directory. Jeff had asked one of the girls in the office to do it. She had phoned the hospital and managed to speak to the chief executive directly, saying it was the Wine Society. She explained they had a case of wine for her and as there was nobody in, could the delivery man possibly leave it with one the neighbours? Before doing so, she needed to verify the address to make sure they were at the right house. The girl sounded very polite and professional and the chief executive was only too delighted to receive the present from a Wine Society member. She presumed it was one of the hospital consultants wanting some favour or other. Leaving the case of wine with her neighbour would be no problem. Jeff would also head out there later. Taking a photograph outside somebody's house always had a big psychological impact. It simply said: We know where you are and we can get you any time we want. Everybody liked a bit of scandal from time to time, so why not if it was on the doorstep? It made the world tick and the chief executive was about to get some very unwanted media attention. To bad about the Englishman's castle being his home; a person could now be prosecuted for beating up a burglar. Press intrusion happened all the time and there was little anybody could do. Political correctness did not extend to shooting them or burglars.

Jeff drove out to the house and parked a little distance away but made sure he had a clear view of the house. From where he was, he could easily see the main door. The detached house was in one of the more upmarket housing developments in Buckhurst Hill, to the east of London. The light was beginning to fade in the October afternoon, long shadows leaning over the leafy neighbourhood. It was unlikely he was going to get a good shot if the light dropped much more, but at least he knew the location for next time. He decided to wait a little while longer, just to see if he could even catch a glimpse of her. Even seeing what sort of car she drove would tell him something about his target.

He may need to follow her around, just snooping a little. She would eventually twig on this, but hopefully not before he had his shots.

It was just after 6 p.m. when he saw the dark blue X-type Jaguar going up the drive, stopping for a few seconds at the double garage doors as they opened by remote control. The car entered and the door closed silently behind it. There had to be an internal door from the garage to the house, he surmised. He could not see the woman at all from where he was and hanging around would be totally pointless. He would return early next day, but it was kebab time now, a large doner was definitely on the cards. It saved time cooking and, despite his age, he didn't have five bellies yet. Defying the laws of the middle-age spread had been his good fortune.

The next morning turned out to be wet and grey. The car was a little steamy on the inside due to the condensation, but he could see the house clearly enough through the semi-open window. Several people in the estate had already left for work well before eight o'clock, and he presumed she would be leaving soon. The garage door suddenly opened and the Jaguar reversed out before closing automatically. This time all he could see was an image of a woman behind the glass window of the car, but he managed to fire off a few shots as she drove past. This was a neighbourhood watch scheme, so his car must have been noticed already. He would try once more at the weekend or perhaps get her photo at the hospital. He decided to come back, but this time, the ubiquitous white van would be used. They were indispensable to painters and decorators but also attracted less attention; just what he needed.

He parked in the same spot on the Saturday. He came prepared for what could be a long wait. A newspaper, flask of coffee and several packets of crisps were piled on the spare seat. This was the most boring part of the job, sometimes mind-numbingly so. It lacked the excitement of being in a war zone but at least it was safe. He did not see any activity at the house and prayed she was in. All he knew was that she was in her late forties and had either been divorced or separated. This information had been given to him by the girls at work, but how they had got it was a mystery. It was their business to know and, just like any good dog, it was their business to sniff out anything whiffy.

Jeff's luck was in. Shortly before 10 a.m., a car rolled up the drive and stopped just outside the garage. He put down his plastic mug of coffee onto the dashboard and reached for his camera; it had a 300 mm lens on. A man in his early fifties climbed out and walked up to the front door. Jeff pointed the camera towards the man and fired off a few shots. As far as he could see, the man was about six feet tall and he had greyish hair, thinning slightly at the top. He rang the doorbell and it was opened by the woman in her dressing gown. She seemed happy to see him and gave him a quick kiss on the lips. The camera went into overdrive as Jeff kept his finger on the button, firing off more than thirty shots. The man turned very quickly to take a last look at his car before going in. Maybe it was his second love. In the space of a split second, Jeff had managed to catch a good shot of them kissing. The door closed.

In total, over forty shots had been taken in only a short space of time. Jeff flicked the camera into replay mode and scrolled through the frames. There were all good shots but the kissing one was the best. That would do very nicely. Having done an easy morning's work, he could now go home now knowing that Ricky would be happy. Yesterday's kebab had worked its way down and he was glad to get away in any case, hopefully home in time before the irritable bowel got to him.

22

Assassin

Jeff breezed into the office on Monday feeling smug with himself. He handed the flashcard to one of the girls, who plugged it into a PC. The images were downloaded and printed off in hard copy whilst he made himself a coffee. Ricky was already there, but he looked somewhat subdued after a heavy weekend of over-indulgence. His hair had only been gelled half-heartedly and he belched loudly, fighting off the indigestion caused by the black coffee on his empty stomach. The headache was something else. The lobster thermidor and champagne for lunch yesterday had unusually started off his stomach problem. Perhaps it was the beginnings of a stomach ulcer and his body was just trying to tell him something. Everything could be abused until it started to fight back.

'Oh bloody hell, my head hurts. Someone get me some aspirins. Jeff, what have you got?' Aspirins may be good for the head but definitely not the stomach.

'I managed to get some shots of the woman but there's a good one of her giving some guy a kiss at the doorstep.' He showed Ricky all the photographs. Despite his sore head, Ricky made a snap decision.

'Oi, Cath, get this to Billy at that trashy newspaper he works for and get him to run the story with these photos. He knows what to do.' Ricky was referring to one of the tacky tabloids.

'How much are we charging for this one?' Cath asked.

'Tell him it's his birthday. He owes me one!' Ricky replied.

'Miracles will never cease,' she said sarcastically, with a smile.

'Talking of miracles, get me one for this bloody head,' Ricky said.

'Miracles don't happen for self-inflicted conditions now!' Cath replied with her Irish wisdom.

'Piss off. Tell the surgeon chap we have got some pictures for him. Email them to him if he wants. Now I don't want to be disturbed,' Ricky ordered.

He pretended to shut his eyes and reclined back on his chair, his short legs resting ungainly on the desk. A cigarette smouldered slowly away in the ashtray, untouched. The poor little bear had a very sore head.

Cath left a message on Nick's mobile. It was his first day back at work and the mobile was deliberately left switched off until he went for lunch. It was only switched back on as he was walked to the canteen; the use of mobile phones was discouraged in hospitals. Theoretically they could interfere with some delicate piece of equipment but in practice everybody ignored it. Computerised syringe drivers delivering intravenous medicines didn't suddenly go haywire whenever a mobile phone went off.

The mobile beeped to indicate he had a message. He pressed 'read' and saw the message. He replied, giving Cath his email address, and scantly thought any more about it until lunch was over. He went to the office which the other orthopaedic registrars used as their base and checked his emails on the computer. There was a message from Glampic in the junk section of hotmail, which had not recognised the email address. It simply said: 'Story running in the paper tomorrow. See attachment.' He opened it; there were no viruses. Immediately in front of him was a picture of the chief executive kissing with the medical director. He had heard she was separated but knew the medical director was married. He had even seen the photograph of his wife on the desk. The image blew him away and all he could think of doing was to print it off. It was only on plain paper but that was good enough. The German word *schadenfreude* meant gaining happiness from somebody's misfortune. Nick thought in English, it was payback. He suddenly understood the power of the media. One simple picture could blow somebody's world apart and that was just about to happen to the two most powerful people in the hospital. The picture was still confusing, as it asked more questions than it answered. They must be having an affair, but it didn't resolve his problem. He still didn't know how to prove his innocence and he had no idea what the media was going to say about this whole business. For now, the day had just got a lot brighter and there was a sense of justice after all. He felt good after many weeks of being 'shafted', as Ricky had put it.

It reminded Nick to thank him, Paul and Jeff for their help. He didn't necessarily want to fraternise with them but it was only fair to buy a drink. He phoned Cath to thank her for the email and said he would come down to the office after work to buy anybody a drink who fancied going to the pub. That sort of offer never got refused. Ricky had shaken off his headache and was definitely game for it. Nick knew he had to drive so it would just be one drink for him, but the euphoria would keep him going. He also needed to know what was going to be in tomorrow's papers. He made his way down to King's Cross but the rush hour traffic was bad and it was after 6 p.m. before he arrived. They decided to go to one of the nearby pubs along the canal. It was already heaving when they got there, despite being only Monday. The trendy London set were drinking wine and champagne by the bottle, loving the thrill of spending money. The office girls were already giggling away from the alcohol and their empty stomachs. They seemed a happy bunch, especially when Ricky was being his generous and boisterous self. The champagne was flowing nicely.

Nick stuck to one just one glass and was relieved when Ricky insisted on paying, although it should have been his shout. He wanted to drink the whole bottle, but having the car was definitely a nuisance this time. Despite his reticence about the paparazzi, they just seemed like any other bunch of people who were out to enjoy themselves. This was definitely not the right time to have a philosophical debate on what they did. Alcohol was a great social leveller and people just liked getting pissed, no matter who they were. Nick found himself to be the man of the moment and the girls were flirting outrageously with him. At one stage, he suddenly felt his head being pulled down onto a young face before receiving a long probing kiss. There was a round of applause for his efforts but he didn't want to pull away. If it had been anywhere other than a pub, he would probably have carried on. That was a spur of the moment thing, but she had definitely done this before. Neither Nick nor the girl showed any sense of embarrassment at all, despite being complete strangers whilst exploring each others tonsils. Nick actually enjoyed the fleeting intimacy and was left with a pressing reminder in his trousers. Taking any further advantage of the young girl would have been wrong, but he suspected it was the other way round. She returned to talk to her friends as if nothing had happened.

He needed to go home because it felt worse not being able to drink. Leaving his car there overnight would be tantamount to stupidity. Jeff had seemed distant from the rest of the group, being somewhat older, but he had quietly got himself drunk without making any fuss. Nick offered him a lift home, which was graciously accepted. He had drunk in some of the dodgiest bars around the world and didn't need to get blind drunk any more. At his age, getting off with one of the younger girls was not a priority any more. His flat was in Finsbury Park, close to the mosque where the firebrand clerics had been feeding the young Muslims with their rhetoric of hatred against Western decadence. Alcohol and sexual promiscuity were sinful.

The traffic had significantly eased off by now and it took no time to get to Finsbury Park. Jeff remained quiet, but he was exhaling alcoholic fumes and Nick was only too glad to get rid of his passenger. He struggled to get out of the sports car but eventually made it out before making a beeline to his door. Nick grinned as he watched him stagger up the path and wondered just how many times he had done that before. The engine was still running and he was just about to set off when he sensed, rather than saw, somebody observing them. It was then he noticed the other man sitting quietly in the car facing him on the other side of the road, just a few yards away. Nick managed to look at him as he drove off. Despite the semi-darkness, their eyes met, but the man's eyes had a flinty hardness about them, something which sent a chill down Nick's spine. He must have been waiting for somebody, but it was none of Nick's business. Nick drove off with U2 and Bono doing his thing. He had even forgotten to ask Ricky what the newspaper article was going to say tomorrow. He just hoped Jeff's head wouldn't be too sore the next day.

An hour later, the Yale lock turned silently, on both the outer and inner doors. The assassin hoped there wouldn't be a second lock on the inner door and there wasn't. The door chain would not have presented a problem, but even that was off. In his alcohol-induced state, Jeff did not hear the quite footsteps approaching his bed. The assassin calmly removed a piece of cloth from his jacket pocket, along with a small bottle of chloroform. He sprinkled a few drops of the liquid onto the cloth and replaced the top on the bottle, doing this expertly in the dark with gloved hands. The cloth was now placed over Jeff's mouth and nose, sending him into a far deeper sleep than before. The assassin then turned on the bedside lamp, knowing that Jeff would not wake up. He went into the kitchen and removed a small polythene bag containing a brown powder from the other pocket. A suitable spoon with the right shape was found. He tipped some of the brown powder into it and added a small amount of citric acid and water before gentle heating this over the gas stove. The citric acid did its job nicely by dissolving the heroin. The liquid was then allowed to cool down a little before it was sucked up into the syringe using a cigarette filter tip. It had to look real. Even junkies didn't want any old crap ending up in the syringe. Using Jif lemon as a solvent instead of potassium citrate was okay, but that caused a shitload of inflammation to the veins. Injecting that bastard into an artery could be bad if the whole thing became gangrenous. Junkies were risk takers and were twenty times more likely to die than normal people. He deliberately left all the paraphernalia on the kitchen table, including the bag of pure heroin.

Returning quickly to the bedroom, he pulled off one Jeff's belts to use as a tourniquet. Finding a good vein on his arm, he inserted the needle and slackened the belt before injecting the brown liquid. Very quickly, the heroin flushed through the blood stream and reached his brain within seconds, switching off his respiratory centre in the brain stem. Jeff stopped breathing and knew nothing about it. Pure heroin was a killer.

The assassin checked Jeff's pulse and eyes to make sure he was dead before slipping out, leaving no trace of his presence. He left the light on, because even junkies had to see what they were doing. Jeff laid on his back with his left arm hanging over the bed, the loosened belt dangling down to the floor near to the empty syringe. His semi-opened eyes looked blankly towards the ceiling, his pupils already fixed. It was an ignominious end to a colourful life. His eyes would never see the horrors of war again.

23

Press Intrusion

'Hospital chief covers up for killer daughter's mistake.'

The tabloid ran its article. It went on to say how the cover-up had occurred, involving the death of a young man in a large London district hospital when a nurse had drawn up a large amount of diamorphine by mistake, as far as it was known. The evidence had been deliberately hidden, implicating a young surgeon who was totally innocent. The nurse in question was the daughter of the chief executive who also happened to work at the same hospital. The cover-up had been in an attempt to save the nurse's job and also to avoid the chief executive from being discredited. More was to follow. The chief executive was also having an affair with the medical director from the same hospital. He was a married man. As scandals went, this was from the top shelf.

Billy Cracknell was a veteran press reporter. He had worked in the newspaper industry for over twenty years and had covered many stories during that time. Originally from Cornwall, he was a quiet and reserved man, which belied his ability to worm the truth out of his unsuspecting victims. Before the article was published, he had simply arranged to speak to the chief executive to get the supposedly official version of the story, mentioning the young nurse without letting on he knew the link between them. It was his newspaper which had originally covered the incident about the young man. On this occasion, he reiterated the rumour and wanted the hospital's version of events to give a more balanced perspective on the matter. The chief executive complied with his request in the belief it would diffuse the situation. She simply stated the cause of death had not been fully explained and that nobody had been found unduly negligent as yet. The matter was still under investigation and that any further findings would be made available at the coroner's inquest. There was nothing more she could say.

Billy had no proof of what had really taken place other than the bits of information he had learnt from the dead man's parents, but he needed to dig deeper. He then asked if the staff nurse was her daughter. The chief executive could not deny it, but was clearly taken aback by the question. He could now write about the link between them and suggest how the whole matter was covered up to save both their positions. It would then be up to the authorities to ask for an inquiry. Even if the truth would never be known, the seed of doubt had been sown and any further actions from the chief executive would be scrutinised in the future. If the nurse was found to be negligent, she could be facing charges for manslaughter and trying to pervert the course of justice. The chief executive would have been implicated, with collusion and tampering with the evidence making her equally guilty. She faced the possibility of having criminal charges herself. Her reputation would then be in ruins, but it was his job to write the article. She should have been more cautious.

Billy had also tried to speak to Bob McLean, but he refused to discuss the matter, referring all press inquiries to the chief executive. He pieced the rest of the story together from Ricky Deans. Ricky usually sold his pictures of the rich and famous to the highest bidder, but had refused to any take money this time. Billy knew he owed him one and had to pay him back with a tip off. It was just how the business worked.

Printing the picture of the chief executive and the medical director together was the icing on the cake, especially when he discovered the medical director was married. It was immaterial what their relationship was and their kiss could have been totally innocent, but it made for good speculation. The picture would tell its own story and the medical director would have his work cut out trying to explain to his wife why he was kissing another woman in a dressing gown at the front door of her house. Both he and the chief executive would also have to explain their relationship to the board of directors at the Acute Hospital Trust and discuss their duplicity in the cover-up. As in most scandals, those at the top had further to fall. The chief executive would have to resign if she was found guilty of covering up for her daughter. The medical director may lose his directorship but could remain as a consultant physician, unless he had deliberately conspired with the chief executive. The nurse herself would be referred to the UKCC, the nursing regulating body, and may also face manslaughter charges. The hospital could only hope to settle any compensation claims out of court. The UK had slowly but unmistakably adopted the American compensation culture. Some people should rightly receive compensation for their loss and suffering if medical negligence was at fault, but many others also regarded this as an easy way of getting money. Only two per cent of all the compensation claims were ever justified and awarded.

There also was a fine line between freedom of the press and abuse by press intrusion, as English law did not adequately protect the individual's privacy. The Calcutt Committee had been formed in 1990 to look into press behaviour in respect of personal privacy, but had failed to find a wholly satisfactory statutory definition of the word. Privacy was not a legal concept which could be directly recognised and therefore no legal definition of the word existed in the English legal system. The judicious use of the press to report on a story that was in the public interest was generally welcomed. The public also needed to be reassured that they were in safe hands, especially when attending a NHS hospital, but this must be balanced against an avalanche of adverse publicity which could literally make people sick with worry about their local hospital. Billy Cracknell merely wrote the story as he saw it. There had been a simple but catastrophic error made by a nurse who then tried to cover up her tracks. This was a scandal of epic proportions, something no self-respecting tabloid could possibly do without. Billy had his story; Ricky had 'his' picture on the front page. The chief executive and the medical director would probably prefer to run a Siberian hospital for the insane right now. Nick had simply had no idea all this would happen when he saw Ricky, but the tide had definitely turned in his favour. Truth always came out in the washing, but he was sad it had to happen like this.

24

Photographs

Ricky Deans came in early as usual. He never missed a day at work unless he was on vacation, but even then he would be on the lookout for a celebrity. His life centred on his work, which sometimes became confused with play. Taking photographs of some busty blond usually involved a mixture of work and play, unless she was less keen on the 'play' bit, but these girls knew who make them famous. Fame had a price. He was still involved in the odd photo shoot, but now largely concentrated on the business aspect of the job. He was very sharp and never missed a trick. Whilst slurping coffee from a steaming mug, he noticed the time and could see Jeff Richards was not in yet. That was very unusual for him. Jeff may have been plastered the night before but he always turned up for work. It was the mark of a professional. Besides, Ricky always expected his photographers to report in, regardless of how pissed they had been the night before, and get on with their assignments. Failing to take photographs could cost the company mega bucks. Celebrities did not wait for the paparazzi.

'Cath, where's Jeff?' he asked.

'He'll be in the country, to be sure,' Cath said, pretending to be deliberately helpful.

'Cut the crap. Call him and tell him to get his arse right here, right now. I've got a job for him,' he barked.

'Yes, boss,' she replied cheekily.

Cath tried to phoned Jeff at home and then on his mobile. There was no answer. It was now 9.35 and the other photographers had already checked in and left a long time ago. Ricky was not going to accept anybody letting him down, especially when he needed to cover a soap star with her new boyfriend in Chelsea. He let the matter stand for an hour before the irritation got to him. He phoned Paul Lewis, who should be trawling the streets in the usual celebrity areas snapping good pictures, even if it was a crotch shot of somebody getting out of the car.

'Paul, where are you?' Ricky demanded to know.

'I'm at Alexandra Palace,' he replied, instantly recognising the gruff, cigarette coated voice.

'What the hell you doing there?' Ricky asked.

'The word is that some American boy band is coming here to check out the views in a limo,' Paul answered.

'What, at this time of the morning? Don't be silly arse, they won't be out of bed at this time of the bloody morning,' Ricky said.

'You never know, Rick. I'll just freeze my balls off a little more, just in case.' It was now late October and the weather was just beginning to turn cold.

'Well, you can stop pissing around and get down to Jeff's place and see what that useless idiot is doing. He's not turned up for work and I'm missing some coverage in Chelsea. Unless he turns up soon, he's out of a job. I don't give a toss if he is some smart-arsed war photographer and you can tell him that,' Ricky shouted.

'Alright, Ricky, just chill, yeah? I'll call you soon,' Paul said.

He hung up and started the car engine before setting off down the hill to Park Road, and then towards Crouch Hill, which was only a short distance away from Finbury Park. Jeff's flat was in one of the small streets with terraced houses which typified London. Some of the houses had been converted into a lower and an upper flat, making them more affordable to buy. There was a communal front door with two further doors inside, each leading into the separate flats. The upper floor was reached through a narrow flight of stairs which a fat person would struggle to squeeze through. Jeff rented the ground floor flat. He had sold his previous flat in Muswell Hill years ago, before the property boom took off in London, and had missed out badly. It was a wasted opportunity which he had always regretted, but there was no point in crying over spilt milk.

Paul arrived outside his flat just ten minutes later. The short journey from Alexandra Palace hadn't even given him time to think about Jeff. He rang the doorbell and simply expected to see him there. After waiting for a few minutes, there was still no answer. He tried to look in the front window but his view was obscured by the net curtain. In daylight, the room inside the flat looked dark and he could not see in at all. The main curtain had been left open, so Jeff was either out or he was asleep in bedroom and had not bothered to draw the curtains last night. He called Ricky back at the office.

'Rick, there's no sign of Jeff. His curtains are open but I can't see inside. What do you want me to do?' he asked.

'It's not like him not to turn up. Maybe he's had a heart attack or something. Is there any way of getting in?' Ricky asked.

'Not really. There's a Yale lock on the outside door, but I reckon there must be two converted flats here,' Paul answered.

'I've got a bad feeling about this one. I'll call a mate of mine who's got a locksmith's business. He'll be able to open the door for you. Are you up for this?' Ricky asked again.

'What, you mean break in?' Paul answered.

'We're checking up on him, not thieving. Don't worry, I take the blame if he gets annoyed. Just sit tight and I'll get somebody there. I'll phone you if there's a delay.' He hung up.

Paul went back to his car and waited for the locksmith to arrive. He was not too concerned about breaking into somebody's flat, especially if it was a workmate who could be unwell. Jeff may have only been with the company for a few months but his work was good. He was never very keen on chasing people in the streets for a photograph, which a lot of the paparazzi did. He was better at stalking, hiding in crafty locations and taking shots without anybody knowing. This job was less risky than photographing Israeli soldiers shooting at the Palestinians, but there was still some excitement when he photographed people secretly; it was a form of voyeurism, he supposed. Usually the subject only realised they had been snapped when they appeared in the tabloids the next day. The art of not getting caught gave him a buzz just like in Afghanistan, when he had hidden the memory stick in his underpants. Sometimes the buzz was really stimulating, which made up for all the other boring times.

The locksmith arrived after half an hour and Paul went up to him to exchange a few words, explaining the situation. It was unlikely that any of the neighbours would ask any questions and besides, there was a bona fide-looking van outside with 'Locksmith' written on its side. People would presume somebody had lost the key or were replacing the lock. The locksmith had no problem opening both the doors and the door chain was not on either, so perhaps Jeff was out after all. The locksmith went away when his job was done and did not step inside the flat. He also did not ask for any money, so Paul presumed that Ricky had sorted it all out. Ricky had lots of friends who always did him favours. He could also get a plumber straightaway if he needed one, and didn't get ripped off either. People did not want to see any nasty photographs of themselves in the papers, which would have been bad for business. Usually they didn't ask for money either. Having had to work hard for all his life, he did not grudge anybody earning their crust for an honest day's graft, especially when he was literally printing loads of the stuff himself. He just didn't like snooty celebrities who treated him like scum.

Paul entered the flat cautiously, which opened into a narrow hall. Jeff was not in the living room but the flat felt a little cold as the central heating had gone off on the timer. He called out to Jeff several more times but got no answer. Sixth sense now kicked in and told him that something was not right, not for entering Jeff's flat but for what he was going to find. He quickly glanced into the kitchen and found it empty except for a few things on the table. The bathroom was also in darkness. As he approached Jeff's bedroom, he just knew something had happened. The door was half opened with a small light shining from inside, but there was definitely a faint sweet odour coming from the room. It was the distinctive smell of bodily fluids, not overpowering just now, but there all the same.

Paul was hoping Jeff was just sleeping off his hangover, but Jeff had not got himself totally wasted the night before, certainly not for an old hand. He was used to drinking with the other hardened war hacks in the dingy bars and hotels around the world. More likely, Jeff may have had a stroke or a heart attack and was now lying in his bed, unable to move. Paul pulled on the door and walked in. He saw Jeff lying on his back, his arms and legs spread out, staring at the ceiling. The pallor said he was quite dead. Paul immediately recoiled at the sight but calmed himself down to look at the body again. There was the leather belt around his upper left arm, dangling down to the floor. Paul also saw the syringe on the floor and a single puncture mark with some dried blood on Jeff's arm. He felt sickened at the sight and had to walk out of the room, trying to control his nausea, which threatened to overwhelm him. A cold sweat broke out on his forehead and the colour drained from him. He reached for his mobile phone with trembling hands and pressed the number he wanted from the memory.

'Rick, I've just found Jeff. He's dead. There's a syringe and needle on the floor. I think he has overdosed on heroin or something. What do you want me to do now?' he asked in a trembling voice.

'Are you sure he's dead?' It sounded like a stupid question but an obvious one.

'Yes, he looks pretty white and his eyes are open. He's dead, Rick. No question about it,' Paul assured him.

'Okay, okay, I'm thinking. Don't touch anything. You'll have to call the police,' Ricky said calmly.

'What! Oh yeah, and I just tell them I busted in and found him like this. Are you kidding me or something, Rick?' Paul was cracking up.

'Hey, just get a grip, alright? Tell them how it is. I'll back up the story and the locksmith will do the same. Just say he was a mate and we were worried about him.'

'Rick, I want to get out of here. I'm not phoning any police,' Paul said.

'Look, you got to! Jeff's dead and he is not coming back. What do you think will happen if you didn't call the police? Somebody will say they saw you. How are you going to explain that? If he killed himself with drugs, than it's his own fault. I want you to take any pictures and camera gear that belongs to this company. Once the police get there, we'll never get them for months. Am I clear on this, Paul? Tell me you heard me,' Ricky demanded.

Rick knew he had to be tough before Paul cracked up and left a load of stuff in the flat. Paul just had to get his act together. There would be a police investigation as drugs have been involved and they would probably go through all the contents in the flat.

'Yeah, alright, Rick. I'll see what there is to take away from the flat. I'll call the police in a minute.' Paul had calmed down; the panic was easing off.

'Good boy. Now, check all his stuff but leave the computer alone if there is one. Switch that on and it will leave a time and date imprint so don't do it. Just pick up any CDs he might have burned any photos on. Bring that lot back with you. I'll see you back here and then you can take the rest of the day off. Just try and not leave any fingerprints around, other wise the police will be asking some hard questions.' Ricky was trying to be helpful.

'Cheers, Rick. I'll see you soon,' Paul replied.

He ended the call and quickly started to look around the flat for what he needed. He went to the kitchen and found a pair of rubber gloves in a bucket beneath the kitchen sink. Jeff must have used them for cleaning the toilet or doing the dishes. The yellow gloves were medium sized and just fitted his hands and no more. He next surveyed the front room, which apart from the ubiquitous TV and armchairs contained a computer with a fairly high spec printer, sitting on a wooden table near to the front window. It was unlikely Jeff was going to have lots of prints lying around when he would have stored his photographs on the computer's hard disk. He would also have backed this up on a recordable CD.

Paul did not switch on the computer, despite the possibility of it having several thousand images downloaded on it. Besides, it would have been impossible to look at them all, let alone identify which ones had been taken whilst he was working for Glampic. The police were bound to look at the computer for any clues, especially any emails which could link him to drug dealers. It was unlikely, as they used pay-as-you-go mobile phones to avoid detection. Instead, he looked at a small pile of computer CDs which were in the rack next to the computer itself. He started to flip open some of the plastic CD boxes and read the handwritten contents. The first disc contained images of some of his recent assignments, and so did the second. Paul took these. Most of the other discs were related to some of his previous work. One had Afghanistan written on the inside label, probably relating to his work there too. It sounded interesting so he pocketed it. He would have a look at them later. Nothing much was known about Jeff, except he had done some war photography around the world, taking pictures of war zones and captured life for what it was. It was a world far removed from the trash that constituted celebrity photographs in today's tabloids, but he had decided to join their ranks. There were some exciting-looking photographs hanging up on the walls, which Paul presumed was his work. Nobody even knew if Jeff had any relatives to inherit what little he had. Everything about him had been a mystery and he never talked about his past or his previous work. Jeff had probably seen some terrible things and it had been his choice not to talk about it. Perhaps he had wanted to hide away from the memories. It didn't matter now; he was dead.

Paul took away the camera gear which belonged to the company. He put them in the boot of his car but stashed the CDs in the glove compartment because he wanted to see what was on them before passing them over to Rick. He also remembered to put the rubber gloves back in the bucket before phoning the police. He was still too upset to sit down and paced the floor instead until they arrived.

Two police officers arrived ten minutes later and took a statement from him. They then radioed back to the police station before more police arrived. This time the police surgeon turned up to declare Jeff dead before the body was removed for forensic examination. Paul was free to go and his statement would later be backed up by Ricky and the locksmith. He was glad to leave the flat and find some comfort back at the office by recounting his story to Ricky and the rest of the team. Everybody needed a support network to help with mental trauma. His mind was still clouded with the image of seeing Jeff lying dead on his bed. People like Jeff weren't supposed to die like this. He was a professional war photographer. It would have been easier to understand if he had blown his brains out with a shotgun, but dying like a junkie was just not his style. Something wasn't right.

25

Subterfuge

The man in the office had a navy blue suit on today, as did his colleague. It was the colour of the senior service but neither were navy men. The leather armchairs were extremely comfortable, especially when taking their Earl Grey tea and biscuits. The weather outside was overcast and a damp breeze blew along the river. The muddy water swirled around the bridgework and slapped against the embankment but it was cosy inside, the room illuminated by a pair of matching floor standing lamps. The senior man was the first to speak again.

'Any word about the inquiry?' he said, stirring his cup of tea.

'Some people seem rather determined that it should go ahead. They want the British police to investigate.'

'Do we know when?'

'Simply can't say. That would depend on the police, and the pressure lobby.'

'What do the French think?'

'They have no wish to drag this on. They have already stated their findings and do not plan any inquiry.'

'Then why on earth dig this all up again?'

'Pressure from parliament, I would guess.'

'Who's involved?'

'Perhaps somebody from the opposition party.'

'Are they receiving funds from anybody in the pressure lobby?'

'Quite likely.'

'Did we do the right thing in Paris?'

'Strategically or operationally?'

'Both.'

'Yes to the first and no to the second.'

'Care to explain that?' he asked, sipping his tea.

'The French have as many as five million Muslims in the country, mostly from Morocco and Algeria. Their colonial past has caught up with them. Already there are riots in their cities and many areas are no go for the ordinary Frenchman. Very soon Holland could go the same way and then perhaps Germany, Denmark and even Sweden. Prominent Dutch citizens have already been murdered in their own country by the Muslim population, which is also rising faster than the indigenous one. The time could come when the western democracies could be dominated by the Muslim radicals. It could be the same over here and certain imams have already preached about waging jihad from the mosques. The richer Arabs, on the other hand, are rapidly buying up western businesses and property with petrodollars. Saudi Arabia alone has over 260 billion barrels of proven oil reserves, about a quarter of the world's total. The non-Muslim world could suddenly find itself being attacked not only by the Islamic fundamentalists but also by rich Arabas. Something has to be done about curbing the Arab dominance spreading throughout Europe. The French have already realised this and their right-wing party has grown more popular recently. It would be disastrous for our country if the Muslims ended up owning everything from the corner shops to the larger department stores as well. The nobility are also marrying into the Muslim culture. Where will all this stop?'

'And operationally?'

'We had six of our own operatives in Paris that weekend and the operation should have been under our control.'

'We invited them to join in as it was a deniable operation. Their hit team need never set foot in Europe again, making them untraceable. They were keen to help, just as the SAS had taken out the drug cartels in South America. Cocaine and organised crime has taken over America, destroying the country from within just as Al-Qaeda is trying to do that overtly. The Taliban are now encouraging the farmers to grow opium crops in Afghanistan in order to flood our countries with heroin. We have a duty to stop the wholesale erosion of our country.'

'I absolutely agree but the Paris operation was just too complicated when it should have been much simpler.'

'Anything in mind?'

'Yes, sabotage the jet.'

'The collateral damage could have been too great, especially if it had crashed over a city. The car crash had looked like the perfect accident, don't you think?'

'Very nearly, except there were too many witnesses around.'

'Any trace of the missing car?'

'The police forensics team found traces of paint belonging to the car, where it had crashed into the back of the saloon. The paint was analysed and the make and model has now been identified as it was unique to that particular model. I believe it has now been crushed and completely disposed of.'

'All traces cold?'

'Yes, except for the first paparazzo and the rider who would be called to give evidence if the inquiry goes ahead.'

'That must be taken care of.'

'Yes, of course.'

'Tell me, whatever happened to the chap who sold the photographs?'

'Apparently he was found dead from a heroin overdose.'

'Taken care of by our American friends?'

'Yes, presumably. We have heard nothing more from them about this.'

'Did the police search the apartment?'

'Yes, there were copies in the hard drive but nowhere else. The computer is secure.'

'Good, at least that's settled but I am still concerned about the Paris situation. The inquiry may go ahead but it is imperative the findings remain inconclusive.'

'We should eliminate our paparazzo in that case.'

'Yes, do that.'

'Any idea how?'

'The French have already sorted their man out and we know the dead driver was one of their paid informants. They were able to pass on some useful information to us when he was still alive so it is a shame to have lost that contact. However, the driver had several traceable bank accounts rather than a Swiss account and any inquiry would look into this. Presumably it could point to the French secret service. It was rather amiss of them but I think the Americans may be able to help us once again.'

'I'm intrigued. Do go on.'

'Just suppose there was another set of photographs. It would be in their interest to remove it from the circulation, would it not?'

'Yes, but there isn't, at least we don't think so.'

'That is not the point. Just say another paparazzo has obtained a copy. They could think they were at risk of being exposed again.'

'I rather like your idea. How should we inform them?'

'Oh, I'm sure you'll think of something. More tea?'

'No thanks. I had better start making the phone calls.'

'Let me know how you get on and do give our friends my compliments,' the senior man said.

The tea break was over. Dirty work was always better done by somebody else.

26

Close Danger

A week had gone by following Jeff's death. Everybody at the agency was shocked by the tragic event as nobody knew Jeff had been abusing hard drugs. Most of the boys, including Ricky, had snorted cocaine, especially after a big deal, but nobody did heroin. They drank a toast to Jeff before almost forgetting he had ever existed. The paparazzi world moved along quickly. Ricky called Paul into his office and uncharacteristically shut the door. The cigarette smoke soon built up.

'Grab a seat,' Ricky ordered. This sounded serious.

'What's up? You're not sacking me?' Paul was not unduly worried.

'Shut up,' Ricky said, in a fatherly manner. 'I've been speaking to a few people. There is something going on which we can't put our finger on. A French motorcyclist was found dead on the motorway. He worked with the paparazzi but was alone when he crashed. Nobody else was involved. There's more.' He paused for a minute. 'Nobody believes Jeff was a junkie. I've spoken to some of the war hacks he used to hang around with. There was no way he could have been doing dope and keep on the ball.'

'So, what are you saying, Rick?' Paul asked.

'I don't know. Somebody not in the business has been asking around about you.'

'What do you mean, Rick?' Paul was definitely switched on now.

'Were you involved in the Paris tunnel crash?' Ricky asked.

'Yeah, I was there. Why?' Paul had turned slightly paler.

'That's what I want to know. What happened in there?' Ricky demanded.

'There was a crash. What more can I say,' Paul answered.

'Don't be an arse. What did you see in there? People are saying it was deliberate, those people were taken out. You had better tell me, this is important!' Ricky raised his voice.

'Oh Jesus, Rick. All we saw was some car and a couple of motorbikes chasing the Merc. Then there was an almighty crash with a flash of light. I don't know what happened. It was all dark in there and I had a helmet on.' Paul looked concerned now.

Ricky stared at the piece of paper on his desk. There was a name on it. He turned it around for Paul to see.

'Was this the name of the French guy who drove the motorcycle?' he asked.

'Jesus Christ! Yeah, it is. What about it?' Paul asked.

'He is the guy who was killed on the motorway,' Ricky answered.

'Oh shit! Did you say somebody was asking about me? Honest, Rick, I saw nothing in the tunnel that could put the finger on anybody. I don't even remember the types of car or motorcycles that were involved. Why would anyone want to get to me?' Paul asked in desperation.

'That's what I need to know. Just try and remember anything. What happened after the crash?' Ricky asked.

'Dunno. I was standing there. Some biker looked into the car. Then the other paps arrived. There was a strange thing. Some geezer on another bike came into the tunnel the wrong way, you know from the exit end. He picked up this bloke who was looking into the car and then drove off. There was also a crashed bike in there. I was too hyped to take much notice and didn't even take any photos. It just felt wrong, you know how it is,' Paul explained.

'Some paparazzo you are. Don't worry about it, mate. God, I need a coffee.' He got up and opened the door before shouting out, 'Oi, someone get me and Paul a coffee!'

One of the newer girls in the office beetled off; it was just Ricky's way of asking.

'Where does Jeff come into all this? He wasn't there,' Paul asked.

'I don't know, Paul. All this is getting a little out of my league,' Ricky answered.

'You don't think somebody got the wrong guy and it should have been me, do you?' Paul asked again.

The coffees arrived which broke up the tension. Ricky took a slurp of the strong black liquid which annoyed his ulcer again. He winced.

'Paul, I want you to give that surgeon guy, Nick, a phone and see what he's got to say after he dropped Jeff off at the flat,' he asked, in a flat tone of voice.

'Yeah, alright. I'll speak to him,' Paul answered.

Ricky was worried. There had been two deaths in a space of a week, including the Frenchman, and somebody was sniffing around about Paul. There must be a reason for all this, and some of the paparazzi had suddenly got twitchy about the whole thing. If there was to be an inquiry about the Paris incident, a lot of paparazzi would be called up as witnesses. But there was no link between Jeff and the Paris incident. Ricky went by his gut instinct; Jeff was no junkie. Something odd was definitely going on. Paul just needed to be on his guard.

Paul went off into the main office and sat behind one of the desks. The telephone was pulled towards him before cradling the receiver between his left shoulder and his ear, dialling the hospital with his right hand. He still had the mug of coffee in his left hand and was sipping it at the same time. He could multitask as well as any woman, except he didn't have to file his nails.

It was now late afternoon and the day got dark quickly in November. The office would still be open for a few more hours yet, despite very little happening in town that week. The celebrities must have gone into hibernation, only to emerge again around the party season at New Year. He phoned Nick, hoping he was working today.

Nick's pager went off and the switchboard number came up, usually signifying an outside call. The operator transferred the call over to him but he groaned inwardly in case this was another call from a GP asking for an admission.

'Hello, Nick Forbes,' he said in his usual fashion, sounding completely neutral but dreading the GP call.

'Nick, its Paul Lewis here. Can we talk, mate? Something serious has happened.'

'Yes, okay, carry on.' Nick sounded rather official.

'Did you know that Jeff died last week? It was in some of the newspapers,' Paul said.

'I'm sorry, I didn't know that. What did he die from?' The news was bad but Nick did not feel emotional, he hardly knew the man.

'That's what I'm phoning you about. It was after the night out at the pub when he didn't turn up for work the next day. Ricky asked me to go to his flat before getting a locksmith to open the door. I found him dead on the bed with a syringe and a needle next to him so it looked like it was a drug overdose. None of us knew he was on heroin. In fact, we still don't think he killed himself.' Paul was recalling the story at a fast pace.

'Slow down, I'm a little confused Paul. Who got the locksmith and how do you know he died from a heroin overdose? What are you saying?' Nick asked, trying to sort the various things going on in his brain at the same time, mostly clinical work.

'I'm sorry, mate, yeah, I'll slow down. Ricky got the locksmith to open Jeff's door because I could not get in. It was Ricky who thought that something was wrong and made me go to Jeff's flat. We have our suspicions that all this could be connected to something which happened some years ago, to do with some crash in a Paris tunnel. I was there when it happened. As far we know, Jeff wasn't there, but he works for our agency. I'm just worried that it was me they were after but they got to Jeff by mistake.' Paul still made no sense with the deluge of information he was giving out.

'Paul, I'm hearing what you are saying but all this sounds a little heavy going. You are making a lot of assumptions. It may well turn out that Jeff had simply overdosed himself because it is quite easy to do. How on earth are you linking all this to something which happened years ago?' Nick asked.

'Nick, I don't know, I'm all confused, mate. Another guy has been killed in France. He was the motorcycle rider I was with,' Paul explained.

'Paul, have you received any threats or received anything to say somebody is after you?' Nick asked logically.

'No, not exactly,' Paul answered.

'Well, I suggest that you relax about all this. There must be some logical explanation. Why don't you meet me sometime this week for a beer and we can discuss it if you like,' Nick offered. There was a short pause.

'Nick, can you tell me what happened when you dropped Jeff off at the flat?' Paul asked.

'There's not much to say. He was a little unsteady on his feet but he wasn't paralytic. He didn't say very much in the car and I saw him go into the flat and drove home,' Nick answered.

'Yeah, okay, Ricky just said to check it with you. It was a big shock to all of us. None of us knew he was a junkie,' Paul added.

'Just tell me something, Paul. What sort of syringe did you see next to Jeff's body?' Nick asked.

'What do you mean? A syringe is a syringe isn't it?' It was not like Nick to ask a daft question.

'No, I mean, was it small, large, made of plastic, what?' Nick asked.

'I don't know, Nick, it was perhaps the size of my little finger. I wasn't trying to be Sherlock Holmes. To be honest, I was crapping myself,' Paul answered.

'That sounds like a five-millilitre syringe. Drug addicts normally used a one-millilitre diabetic syringe. It would be a little strange if Jeff had used a bigger syringe. Look, I would advise you to speak to the police if you are really concerned about Jeff's death. Why don't you keep me informed if anything else turns up?' Nick offered.

'Okay, I'll be in touch. Thanks for listening, mate.' Paul hung up.

He went back to Ricky's office and told him about the conversation. The girls were packing up for the day and would be leaving soon. Ricky and Paul chatted for a while but the conversation was going around in circles. Neither really knew what was going on and there was no point speculating what could be happening. They also decided to leave and switched the lights off, before locking the main door behind them. It was totally dark by now, save for a small light in the courtyard. Ricky jumped into his metallic purple BMW M3 coupe and drove out of the mews compound. Paul got into his car and turned the ignition. The starter motor was dead. The car just wouldn't start, it didn't even turn over. He desperately wanted to get home and not get stuck in the dark courtyard. He now regretted not taking out breakdown cover when the leaflet had come through the door. It was a little short-sighted when his job depended on having a car. He was all alone now in the car park which was nearly in the darkness. Some light was coming in from the street outside, which silhouetted the arched entrance. The car felt cold inside and there was no other option but to leave it there overnight. There was no way he was going to look around in the engine bay, even if he could see what he was doing. Somebody could fix it tomorrow. There were enough garages around the area, no doubt some dodgy ones too.

Before abandoning the car, he had a quick look around to make sure there was no camera equipment or anything else which somebody might take a fancy to. He opened the glove compartment and saw the three CDs he had picked up from Jeff's flat, something he had almost forgotten about. He took them with him. The mews compound was not locked at night so the car was an easy target for any passing yob with a penchant for breaking into cars. He was satisfied the car did not have anything worth stealing in it. It had an immobiliser so hopefully the car itself won't be stolen. As he was about to leave, a sudden movement caught his eye. The mews was enclosed by buildings on all sides with only one exit to the street. He also heard a tiny sound coming from the corner of the compound which stopped when he peered out of the car. The car park felt very deserted but he was unable to see or hear anything now. An icy chill ran down his back. Perhaps it was just a cat or a wino looking for somewhere to doss down for the night. It would not be the first time these people were evicted in the morning.

He started to reassure himself with this possibility but the fear would not go away. What if there was somebody out to kill him? The car offered a margin of safety but it would be terribly cold in there. Besides, an axe-wielding maniac would soon make mincemeat of the car and him. There was no other option but to get out and run for it.

Without moving any muscle in his body, he eyes strained to look for any movement within the compound. His imagination started to play havoc; he thought he could see shapes where there were none. The menacing presence remained. The exit was only twelve yards away but it seemed a long way.

Just then, a rowdy bunch of lads appeared, walking slowly along the main road and heading for another pub. They were all Jack the Lads, with the herding instinct of sheep. Without thinking, Paul grabbed his chance to escape and quickly dashed out of the car. He slammed the door shut and used the ultrasonic key to lock it. There was no way he would he have stopped to lock the car with a conventional key. He almost ran from the car and smacked into the middle of the boys without caring if they were going pick on him. Being called a wanker was a small price to pay but he just smiled with relief. He made his way to King's Cross station and arrived slightly out of breath. His legs were trembling, from a mixture of fear and the rapid walk. It was a sense of relief; he almost felt stupid. For the first time since leaving the car park, he turned around to see if anybody had followed. Everybody in the street looked absolutely normal. Nobody looked remotely like a murderer, except he didn't know what one looked like. He now felt like a complete fool, but Jeff's death, and what Ricky told him today, had totally spooked him. The others would think he was totally daft if he recounted the story to them. Still, he needed to speak to someone and the only person he could think of was Nick. Before buying a tube ticket, he phoned him from the main entrance area where people were still milling around.

'Nick, I'm sorry for phoning, mate. I know I'm a nuisance but the truth is I think someone is out to get me. My car has suddenly gone dead when it has never broken down before. Is there any chance you could pick me up and let me stay at your flat until we get this sorted out?' Paul sounded desperate again.

Nick had had a busy day at work and was really looking forward to doing absolutely nothing that night. He sensed the urgency in Paul's voice and knew something was going on. Paul had walked into his life at the time when everything had gone pear-shaped, but it had probably saved his career. He felt obliged to help him.

'Okay, where are you?' Nick asked.

'I'm at King's Cross station. I'll stand at the main entrance and wait for you,' Paul replied.

'No, I'll tell you what, it would save a little time if you jumped on the tube to Wood Green. I'll pick you up outside the station in, say, fifteen minutes?'

Wood Green was just down the road from Nick's flat and it made sense not to drive all the way into the centre of London. Curiosity had now taken over. He didn't want to get involved with any shady dealings involving the paparazzi. He never knew Jeff as a man, so what if he was a junkie? Paul only got involved with him because he wanted to sell his photograph and that was not a good enough reason to help him now. No, he was intrigued as to why Paul felt it necessary to ingratiate himself in this manner. Surely he had his paparazzi mates to call on. He just hoped Paul wasn't gay. Something in his voice said trouble. Paul had mentioned about being in the Paris tunnel and that some Frenchman had also been killed. Somebody was now coming after him and the whole thing seemed linked to the Paris affair. Except Jeff; he had been some ex-war photographer who had joined the company to make a living towards the end of his career. Nobody knew or believed he had been a junkie. Experienced junkies knew what they were doing and never used pure heroin or shared needles. Jeff had looked too fit and healthy to have been a junkie; he hadn't had that doped-out look. If Paul had been right about the size of the syringe, it was too big for injecting heroin unless it was for a big amount. That would be suicidal or deliberate murder. Nick was sure he would hear more about this.

27

Freefall

There was a definite buzz going on at the hospital following the newspaper article. The scandal of the cover-up had been bad enough, but the speculation was rife as to how the newspapers had managed to link the nurse with the chief executive. The usual reason could be jealousy, with some nurse spilling the beans after failing to get the job, stating it was a fix. The affair itself was the cherry on the cake which hit everybody like a bomb shell. There were too many secrets knocking about. Who else was having an affair? The nursing profession was not incestuous in the way the medical profession used to be when children were expected to follow in their parents' footsteps, especially sons of male doctors. Nursing had been a popular profession amongst women until the long years of poor pay and conditions put pay to that. The profession was now infused with males, just as the medical profession was slowly becoming dominated with females. The world order had changed very quickly and men were even staying at home to look after the children.

Brenda Hawkins had gone on immediate sick leave after the newspaper article was published due to stress, leaving her mother to brazen it out. Quite rightly, the chief executive had pointed out that her private life was her business, except to Bob's wife perhaps. The medical director sheepishly said that he met up with her to discuss hospital matters, but some people may have been gullible enough to believe it. The story ran for another day, giving more information about their lives, speculating on the affair at a time when the hospital was already in a blaze of publicity. Rather than causing widespread despondency, the whole hospital was actually thriving with excitement because it was their hospital that was making the news. Even the members of staff who have never spoken to each other started up conversation for no other reason. The patients tried to grab a slice of fame too, just for being there. The chief executive became the butt of jokes and people watched as she fell from her perch. The medical director was the dirty old man who had to keep both his wife and the chief executive happy, and speculation extended as to whether the boardroom table had been used for extracurricular activities. Life for the chief executive had become intolerable and her position was now untenable; there was no other option but to resign. The medical director reverted to his role as a hospital consultant but the stress was telling.

Brenda Hawkins' own resignation came within a few days, which was a great source of relief to everybody. To celebrate the occasion, Meg suggested going out for a meal, but Nick suggested she came over to his flat later to meet Paul and stay for dinner. He briefly mentioned that Paul was in some kind of danger, without elaborating on the details. She accepted the invitation.

Nick was always a little wary when it came to dating women in case he wasn't up to the mark. As an impoverished medical student, he had learnt the harsh realities of life when all the gorgeous female students only seemed to go out with guys with fancy cars. All that had changed when he had qualified and cars did not matter any more. Every young male doctor at the Western General in Edinburgh had tried to get off with the most gorgeous nurse working there but had failed, despite their public school background and fancy cars. She had just asked him back to her flat in Leith one night after a few drinks with the other medics and had wondered why he had never come on to her. It had felt too foolish to say it was because he had a little rusty VW. Perhaps it was his unassuming attitude which endeared him to women, often making other men jealous. The evening he had spent with Meg at the Indian restaurant had been magical, but he was afraid she may say no if he asked her out. She desperately wanted him too.

Meg was not naive. She was a sensible woman and knew a lot about men. She just felt too reserved to ask Nick out again and had wrongly presumed that she was too old for him, despite being only thirty-six. Besides, many of the younger nurses fancied their chances with him and she knew that only too well. She was intrigued by him and could not understand why he had chosen to go out with Emma, apart from the fact she was pretty. Emma had frequently come down to Casualty to deal with gynae cases, but her attitude stank. She made it known she was the doctor and Meg was the nurse. Perhaps it was a mutual dislike between the two attractive women. Meg had identified Nick's deep-seated sadness long before they became friendly and now understood it was due to his lack of childhood. Emma could never understand that. She would love to go to his flat, meet Paul, have dinner and then go home. They agreed on a time; 7 p.m. was only a few hours away.

Nick had to think what was in his fridge. All he had were some chicken breasts again and it was time he stocked up with some decent food. He would worry about that later, but curry seemed the best bet, yet again. He still had a mountain of dictation to do.

After work, he parked the car at the back and flew up the steps. The kitchen and the rest of the place did not look too untidy, but he wasn't unduly worried. He helped himself to a whisky and prepared the curry, which only took half an hour to cook from start to finish. He turned the heat off and added some garam masala, the highly fragrant spiced powder which made it smell nice. He went for a shower to freshen up.

Paul arrived just after he came out of the shower. The whole flat stank of curry, shower gel and aftershave, a heady mixture which smelt like some eastern bazaar, except the flat was less exotic.

'Blimey, Nick, this place smells like a brothel!' Paul pretended to be offended.

'How's your day?' Nick grinned like a silly schoolboy.

'I got some guy from a garage to have a look at the car. The electrics were stuffed. Apparently, somebody had managed to get in the car and then cut the ignition wire. They got in despite the car alarm. It was a professional job, Nick. Somebody was in the car park,' Paul said.

'How could someone have got in if it was alarmed?' Nick asked.

'Apparently one of the rear lamps was deliberately broken and the car was short-circuited, putting the alarm out of action. Then, they got in and cut the wire beneath the dash. I made sure one of the other boys came out with me into the car park tonight; it's scary stuff, mate,' Paul added.

'Have you reported it to the police?'

'Nah, the police aren't going to find who did this. There was no CCTV there. I can only think that somebody slipped in and tampered with my car when it was starting to get dark. Whoever it was then hung around waiting to do me in whilst I figured out what was wrong with the car. If he was a professional hit man, he could have sorted me out without leaving a trace,' Paul said.

'Why would he kill you in the courtyard?' Nick asked.

'Does it really matter where he did it? Maybe he was just playing with me, like cat and mouse. Who knows, Nick? Maybe he is a nutter. We presume he killed Jeff and made it look like a heroin overdose. These people are good. That's what scares the shit out of me,' Paul said.

'Okay, give me one good reason why he wants to kill you?' Nick asked.

'How much did you read about the crash in the Paris tunnel a few years ago? The official version was apparently fabricated and the evidence was covered up. The French police said the driver was drunk and he crashed into the metal pillar, but there was no evidence that he had been drinking that day. His blood sample could have been tampered with when they got it to the lab. Nobody really knows the truth, but why did the electricity stop working just before the crash? Why was there no evidence on CCTV? There was also the flash of light which we saw. People are saying that it was some kind of a strobe gun used by special forces to blind people, but I thought it was metal sparks when the car hit the pillar. Everything happened so quickly that I don't really know what I was looking at. Somebody clearly thinks I saw something and doesn't want me to give evidence.' Paul was giving an oratory, perhaps it was out of genuine fear.

'Hey, it's okay, Paul. If you feel this sure about things, you have got to go to the police,' Nick said.

He could see just how upset and scared Paul was getting. Perhaps what he said was true and the questions surrounding the Paris crash was still not resolved, despite numerous attempts by both French and British authorities to end the speculation. The official verdict maintained that the driver was drunk and had crashed the car, perhaps as a result of being chased by the paparazzi. Nobody had actually asked the question why anybody wanted to kill the people in the car. Was there some political conspiracy involved? This was not the right time to go into that.

There was nothing Paul could do about this situation tonight so he might as well try and relax. He should see the police in the morning and perhaps get some protection until this business was over. Meg would be here soon and he just wanted to relax. His career was difficult enough, but problems just kept following him and it was starting to grind him down. Some people believed in fate but others believed you made your own luck. Nick never knew what to believe, but he was due a lucky break. Perhaps working with Meg had been it. She was there for the taking but he had not seen it. He fetched Paul a lager and poured himself another whisky rather than think about the meaning of life. He told Paul they had a guest coming that evening.

The doorbell rang just after 7 p.m. and Nick walked to the front door in a nonchalant manner, trying not to appear to be too eager. He opened the door and saw this gorgeous person standing there.

'Hello, Nick. Brought you a present.' She held out a chilled bottle of champagne.

'Wow, you had better come in. You only brought one?' He was teasing.

'I'm only a poor nurse! Something smells good. Not sure if champagne goes with curry but I'm not fussy if you're not.' She entered the flat, quickly taking in the scene. She didn't say it was nice because that would be lying.

'This is Paul,' Nick said, as Paul walked into the hall from the living room.

'Hi, I'm Meg,' she introduced herself.

Paul said hello. They made small chat whilst Nick opened the champagne and emptied the whole bottle into three large wine glasses. He brought them through into the living room whilst the bubbles fizzed away like crazy.

'Hey, steady, I'm driving later. Cheers.' Meg giggled at the size of the glass.

Nick excused himself again to go sort the meal out. Meg and Paul talked about their jobs and their involvement with Nick, who popped in and out trying to join the conversation. The rice was cooked in twenty minutes and Nick served the curry on three large plates with spoons, as it was easier to eat rice that way. He was not the type to stand to ceremony and just hoped Meg was not put out by his lack of decorum. Moby was played away on the CD as they ate their meal. Nick explained he was not a great pudding fan and there was none. Paul excused himself and went for a shower. Meg came through into the kitchen with the plates as Nick made the coffee. They could talk as Paul was out of the room.

'So, how are you, Nick?' Meg asked.

'Good. And you?' he replied.

'Relieved Brenda has resigned!' Meg said.

'Was it bad when I was away?' Nick asked.

'Yes it was. First the press were there trying to get people to tell them what they knew. Then, after we discovered what had happened, I got a hard time from the senior nursing officer. I can only presume she was being leant on by the chief executive. Brenda became impossible to work with, just ignoring everything I asked her to do. I could only imagine what you must have gone through. Thank goodness this madness is all over,' Meg replied.

'I always knew the truth would come out eventually. The hospital will have to pay some compensation and I just feel sorry for his parents.' Nick was now making some very small talk.

'It was an easy mistake to make. I can't understand why the manufacturer of the diamorphine simply didn't think of putting different coloured labels on the vials according to the strength. It would be the obvious solution.' Meg sounded sensible.

'That would be too much like commonsense. I suppose this whole thing has come on the back of the Harold Shipman murders and the memory is still fresh in people's minds. It's only too easy to kill somebody with an injection. Even drug addicts die when the dealers screw up and don't cut the drug properly. Apparently, one of Paul's colleagues was found dead in his flat last week from a heroin overdose, except Paul doesn't think he was an addict. He seems convinced that somebody is out there to kill the paparazzi,' Nick said.

'Why them?' Meg asked.

'It's a little complex to explain. You're not here to talk about that.' He spoke softly, looking into her eyes.

Paul walked into the kitchen after his shower. He had a fresh set of clothes on so he must have either been back to his flat or had bought them new today. He smelt of aftershave too, his own rather than using Nick's.

'Nick, okay to use your computer? Need to check the emails,' Paul said.

'Yes, help yourself,' Nick replied. The computer was in the spare bedroom where Paul was sleeping.

The music had finished; so had the coffee. They went back to the living room and Nick changed the CD to Groove Armada. The funky beat started to gently pound away from the floor-standing speakers, as they settled on the settee. Meg still had some of her champagne to drink. They sat listening to the music as Nick slowly soaked his brain with more whisky. He was feeling relaxed, happy and acutely aware that Meg sitting next to him. Her presence so close to him was like a form of exquisite torture, both mentally and physically, not knowing if he should make some move to establish physical contact or not. He slowly sipped away at his whisky, feeling the glow descending down his gullet. Willing himself on, he slowly reached out and touched her hand. He felt her stiffen and thought she might pull it away but instead, she held on to it. She lent across and kissed him on the lips. He could smell her perfume and the warmth of her body as they pressed against each other, kissing slowly but passionately, their lips communicating in a blissful manner. The magic didn't last.

'Nick, come and see this on the PC! Oh, sorry.' Paul burst in on them but was too excited to be embarrassed.

They pulled away as if they had been caught in the spotlight, confused for a split second by the suddenness of the intrusion. Meg immediately reached out for her glass of champagne in order to cover up for her embarrassment.

Paul had something important to show him. Nick followed. On the screen was a group of men being killed by a couple of Mujahadeen, judging by their clothes, but there was also a soldier in combat fatigues looking on. The people who were being shot were all tied up. They had been murdered. Paul clicked opened several more images on the computer until the last one showed a soldier looking up straight up towards the photographer, who was presumably in the helicopter. The same helicopter was pictured on the ground unloading supplies. They could only presume it was Jeff who had taken these.

Nick had seen some horrible injuries without flinching but it was the image of seeing people being killed which made him feel very uneasy. These people were human beings, regardless of who they were. As a doctor, his integrity was based on the sanctity of life, to save people and to heal the sick. The thought of one human being taking the life of another was a complete anathema to him. He was just as upset as Paul was.

'What are these pictures, Paul?' Nick asked.

'I was just going through a few of Jeff's discs that I took from his flat in case they were work related. I think these must have been taken in Afghanistan, it says so on the label. That soldier is Caucasian, so he could either be British, American or Australian. They must be special forces because that is not a standard army-issue rifle. The SAS or the Yanks would use something like that,' Paul said.

Nick looked at the image of the soldier staring back at him from the screen. The man had hard, piercing eyes; killer's eyes. It was like déjà vu.

'I think I have seen that man before, but don't ask me where,' Nick said.

'Nick, you're freaking me. What do you mean you've seen this man before?' Paul asked worriedly.

'I don't know, but I have seen him somewhere,' Nick answered.

'Christ, if you have seen him he must be close! Nick, just remember! Where did you see him?' Paul begged.

'I don't know, maybe it was outside Jeff's flat. It was dark but there was somebody in a car. Yes, that was it. I can't swear that it's the same man,' Nick said.

'Oh Jesus, he must have been the guy who killed Jeff. He looks really mad in the photo. Jeff must have caught them shooting a bunch of guys when he shouldn't have been there. Maybe they came to retrieve the pictures to stop them getting out. What should I do with this stuff, Nick?' Paul started to panic.

'I don't know. Get it to the police as soon as possible. Why don't you go there now? Tell them you think somebody is stalking you. I'll drive you up to Enfield now if you want.' It was the most sensible advice he could come up with.

'Yes, but how am I going to convince the police that someone is after me?' Paul asked.

'Well, just say that you suspect Jeff was murdered rather then killing himself with an overdose. Show them these photos and let them work it out. Also say that your car was sabotaged. I think you need police protection. If we are dealing with a professional killer, it will only be a matter of time before he discovers you're here. Go to the police tomorrow if you don't want to do it tonight.' Nick knew just how easy it was to be traced. He didn't relish the thought of going out to the back where the car was even with Paul, in case the man was watching the flat.

'You're probably right, mate. I'm sorry if this has put you in any danger. I promise to go to the police station tomorrow and tell them about this. I don't know how to thank you, mate. Just believe me, there was somebody in the car park yesterday.' Paul was nearly losing his nerve now that a connection had been established with Jeff's possible killer.

'Okay, I'm just going to have a quick word with Meg. Put the stuff away and turn the PC off. It won't do you any good looking at these pictures,' Nick suggested.

'Sorry for barging in on you just then, mate. She's a real cracker. Let me know if she has a sister!' At least some of his cockney sense of humour had returned.

Nick smiled nervously. Somehow, he would be happier if Meg was away from the flat just in case they were being stalked. He did not tell her about the photos he had just seen but Meg had presumed something was wrong anyway, especially when Nick insisted she left quite soon and saw her down to her car. He also stayed there until she was well on the road. It hadn't been the most romantic of nights but Nick certainly had a different way of entertaining his women, she thought. She laughed at the thought of referring herself as his woman.

28

Police

Paul left the flat in Palmers Green the next day and drove down to the police station in King's Cross. He had phoned the office to say he would be in later that morning. The duty sergeant took his personal details and also noted his concerns. Paul explained about Jeff, his car, the Frenchman, the Paris incident; the whole lot except the Afghanistan photographs. He missed out the vital link and simply stated he thought somebody was out to get the paparazzi in general and him in particular. He was also scared after somebody had broken into his car. He did not report the incident at the time because he thought it would have been a waste of time. He also didn't think to claim against his insurance because the repairs had not cost very much and nothing had been stolen. The police failed to ask the link between Jeff and the Paris incident, which Paul would have been unable to answer anyway as there wasn't one. At least there was no apparent link that he knew of. He wanted Ricky to see the photographs just in case there was money to be made from them, but he also wanted the police to look after him. He was creating a confusing situation for himself.

The sergeant tried to reassure him it was a local gang out stealing cars in the area. He also thought that there was no real evidence to suggest that the paparazzi were being specifically targeted by anyone. Without disclosing too much detail, the sergeant also said that the word about the bag of pure heroin in Jeff's flat had been circulated to all the police stations in case more was found in London. Pure heroin was lethal if sold to unsuspecting drug addicts. He concluded that Jeff had a habit unknown to anyone and had somehow obtained the heroin in its pure form. The sergeant had no idea regarding the autopsy report, as the case was being dealt with at another police station and besides, he could not reveal confidential information. As far as he was concerned, Jeff's death was unnecessary but was not suspicious.

Paul left the police station thinking it had all been a waste of time and he was totally unconvinced by the sergeant's take on the situation.

He had not said anything about the photographs as they would have been taken away due to the nature of the material. They could be sensational and make a lot of money if they were touted to the right people, perhaps to one of the big Sunday newspapers. The insurgency in Afghanistan was still topical at the moment and troops were dying out there. Some Sunday newspaper may jump at the chance of doing an article about the special forces murdering their prisoners. This would set alarm bells ringing in the Pentagon and Whitehall. Amnesty International would also be aghast. People may well watch reality TV these days but the odd massacre still managed to hold its fascination. The photos should sell easily.

He thanked the sergeant for his advice about keeping a low profile. The police would look into the matter, which really meant they would do nothing unless some new information came their way. Perhaps they would take this seriously when his body was found floating in the Thames. It was nearly eleven o'clock when Paul arrived back at the office. The other paparazzi were out on the streets and the girls were busy doing their work. After saying a quick hello, he grabbed a mug of coffee and went to Ricky's office. He was met with the customary greeting.

'Where the fuck have you been?' Ricky asked bluntly.

'Been down the nick haven't I?' he said, using the curious cockney phraseology. 'Don't worry, I'm not in trouble or anything like that but I'll tell you what he said about Jeff before I show you something,' Paul answered.

'Yeah, go on,' Ricky urged, pretending to be annoyed by his late appearance.

'He reckoned that Jeff had a habit and topped himself by mistake after shooting up too much pure heroin,' Paul said.

'Is that it?' Ricky asked impatiently, as if looking at some moron in front of him.

'No, he also said that my car was done in by some local lads. Rick, I know Jeff was murdered. I don't think he was a junkie. That was pure heroin in him, but junkies never use the pure stuff. Somebody put the stuff into him and planted the smack to make everybody think he was an addict. Now, why would anybody do that unless somebody wanted him dead but to make it look like an accident at the same time? Also, when I was in Jeff's flat, I had a look around and found some CDs that he had burnt. This is going to blow your socks off.' He produced the Afghanistan CD from his pocket and waved it around in the air like a trophy.

'What's that?' Ricky asked.

'It's some of Jeff's photos taken in Afghanistan. The pictures showed a bunch of people getting murdered. They were all tied up. A couple of the people in it look like American or British special forces soldiers and the rest look like Mujahadeen,' Paul said cleverly.

'Let me see it.' He snatched the CD from Paul's hand and flipped the lid open. The CD drawer slid open on the computer with a gentle whirring noise. He popped it shut and then double clicked on the 'My Computer' icon. A list of entries appeared on the screen and he clicked them open. The pictures were as Paul described.

He saw the picture of the soldier shooting a man in the head at point-blank range. He then opened the other pictures and saw a sequence of photographs portraying the deaths of more men. The final photograph showed one soldier looking upwards, with some dust swirling around his feet, indicating that he was looking up towards a helicopter. Even with his eyes partially closed to shield them from the downdraft of the helicopter, the hardened stare was that of a pure killer. Ricky let off a soft whistle.

'Do the police know about this?' he asked.

'No. I only discovered them yesterday. I was staying with Nick Forbes and I popped the disc into his computer. What do you think?' Paul asked.

'What's up with you and this guy? Are you a couple of poofters or what? Yes, I think this stuff could sell. I'll put it around,' Ricky said quickly.

He looked like a thoughtful Robbie Coltrane, psychoanalysing the ramifications of this material which could stir up a lot of trouble, but it was sensational stuff. He would not be the self-styled Paparazzi King if he simply did not try to get this type of material out into the public arena. The others would be gob-smacked, wondering how in hell he got his hands on them. He never divulged his source, creating an aura of mystery which further boosted his ego.

'Just two things, Rick, what's my cut and what do think will happen when this gets out?' Paul said, trying to do a deal with concerns for his own safety.

Ricky thought carefully for exactly three seconds.

'You'll get twenty-five per cent plus a good bonus at Christmas. Once it's out, nobody can touch us, freedom of the press and all that.' That was Paul's reply.

'I don't want to argue, Rick, but it was me that got the disc. I want fifty per cent on this one,' Paul stated.

'Listen, mate, if you tried to flog it without me, you'll get a lot less. Trust me. I'll get a good price on this, maybe fifty or sixty K. Flog it yourself if you want, but I can tell you now you'll be lucky to get ten, maybe fifteen K. People buy from me because they know I only sell the dog's bollocks.' Ricky was being ruthless; again it was just business.

'Alright, Rick, are you happy if we settle on thirty per cent?' It was Paul's last throw of the dice.

'Yeah, alright, I'll give you that one. If some people are going to get pissed off with this stuff, they will come for me, not you. I need the danger money. Now, piss off and do some work,' Ricky said.

Business, as far as Ricky was concerned, had been concluded, but Paul still had some burning issues in his own mind. He was a worried man.

'Rick, the police want me to keep a low profile, away from the job a few weeks until they know more about what's happening. What do you reckon if I stayed off?' he asked.

'The best thing you can do is to be right in there, amongst loads of people, if you think some psycho is coming to get you. Don't stay alone, so why don't you go and pull a bird or something, but I want you on the job and I don't just mean shagging. Now don't piss me about. There's some stupid little twat staying at the Dorchester who thinks he is a pop star. Go and piss him off and take some pictures.' Paul could see that Ricky was not in a good mood today.

'Alright, Rick, I hear you so keep your hair on. With all this money you're going to throw at me, how about a party at my place this Saturday?' Paul asked, trying to pacify his boss.

'Yeah, good one. Make sure you get plenty of birds and booze otherwise you can party by yourself. Get your mate Nick to come. The two of you seem close. He needs to get out of his face, so get him pissed. Just don't poof around in front of me,' Ricky said.

'Actually, Rick, he's got a nice bird, so why don't you back off about this poofing lark. Anybody would think you're hiding something yourself, mate,' Paul answered.

'Get some work done. I don't pay you for nothing!' Ricky bellowed.

'Saturday, don't forget!' he reminded Ricky.

Paul could just see that there was going to be a lot of drinking to be done, amongst other things. If the photos did sell for sixty thousand and his cut was thirty per cent, it would mean a lot of booze and charlie. He felt less worried already. The booze would come from one of the local wine merchants and they supplied the glasses too. The food was easy, Marks was round the corner. He had better order some lobsters for Ricky, just in case. The charlie would come from one of the black guys dealing right outside King's Cross railway station. Life could not be easier. He just didn't want to lose it too soon like poor old Jeff. Where's the fun in that?

Ricky went on the phone and personally contacted several newspapers. He whetted the appetites of the large national newspapers by mentioning human rights abuses conducted on prisoners of war by the coalition forces fighting in Afghanistan. He promised that the photographs were highly revealing and his price was for offers over £60,000. All they had to do was to decide if they wanted an exclusive package. He just waited for them to call him back. It was a game he enjoyed playing and he was the champion. Once the interest had been generated, he could play them off one against the other, saying how much he had already been offered. If nobody was interested, he would simply drop the deal and move on to another. The trick was not to seal the deal too quickly, because that would indicate panic-selling of something that was no longer hot property, but to delay things indefinitely could make the buyer lose interest. Today's picture was only as good as something else which came along. He had until Saturday morning to sell the photos, ready for publication on Sunday when people had the time to read about a major world situation. Time was on his side, but he would even consider an offer of less than £60,000 because the subject material would only have a limited audience. It was now Friday and he was getting a little weary of haggling all week. Making money was now no longer such a big deal any more and he could afford to lose out on a few thousand, but it would be a nice way to end the week. Paul had the right idea of having a party. What's the point of having money if you don't spend it? He was going to thoroughly abuse his body tomorrow night; it was worth the suffering the next day.

Paul phoned Nick later on that day to thank him for his hospitality and to ask him to his party. He also said he had been to the police station and recounted what the sergeant had said. Nick tried to clear one of the points Paul had made.

'Did you say that the police found a bag of heroin at Jeff's flat, indicating he was a heroin addict?' he asked.

'Yes, that was what the sergeant said,' Paul replied.

'Did the police say he had any other puncture wounds on his arm or other parts of his body to indicate that he was a regular user?' Nick asked again.

'No, the sergeant said the post-mortem report was at another police station, but he wouldn't tell me even if he knew the details,' Paul said.

'Did he give you any other details to be so sure Jeff wasn't killed?'

'No. He just said there was nothing suspicious,' Paul reiterated.

'Forensic toxicology is not something I know very much about but drug addicts have a higher risk of dying from different things, such as HIV, Hepatitis or even from general neglect, but not usually from using pure heroin. They usually know what they are doing and dealers usually cut the heroin with something else to make more profit. Some even use talcum powder. I have my doubts about Jeff's death. Junkies use the little insulin syringes which they get free of charge from the needle-exchange programme, to stop them sharing needles. Jeff didn't do that,' Nick said.

'I think you have just confirmed my fears, Nick. What do you make of the car break-in?' Paul sounded subdued. Everything Nick said had made sense so far.

'The Golf, like the Audi, has an immobiliser built into the engine management system. If the key was not in the ignition, it would be impossible to start the engine, even by hot-wiring it. The engine management system has to recognise the microchip in the ignition key to fire up. Anybody who breaks into cars for a living will know that. That is why it is usually the older cars which get broken into. I think somebody wanted to disable your car and then attack you while you waited for a mechanic to arrive. I guess whoever did it had not reckoned you didn't have any breakdown cover. It was just as well you left when you did that night,' Nick said.

'Nick, you are knocking the crap out of me. I'm going to go out with the lads tonight and crash on somebody's floor. Look, come to the party tomorrow. It will be good to see you at my place for a change and you have my address. There will be plenty of people there. Why don't you bring Meg with you? Ricky says you need to get pissed and forget about all that crap at the hospital,' Paul urged.

'That's good of you to ask. It's short notice but since I have made no plans whatsoever, I shall look forward to it. I'll see if Meg can come but I've not spoken to her today,' Nick replied.

'Yeah, it will be good, I promise! Let's have some fun, mate. The boys get a little wild but they're good blokes. Just come along with Meg. Rick's an animal when it comes to women but I'll keep him under control!' Paul sounded really excited about his party, having forgotten about his stalker, at least for now. He lived in Islington which used to be a dive, but not any more since the yuppies had moved in years ago. It had become a chic little area, just affordable to most working people, unlike some of the more expensive areas.

Nick felt a little uneasy about going to a party surrounded by the paparazzi, but perhaps his preconceptions preceded him. The word paparazzi actually originated from the Italians, which translated loosely as buzzing insects pouncing on their victims. It was coined in the 1950s when photographers riding on Vespa scooters deliberately went around taking photographs of the rich and famous as they debauched themselves in the Via Veneto in Rome.

The public had, until then, only seen their screen idols in airbrushed photographs produced by the film studios in order to promote their films. The paparazzi now showed the same people in unguarded poses, often revealing an unprecedented amount of flesh, unlike the sanitised Hollywood version. Richard Burton and Elizabeth Taylor were caught kissing through a telephoto lens when she was still married to her previous husband. The public wanted more of this type of intrusive photography and the age of the paparazzi was born. Had the public turned away from the paparazzi, they would all be out of a job.

Nick decided he would see Paul Lewis once more at the party before casually dropping his acquaintance. The people at the hospital people still had no idea who had taken the story to the press and Nick wanted to distant himself from now on. He was still intrigued enough to ask about Jeff's photographs.

'Paul, what did you do with the photographs?'

'I gave them to Ricky. He is trying to sell them. It should fetch a bob or two.' Paul gave a straight answer.

This was exactly the aspect of the paparazzi which Nick hated. Everything came down to money. Out of curiosity, he wondered how much pictures like that could fetch. He asked Paul very bluntly.

'How much is he going to sell them for?'

'Ricky is going for £60,000, give or take a few thousand,' Paul answered.

'That is more than I earn in a whole year for making life-and-death decisions. How can anybody justify that kind of money?' Nick was incredulous.

'I can hear by your voice that you're not in favour of this sort of thing, Nick. Just think of it this way, if some people are being shot at in cold blood, don't you think the world has a right to know about it? What if your father had been one of those men getting killed, wouldn't you want these men to be brought to justice?' Paul tried to defend himself. Nick thought about the matter for a few seconds before replying.

'I'm not going to argue about that; people need to know about the truth. Perhaps I'm not so bothered about the exposure of bad deeds or corruption, but I just think it is wrong that people can have their private lives so blatantly exploited by the media. Take, for example, the photograph of the socialite who had her toes sucked by her financial adviser. They were on holiday together when she was still married to her husband. That was a very private matter which has not benefited anybody except for the man who took the photos. Who needs to see toe sucking?' Nick asked.

'Nick, just consider this. How many people have got famous because of us? I can tell you: loads. When the movie stars get some coverage, their earnings go up because people go to see their movies. When one famous actor started to sound off about the paparazzi, nobody took his photographs, he didn't get the coverage and the movie flopped. It's not all one-sided.' Paul explained his side of the story.

'Yes okay, Paul, you have made your point and I don't want to fall out with you about this. I shall see you tomorrow. Bye.' He hung up.

Nick stopped the conversation before it got heated. One fight was enough. He tried to see Paul's point of view and he could understand why some people needed the paparazzi to promote their careers, but he still didn't agree with the intrusion of people's privacy. Perhaps celebrity status and personal privacy were mutually exclusive events. He was just glad he had managed to preserve his anonymity without getting his face plastered across the newspapers as the surgeon who killed his patient with diamorphine. No matter how much of the story was retracted when he was found innocent, his face would have been etched on some people's minds. Who could ever forget the bearded face of Dr Harold Shipman, the most prolific murderer in British history? Perhaps being associated with just one death would not have mattered too much in Nick's case. Fame was exponential to the amount of exposure one received and tomorrow would be another day. Nobody could ever know what it would bring, which surely was the whole point of staying alive.

29

The Party

Meg agreed to come along. Nick was relieved he didn't have to go to the party by himself. There was nobody there he knew well enough except Paul, but even he wasn't exactly a friend. The girl he'd snogged in the pub didn't count. These people were merely acquaintances that fate had brought to him. Nick offered to pick Meg up from her flat but she suggested he came for dinner first, to repay the compliment. He looked forward to that after a gruelling week at work, taken up with ward rounds, outpatient clinics, clinical meetings and operations; he just needed to unwind. He could quite easily become a couch potato and sit in front of the TV but life was for living. Going out on a Friday night could be tiresome when his mind said yes but his body said no. Saturday nights were different unless he was working. It was his party night where he could easily flirt and captivate some woman with his chat rather than giving it large with the drink and talk about football. That was definitely not his thing.

It was just a notion but he already suspected he would be waking up next to Meg in the morning. It wasn't overconfidence on his part, but ending up in bed with a pretty woman had never been a problem, even as a medical student. It was only the high maintenance girls who went out with the guys with money. There were enough pretty nurses at the doctors' parties who never once asked what sort of car he drove. Dating several of them at once did become a juggling act, especially when he was working 120 hours a week, but it had been good training for mental stamina and physical resilience.

He arrived outside Meg's modern flat in Southgate just after 5 p.m. with a box of Thornton's chocolates, something Emma hated. It would make his day if Meg liked them. Chocolate had wonderful antidepressant properties until people got too fat from eating them. Depression really set in then. Meg would never allow herself to get out of shape. She was the type of woman other women hated, the ever slim goddess who looked good in anything she wore. Nick felt like he was some big kid visiting Willie Wonka's factory just then. There were four flats in the building. He pressed the buzzer before the door buzzed open to let him in. Her flat was on the upper floor but the door was already opened by the time he climbed the stairs. Meg stood there leaning against the doorframe with a big smile on her face. It was the simple but stunning yellow dress which did it for him.

'Hi. You look good!' he said, giving her a peck on her lips.

'Thank you! So do you. Love the smell. What is it?' Meg asked.

'Davidoff.' He smiled back before giving her the chocolates. It was goodbye to Emma, for ever.

The flat was modern and feminine just as it was bright and clean, with off-white emulsion paint on the walls. Pale blue curtains hung from the metal poles which looked stunning, unlike those in his flat which were prehistoric. The linen-covered settees looked comfortable and the glass-topped stainless steel coffee table matched the style perfectly. The ubiquitous *Cosmo* was there. Ornaments dotted around the flat.

'I suppose I should give you the grand tour,' she said.

'Okay.'

'This is the living room, obviously! This is the kitchen, excuse the smell, I've using cumin in the recipe but it's not curry, and this is the bathroom, the spare bedroom and my bedroom!' she exclaimed in an exaggerated voice.

She had basically stood in the hall and moved very little, pointing to the various rooms which Nick quickly glanced through. It had been a whirlwind tour. Nick could only mumble how nice it was after whizzing from one room to another all in the space of seconds. It didn't matter. They ended up in the kitchen where Meg poured him a glass of wine before picking her own glass up. She had already put his chocolates down onto the worktop, delighted with the gift. They stood in front of each other for a few seconds and spontaneously started to kiss. Nick could feel her toned body stiffen as his tongue touched hers. She was running her fingers through his hair and pulled him tighter to her. Nick felt the curves in her body before running his hands down to her buttocks. They were locked in a passionate embrace, finally giving in after so long. Their relationship had been purely professional until now, which neither had wanted to destroy by getting too personal. It was too late; they both suddenly realised just how much they wanted each other. Their career paths had intertwined over the years but recent events had made their bond even stronger. Meg had desperately wanted to hold him when he was going through all the hell but hadn't known how to tell him. She had seen him fight for his career and go through the break-up of his relationship. He needed all the love he could get and she would give it to him, unconditionally. She would not ask for anything back. All that mattered now was that they needed each other, to be united as one.

Nick reached beneath her dress, and gently slipped his fingers through the side of her knickers, teasing them down. She unbuckled his belt and frantically tried to free him. They staggered towards the dining table with their lips glued together, their breathing rapid, their pulse racing faster and faster. Meg leant back against the dining table, kicking off her underwear. He entered her, feeling her tightness. They were now united at last and abandoned themselves to each other. His emotions surged to overwhelming levels; there was just an incredibly deep-seated love for this woman. He did not want the feeling to go away but wanted it to last for ever and ever. Meg gave herself freely to him; it was the most intense climax of her life. All she could do was to utter his name, again and again.

Their passion spent, they held on, kissing tenderly. The two pounding hearts gradually slowed down but their bodies trembled gently from the emotional and physical assault they had given each other. Nick felt moved enough to say something he had never said before.

'I think I love you.'

She didn't want to spoil the moment by saying she thought he said it to all the girls. She knew he meant it. The saucepan lid rattled away to let off the steam. The food was definitely ready. It was minced pork with paprika, cumin and tomatoes. Meg eased herself off the table and slipped her knickers back on and felt a little self-conscious as she smoothed her dress out.

'I hope you are hungry, Nick,' Meg said.

He looked at her in a lustful way whilst zipping his trousers. She burst out laughing.

'Not that you beast!' She was in love with him too.

After dinner, it was party time. They felt emotionally close and wondered why this had never happened long before. Meg's last true relationship had broken down when she simply fell out of love. There had been other men, including yuppies in their Porsches, but they had all lacked any real character. Nick was different, not only was he six years younger than her but he was a gentle person with a strong and determined mind. His smile could disarm even the most formidable senior nursing officer just as his stare could reduce a pompous idiot into a mumbling wreck. He was the kind of person who did not like fools or backstabbers and he made this very clear in his own irremissible way. Tact and diplomacy was not his strong point but he could also turn on the charm when it suited him. It was his lack of diplomacy which sometimes rubbed people the wrong way but he spoke his mind without the preamble. That same quality also endeared him to others in equal measure; the yin and yang were balanced. She didn't care if he was a little arrogant at work because his bedside manner made up for that. He treated his patients with respect and always tried to explain things in a simple manner. She had probably been in love with him for years without realising and now she didn't want the evening to end.

They climbed into the Audi TT. She loved the denim blue colour. Nick punched in the number of the CD he wanted from the stacker and Guns and Roses started as they set off for Islington. The weather was chilly but the night was clear. He turned the heating up to exactly twenty-two degrees on the climate control as Axl powered his way through the speakers. Life couldn't get better just then.

Meg struggled to keep her hands off her newly found love as he drove. Nick just kept his boyish grin on his face and had to concentrate on his driving. He managed to find the place without too much difficulty and squeezed into a tight parking space. Paul answered the door and showed them in. The party was definitely on. Just like any other typical London terrace house, the living room was off the narrow hallway with the dining room next door and the kitchen at the back. There was also an outside toilet in the backyard, a reminder of the days when toilets were cold places to be in. The stairs led up to two bedrooms with the bathroom with toilet at the back of the upper floor. Paul indicated they should leave their coats in the bedroom. After doing so, they went down to the kitchen to get a drink, the usual meeting place. Nick was driving again so it would have to be a couple of beers only. They had to push past people in the narrow corridor to get to the front room where they met up with Paul again. The music was punching out but it was just possible to hold a conversation. Ricky was there with his usual entourage of young women and the paparazzi boys were being very loud. They would normally be hanging about outside Stringfellows or Annabelle's, waiting for the celebrities to make an arse of themselves, but tonight was a rare Saturday night off. Ricky was in a generous mood. He saw Nick enter the room with his blond.

'Oi, Nick, come here, mate!' he shouted, blowing cigarette smoke out from his nose and mouth at the same time.

Nick stuck his hand up to give a friendly wave. He held on to Meg's hand as they went across.

'How are you doing, Nick? Who's this absolutely gorgeous creature?' he said, eyeing Meg up.

'This is Meg. We work together at the hospital. So what's new, Ricky?' Nick asked.

'Hiya, Meg. Nice to meet you.' He made a big show of standing up and kissing her hand before finding it easier to sit down again. The alcohol had weakened his legs.

'I'm Ricky. I'm afraid Nick does not like what I do for a living!' He burst out laughing. 'I suppose we all need surgeons but Nick can make a lot more money in this job. Sorry, mate, just winding you up,' Ricky said exuberantly, almost relishing his self-confidence that only new money could buy. Cleary, the focus was on himself, the feel-good factor coming from the Krug champagne.

Nick took the banter well. He could see that Ricky was well oiled, clutching onto his bottle of champagne. Ricky very much lived in a world of his own and if one could accept his character was larger than life itself, there was no reason to dislike him. Nick just wondered how he'd got on with Jeff's photographs. At least that was something to talk about.

'I heard from Paul that you were trying to sell Jeff's photos?' Nick asked.

'Yeah, some newspaper actually bought them this morning. It should be out tomorrow and all the tight-arsed war ministry people are going to scream blue murder! That would be fun, but what are you and Meg drinking? Have some champagne, not that lager crap. Oi, Paul, get us a couple of glasses will you? I'm looking after your guests here, you daft sod!' Ricky was on top form as he belched.

Paul returned with two clean glasses and another bottle of champagne. He passed them on to Nick before disappearing again. Ricky beckoned Nick to open the champagne as he couldn't be bothered to do it. It was definitely nicer than the lager. Nick tore off the metal foil and undid the wire holding the cork in place. With a quick twist, the cork came out easily but he controlled the pressure. There was no sense in wasting champagne. He poured out two glasses and topped up several more. The girl he had kissed in the pub was there but she hardly acknowledged him. Nick felt smug anyway. Meg was talking to Ricky but kept giving him a furtive glance from time to time to say that she was going to 'have' again him later. He had his boyish grin on again; in fact he wanted to laugh. He just felt incredibly happy, knowing he was there with probably the best looking woman in the room. He also knew that as a surgeon, he could probably have just about any other single woman there, perhaps even some of the attached ones. Confidence was a great aphrodisiac.

The party was going well. The office girls were in their little corner and Ricky was playing the local ringmaster. His easygoing manner, cockney accent and peroxide-blond hair somehow pulled people to

167

him like a magnet. The expensive aftershave and money just added to the appeal. Nick needed to go to the toilet but he knew Meg was in safe hands. Despite his rough diamond character, Ricky lived by a certain code and wouldn't tread on Nick's toes. Nick signalled to Meg where he was going as he pushed his way through the bodies. There was a small queue for the upstairs toilet. Not everybody knew about the one out in the backyard, which would have been too cold for the ladies. Nick made a note to speak to Paul as he had not seen him for a while. He would stick to his earlier decision of ending their acquaintance as they had absolutely nothing in common. The fight they had had at the supermarket was now history, but Paul had helped him out of a tight corner regarding his career. Apart from that, they had divergent views about life and Nick found it hard to think of Paul as a true friend.

He was still thinking about it as he made his way back down the stairs after going to the toilet. There was just a glimpse of a tall man with dark hair making his way to the front door. Somebody had said something to the man, who turned his head to reply in a friendly manner. His accent was definitely American. Nick immediately knew there was something strange about him. London may be very cosmopolitan with nearly half the population in central London speaking with a foreign accent but this man was different; he was familiar. Nick had seen his face before, particularly his eyes. A chill suddenly ran through him as the man briefly looked up and locked eyes with him. Nick quickly averted his eyes and pretended to concentrate on the stairs without stepping on anybody. By the time he got to the bottom, the man was gone. He immediately thought of Paul as he pushed his way into front room. He caught Meg's eyes and beckoned her to come to him as he scanned the room. Meg followed him out of the living room where they could talk without the music getting in the way.

'Nick, what's the matter?' she asked, seeing the concern on his face.

'I don't know. I thought I saw the man in the photographs. Paul was being stalked by somebody and it could be him. We have got to find Paul. You look down here and I'll go back upstairs,' Nick said, without going into too much explanation.

He rushed off without telling Meg he thought this man had also been outside Jeff's flat. She had not been told much about Jeff, his photographs or about his death but she could see Nick was fired up about something and that was enough. Explanations could come later but she knew Paul was in danger. Nick quickly climbed the stairs again and didn't care so much who he stood on this time. He searched the two bedrooms and did not find Paul. He bombed down the stairs and found Meg in the kitchen. Most of the people were chatting happily, some smoking cigarettes, others a sweet-smelling resin. Somebody volunteered they had seen Paul going out to the outside toilet, followed by another man. Nick's blood ran cold. He grabbed Meg's hand and pulled her out of the back door. It was freezing outside. They shivered in the thin clothes.

The backyard was dark except for the light coming from the dining room window. The small outside toilet was to the rear of the kitchen. Most houses had been converted to have them indoors, so this was a relic of a bygone era. Paul had clearly not bothered to modernise his house. Living alone, he obviously didn't feel the need to. What mattered was the need to find him quickly. Nick could see the closed door and the toilet appeared to be in darkness. No light seeped from the gap above the door. Instinctively, he knew something bad had happened in there. He grabbed the door handle and pulled the door open, revealing a slumped body on the lavatory seat. Even in the semi-darkness, he could see it was Paul. The light switch was just inside which Nick clicked on. Paul's shirt sleeve had been pushed up and the right arm had a purplish swelling in the middle where the vein had been punctured. A five-millilitre syringe was on the floor. Nick quickly looked at his other arm and found no other needle marks. He suspected it was the same for Jeff. There was a weak pulse, barely beating and Paul's breathing was shallow. His pupils looked constricted, a sign of morphine toxicity. Paul needed to get intravenous narcan into him very quickly, before the heroin killed him. Nick fumbled for his mobile and dialled 999.

Meg went in to clear the kitchen and asked the people there to give Nick a hand. They quickly carried Paul in and laid him on the floor. His pulse was getting weaker, as was his breathing. He would have to be resuscitated immediately if either stopped. People still milled around trying to be helpful but drunken people with no first aid skills were a menace. Nick had to get a grip of the situation before it got out of hand. He tried the diplomatic way.

'Listen in! I want all of you to piss off! Paul will need to be resuscitated and we need the space, now! I also want you to clear the hallway to let the paramedics get in. Move it!' he shouted.

The crowd did as they were told but a dozen heads still poked into the kitchen. Meg had already ripped Paul's shirt open ready to do CPR as Nick had his ear to Paul's mouth and nose to hear him breathe, keeping a finger on his carotid pulse at the same time. Paul was still alive but it seemed like an age before the paramedic arrived, the seconds ticking away very slowly. The paramedic has got there in under ten minutes, using a powerful motorbike which was much quicker than an ambulance. Nick and Meg quickly introduced themselves and explained the problem. The paramedic inserted a Venflon as Nick drew up two millilitres of narcan. He quickly injected the solution into Paul as Meg strapped the oxygen mask on and gave him full flow. Almost by miracle, Paul started to revive almost immediately. He became agitated initially and started to pull the mask off. He looked at Nick, then at Meg and the paramedic in a very confused way. He kept asking what was happening. Nick calmed him down by talking very slowly, almost as a father would to a child. It had been a close shave.

The ambulance arrived shortly afterwards and the crew strapped him into the chair before wheeling him out. Nick went in the ambulance to make sure Paul was okay. He quickly explained the situation to the crew and said it had been a murder attempt. Paul started to gibber as if trying to come to terms with the situation but his mind was clearly confused. The ambulance crew attached a heart monitor; his heart was beating normally. Nick reassured him everything was back to normal; it was all over.

The party was over too. Some people had gone away but others remained and mingled in the house or the streets, talking about the drama. Ricky went around telling everybody to go home or find another party. He seemed to have sobered up very quickly and saw Nick walking into the house from the ambulance.

'Nick, what happened?' he asked.

'Paul muttered something about being followed when he went to the toilet outside and this guy just stuck a knife up to his throat and then made him inject heroin into himself. The man, whoever he is, must have seen people go in and out all evening and found the ideal place here to do Paul in. He must have been one cool customer to do that amongst all these people. Paul was right, he was being stalked. Jeff was probably killed in the same way. Rick, what are these photos all about? Who did you sell them to?' Nick asked.

'It doesn't matter now. They have already been printed in the Sunday newspaper. Somebody tried to stop this getting out but they were too late. Jeff must have tried to sell them before we knew anything about it and they killed him thinking they had all the copies. When we touted them around again, Paul nearly gets it. You tell me, I don't know what is going on,' Ricky said, suddenly feeling quite traumatised that another paparazzi had nearly been killed.

'Sorry, Ricky, I don't get it myself. Jeff was killed because he tried to sell these photographs. Paul said he thought he was being stalked even before he found them. So why was Paul being targeted? Apart from the fact that they both worked for you, there was no link between Paul and the photographs until Jeff had been killed. I think you know more about this than you are letting on. I asked Paul to hand them in to the police, but you had to sell them to the newspapers. Nothing makes any sense except you've made some money out of this and Paul was nearly killed,' Nick said, feeling slightly angry that greed had started to cost people their lives.

'I am trying to think, mate. Just lay off about me making money. You're absolutely bloody right that it doesn't make any sense. Paul thought it was to do with the Paris incident. He said somebody probably wanted to shut him up in case he had to give evidence at the inquiry, if there is going to be one. That must be the link. Whatever it is, Paul is still in trouble until this guy is caught. We'll hand over all the photos to the police but if this guy is a professional killer, he will know how to keep a low profile. Paul must go under police protection tonight, and speaking of which, I think the boys in blue have just arrived. Do you want to speak to them or will I?' Ricky offered.

'Could you do it? I have given enough statements to the police recently. Just tell then there is a syringe and needle in the toilet for their forensic people to look at,' Nick said wearily. 'They will probably ask who found him. Just say you don't know.'

'Yeah, off you go, Nick. I'm still too pissed to think straight about this. Keep in touch,' Ricky said as he held out his hand, still feeling the effects of the Krug swilling around his brain.

'Thanks.' Nick shook his hand. It had been quite a dramatic day and he just wanted to walk away from all the mayhem.

He found Meg sitting on the stairs and suggested about going home. They picked up their coats and left. Guns and Roses stayed silent as they drove back to Southgate. Meg asked if he wanted to stay and he felt he couldn't say no. Too much had happened for either of them to be alone. They cuddled up and fell asleep in her cosy bed where it felt safe. The bogeyman wouldn't get them there, at least it seemed that way.

30

The Reckoning

Nick woke up in a strange bedroom. He had to think where he was until he saw Meg lying there with her back towards him. In the half light, he observed her bare shoulders as they moved gently, in time with her breathing. The wintry sun tried to fight its way through the pale patterned curtains, giving a gentle glow to the Sunday morning. It felt good to be in love. In fact, he loved everything about her, from her delicate freckles, her blond hair, to the way she laughed. It was all so indefinable. He moved closer and held her. She moaned gently as she felt his hand rest on her breast. He could feel himself stirring again as she responded. This time, they made love gently, less frantically but equally satisfying. She kissed him tenderly as if to cement their new-found love. What had happened yesterday at the party seemed like a bad dream, almost as if it had never happened.

'Do you want tea or coffee?' she asked, running her fingers through his hair.

'I just want you,' he muttered in jest. She sat up and threw a pillow at him, making him giggle in the process.

'Tea or coffee I said!'

'Oh alright, I'll have a cup of tea with my crumpet then.' Nick then burst into laughter at his own joke. Yesterday's nightmare had almost been forgotten.

This time she got out of the bed and pulled the duvet off in mock disgust. Nick had to retrieve it, feeling rather silly lying there all naked. The tea soon arrived, followed with another kiss. Meg went for a shower in the en suite bathroom.

'What are your plans today, Nick?' she shouted out through the half-closed door.

'Nothing much. Need to do some shopping and iron the shirts,' he shouted as the shower switched on.

'I'm going to the church today. Are you a churchgoer, Nick?' Meg asked.

'Nope. I'm not that type. I didn't know you were religious,' he replied.

'You hardly know me!'

'Oh yes I do!' he said in a cheeky tone of voice.

'Nick, you have a one track mind and I'm going spank you for that,' Meg promised.

After showering, she came out wrapped in a large white towel, dived on top of him and pretended to pillow fight. He fell into hysterics again as he felt the water drip from her wet hair. She kissed him once more before jumping off to finish what she was doing, sticking her tongue out for good measure. She didn't look thirty-six; more like some impetuous teenager. The events last night just made them glad that they were alive.

The smell of bacon and eggs wafted through the flat as Nick came out the bathroom. He decided to give Paul a quick call. As it turned out, Paul had suffered no lasting effects from his ordeal and was free to leave the hospital except the police had now taken a major interest in the matter. A policeman had been assigned to guard the ward all night and he was now going to a safe house until his attacker had been found. It was reassuring to know. Paul would keep his mobile on. Also, if anything came up he would be in touch with Nick.

Meg had agreed to come over later that afternoon after she had been to church and done her own shopping. Nick left after breakfast and stopped at one of the big supermarkets. Sunday wasn't Sunday without the newspaper. It was an essential item in the trolley. At home, he plopped it on the worktop, still wrapped up in the clear cellophane bag. The flat looked exactly the same as when he'd left; the few unwashed dishes still remained by the sink. He whistled a nondescript tune as the shopping was put away, feeling very satisfied with life. The newspaper headlines then caught his eye; there was an article on Afghanistan. He ripped the cellophane off and unfolded the paper. The article ran onto the second page. Turning over, a picture of the massacre was there. It had been too much for the front page. Ricky had sold the pictures to a classier broadsheet.

The article described the incident and implicated the role of the special forces in the dirty war going on in Afghanistan. Several of the pictures showed men being shot by a soldier and two Mujahadeen warriors, but there was no picture of the soldier beneath the helicopter. He would read the article first; the shave could wait, having already showered at Meg's. After making a mug of coffee, he wandered into the living room with the newspaper. Something was different there; he sensed another person in the room. The man sat very quietly in the armchair, his gaze unwavering. A small automatic lay on the armrest; it was a Walter. The silencer on the end made it even more menacing.

'Jesus! Who the hell are you?' Nick shouted in a startled manner.

'Shut up! Sit down and be quiet!' The man spoke with an American accent.

Even without moving a muscle, he looked menacing. There was a commanding authority about him which demanded immediate respect. Nick remained in shock, unable to comprehend what was going on at that confusing moment.

'How is your friend?' the man asked inquisitively.

'He seems to be okay.' Nick immediately presumed Paul was the subject matter.

He recognised the man from the party yesterday; it was also Jeff's killer. His brain remained frozen, unable to think beyond the simple reply.

'I presume you were the guy that found him, right?' the man asked.

'Yes, and I presume you tried to kill him,' Nick said.

The man gave him an icy stare and said nothing for a minute.

'I ask the questions, you answer, okay? I told you already, sit down.' Nick didn't have to be asked again.

'Yes, sorry.' Nick played the underdog to his uninvited guest.

'Good, now we understand each other. I believe you work as an orthopaedic surgeon?' the man asked.

'Yes, I am. How did you know that?' Nick was curious to know.

'Like I said, I ask the questions.' His voice remained icily calm.

'Okay, sure. I don't want to cause any trouble. Just tell me what you want,' Nick said quietly.

'I want you to get your friend here.' His voice remained flat, unemotional and straight to the point.

'At least tell me why.' Nick needed to know.

'Just know this: I will have to kill you later, but you can choose how you die. The painful way is through a bullet in the stomach and I have seen a man take more than thirty minutes to die like that. The easy way is through a nice injection of the good stuff. It's up to you, but for that, you need to get him here.' The offer was made in a very seductive way. It almost sounded too good.

'I don't even know who you are. Are you planning on killing him too?' Nick asked.

'Yes.'

'The pictures have been published. How would our deaths change anything?' Nick asked in desperation.

'It's simple. I will kill your friend because I have to. I will kill you because you know me,' he explained.

'Just tell me one thing – did you kill a guy called Jeff Richards?' Nick asked.

'Yes.'

'Why? Was it because he was trying to sell the pictures?' Nick asked.

'Yes and no.' The man was being deliberately vague.

'No?'

'Let's just say the 'no' was for payback,' the man said.

'Could you just explain that?' Nick asked.

'Sure, since you're not going to be alive. That photographer was in the wrong place at the wrong time. We didn't murder anybody. The man you see in that newspaper today was my buddy. The Taliban went for his gun and he had to put him down but the pictures told the wrong story. We just tried to take the pictures out of the circulation but there must have been other copies. My buddy blew his own brains out because the stress got to him, not just about this, but about the whole goddamn war,' he explained.

'So, you killed Jeff for revenge?' Nick asked.

'We didn't want him to shoot his mouth off. Let's just say I enjoyed killing him. Our guys out there are risking their lives every day to take out these terrorists and some photographer comes and screws things up. Do you know how many GI Joes have killed themselves after Iraq or Afghanistan when they just couldn't take it any more?' he asked.

'No.'

'Let's just say the world owes them. Now I want you to get your friend here.' His eyes pieced through Nick.

'He didn't sell the pictures; his boss did,' Nick pleaded.

'Phone him.' It was an order.

'How did you find me here?' Nick asked.

'I followed your friend from Kings Cross on the tube and then your car in a taxi. Now just call him!' He was getting annoyed with Nick's questions.

So Paul had been right all along. This man had been in the car park that night. Nick tried hard to find a way out of this mess. He figured the man would not shoot him just yet, not until Paul was here. He had no idea how to persuade Paul to come over when he was under police protection. Perhaps the man already knew Paul was in a safe house and this was the only way of getting him. But how had he known that?

'Look, for what it's worth, I did not think it was a good idea to publish those pictures. I don't know what went on in Afghanistan and

I don't agree with what the paparazzi do but that is not a good enough reason to kill us. Besides, this whole thing has nothing to do with me.' Nick tried his best to delay the inevitable.

The man was untouched by Nick's sentiments and stared blankly back at him. He reached out and casually picked up the automatic, pointing the business end towards Nick.

'I'm going to shoot you now unless you call him.'

The talking was over. Nick sweated beneath his shirt, acutely aware that it was still the same shirt he had on last night. He figured he had just about established a good enough rapport to ask a couple more questions.

'How did you know he was alive and that it was me who'd saved him?' Nick asked.

'I waited. I guessed it wouldn't take long for somebody to find him. Let's just say, I know about these things,' the man replied.

'You didn't want the pictures did you? There was no way you could get them at the party. It was simply to kill him and make it look like an overdose gone wrong. Why?' Nick probed.

'You know, in another time, another place, Nick, we could get along. This is nothing personal but I have a job to do. Let's just say your friend saw something he shouldn't have done, or at least he should have kept quiet and not said anything to the French police. That sort of thing could be unhealthy.'

'So this is about the Paris thing. Who are you working for?' Nick asked.

There was complete silence but at least the man smiled.

'Hey, you've got a lot of balls. This gun doesn't scare you, huh?' he asked in a mocking tone.

'If I'm going to die it won't matter would it? What was the big deal about the Paris incident anyway? The couple died and the driver was drunk. Was there something else to say about it?' Nick sounded off, the bravado creeping in.

'You know, Nick, there are a lot of bad things in the world. One of them is that you Brits still think you can pull the strings, but the really bad thing is that the Arabs are taking over. The have the oil, they own the shipping ports, airlines, hotels and some of the best real estate in your country and mine. The Saudi government alone wants to spend three hundred billion dollars from fighter jets to shit pans. They could buy foreign governments for that. They already own castles in your country. Do you want them to take over your royal family? Huh? Think about it man. The other half of the Arab world wants to blow everything else up. And now the British police want an inquiry on this

Paris thing. You Brits gotta get real man. So what if some Arab got iced? Just understand this: the Paris crash was an accident. Your friend ain't gonna say otherwise because he's a dead man already. You just call him now or I'll put a slug in your knee. It won't kill you just yet but it will be messy. What's it gonna be, Nick?' It was an ultimatum with no get-out-of-jail card.

'Okay, I'll call him. You already know he is under police protection, don't you?' Nick said it a deflated tone.

'I guessed you could be useful. Get him to lose the police.'

Nick pulled out his mobile and pressed call against Paul's name. Thank God he answered.

'Paul, listen its Nick. I need you to come over to my flat right now.'

'What's up, mate? You sound nervous,' Paul answered.

'We have a mutual friend who wants to meet you. I can't spoil the surprise. Can you come?' Nick asked.

'Is she nice, mate? It's a bird, right?' Paul joked.

'You'll see when you get here. Can you leave the police behind?' Nick was hoping for the opposite; he would be extremely glad if they did come.

'Yeah, no problem. I'm just stuck in some place they use as a safe house with PC Plod, except he is not in uniform. I'll ask him,' Paul offered.

'Thanks, Paul.' Nick waited anxiously.

'He says no can do, mate. Too risky. They reckon this man will have a firearm and they ain't got the men to take me round to yours. Something about a full protection squad. Sorry, mate,' Paul finally said.

'Cheers, Paul. See you when you get here,' Nick replied.

'Eh? I said, I can't come.'

'Yes, I heard you. Leave the police behind.' Nick said that slightly louder for the benefit of his guest.

'You're being daft, mate. I can't come. Just told ya,' Paul repeated.

'See you later.' Nick rung off.

'Your buddy coming?' The man asked.

'Yes.' Nick now had to think fast. He only had a few hours until Paul failed to show up. Always buy time.

'Okay, so we have a little wait. Relax.' He placed the gun down again on the armrest.

'Do you mind if I called my girlfriend? She was going to come round but I don't want her to get mixed up in this,' Nick asked.

'That pretty little thing. Yeah, sure. I'm listening.'

It was a precautionary reminder for Nick to watch what he said. The man had obviously watched them at the party yesterday. He just prayed Meg was in and that she would pick up on his distress. Paul was not going to come here with the police and Meg was his only chance left.

'Hi, Meg. How are you?' he asked.

'Okay. Church was good. What's up?' she replied.

'Look, something has cropped up so I don't want you to come over today. Is that alright?' Nick said.

'Nick, is that a brush off or are you teasing me?' she laughed.

'I'm being serious.'

'I thought we were having a good time or was that just a one-night stand?' she asked.

'No, it wasn't a one-night stand. I love you but I just can't see you today, that's all,' Nick tried to explain.

'Has one of your 'girlfriends' suddenly turned up and this is awkward for you? Just tell me honestly. Well?' Meg asked.

'No, it's nothing like that, believe me. My eyes really hurt. It happened all of a sudden.' He tried to sound as obscure as possible, trying to make her think.

'There was nothing wrong with you or your eyes earlier on. Is this some kind of bullshit, Nick?' Meg really didn't know whether he was joking around, trying to wind her up for a laugh.

'They're painful in a really piercing way. It is going to kill me unless I can do something about it,' Nick said. He saw the man stiffen up. He had gone over the edge and he knew it.

'Look, I've got to go. Just don't come, okay?' His voice was just about to break down. He was sure Meg hadn't picked up on what he was really trying to say. He was dead meat.

'Okay, Nick, if that is what you want. I hope you have a good time too!' She rung off in a sarcastic tone of voice.

Damn him. That bastard had another woman there. There was nothing wrong with his eyes which she hoped was killing him. What was that about the piercing pain? Good. Meg was still furious and thinking obscenities when her landline rang again. She thought it was Nick again.

'Hello!' she almost shouted.

'Meg?'

'Yes, who's that?' she asked.

'It's Paul here, Meg. Sorry to call you. Got your number from the telephone book. Is Nick with you by any chance?' he asked in his smooth London patter.

'No.'

'He was just on the phone to me a few minutes ago. It was a weird call. He asked me to come over to his flat straight away but said not to bring the police with me,' Paul explained.

'I just received an even weirder call. He asked me not to come over because his eyes were hurting him. There was absolutely nothing wrong with him earlier on,' Meg said, in mock disgust.

'What else did he say?' Paul asked.

'He mentioned that his eyes were piercing with pain and that it was going to kill him. I think that was what he said,' Meg replied, trying to make some sense from all this nonsense.

'Oh my God!' Paul exclaimed.

'What is it, Paul?' Meg asked.

'He is there! You wouldn't know unless you saw the pictures and that was what Nick meant. This man had weird eyes, you know, cold icy eyes like a killer. He didn't want to put you in danger but the man wanted me there because he knows he can't get to me with all the police protection. Hell, he is still after me! Listen, Meg, I'll get the police onto this straight away. Just stay by your phone and I'll be in touch. We will keep you informed, okay?'

'Alright, Paul. Phone me as soon as possible.'

The phone went dead. Paul had to speak to the police.

A squad of patrol cars rushed up to Palmers Green with their sirens blazing. The firearm team readied their weapons, using Heckler and Koch MP5s, which were superb submachine guns, reliable and very deadly. They also had Remington shotguns to blow off door hinges if necessary. Nick's flat was surrounded within fifteen minutes. The police helicopter flew overhead as the streets below were cordoned off, the traffic diverted away from the area. Both Nick and the killer had heard the sirens approaching but it could have been for some other emergency up the road. There was no mistake about it when the squad cars stopped around the flat. Marksmen positioned themselves behind the cars with their weapons pointed towards the flat. The man watched them arrive from behind the curtains. Nick had somehow managed to alert his girlfriend and a sneaky suspicion crossed the man's mind.

'Hey, Nick, I guess your friend was never coming, was he?' he asked.

'No,' Nick replied.

The man walked across the room and punched him straight in the mouth. Nick saw a kaleidoscope of colours and felt totally dazed, making him fall back onto the settee. He tasted fresh blood in his mouth. The initial numbness in his jaw slowly turned into pain.

'You're pretty smart but to me you're a real pain in the ass, mister. Do you want a fucking bullet in you right now? Well do you?' He'd lost his temper and that was dangerous.

Nick could see the man standing above him, with the automatic held very tightly in his right hand. His finger was on the trigger, the slack taken up, and any slight pressure would send the hammer down onto the percussion cap, sending a 9 mm slug into his brain. Nick shook his head meekly with the blood trickling down his chin. The man quickly assessed the situation. He pulled Nick roughly from the settee, pointing the gun straight into his face. The time for explanation was over. Nick was now a hostage and they were going to make it out of there straight away. The man knew that hostage negotiations were a load of bullshit. They were for hot headed radicals who hadn't started to shave yet.

'We're leaving by the back door,' he said and Nick nodded. 'We're going to use your car, but you drive.' He grabbed Nick roughly and pulled him through to the kitchen.

'My car keys are in my coat pocket. Okay to put the coat on?' Nick asked.

The man agreed. The coat was where he had left it, on the back of the chair. He felt in his right pocket and found the car keys along with his pen. It was one of those chunky plastic pens which drug companies gave out as a free present, their logo clearly printed. Nick felt a shove in the back as the man pushed him towards the door. There would be police covering the back stairs, probably even from the landing just outside. Several guns were probably pointing towards the door right now. The man knew the drill. He opened the door slightly, to tell them what he was doing. He didn't have to look.

'Coming out! Don't shoot. I have a hostage and there is a gun pointing right at his head. I said, don't shoot!' He spoke clearly and loudly. There was no sign of panic.

He didn't trust these people. The police marksmen were highly trained but they didn't have combat experience. It made their fingers itchy and more often then not, they got it wrong. Innocent people had been shot by the police by mistake, but there was no need for his hostage to die yet. If they took him out, the spasm in his hand would also set his gun off, killing Nick in the process. That would be a shame and a very unprofessional thing to do.

He slowly opened the door with his foot, keeping Nick in front of him. He grabbed a hold of Nick's coat and pointed the gun into the back of his neck. He could now see the police marksmen with their guns trained on him. They had all been issued with his photograph, downloaded and sent electronically within seconds so there would be no mistake. Nick walked out with his arms in the air. Very slowly, they emerged together. The policemen did not say a word. The hostage negotiator had not arrived and was still being briefed about the situation. The police knew they were dealing with a special forces soldier, who also happened to be an assassin, probably paid or otherwise. It was better to avoid a stand off.

They advanced slowly down the stairs until they got to the car. The guns followed them every inch of the way, with red laser beams coming from different directions as they pointed to the man's head. Nick unlocked the car ultrasonically. They both got in from the passenger side and Nick had to climb over onto the driver's side. The Walter never moved from his head. Nick put on his seat belt but noticed the man did not. It wasn't the right moment to say 'clunk click every trip'.

'Where to?' Nick asked.

'The North Circular, heading towards Hertfordshire.'

'Okay.' Nick started the car and slowly drove off. The police scrambled into their patrol cars and followed a hundred yards behind. They knew the automatic pistol was only accurate up to fifty yards but it would be hard to shoot at any target behind the Audi anyway.

Nick drove out into Green Lanes and turned left towards the city. He picked up the North Circular Road about a mile further down and turned right. A long line of police cars followed, including the helicopter above. They knew they were relatively safe, but they had to keep the public out of the way.

'Where now?' Nick asked.

'There is a small aerodrome at Elstree. Go there,' he replied.

'Where is that?' Nick asked.

'Don't you have sat nav in this car?'

'No.'

'You're a really useful guy, Nick. Where's the map?' the man asked.

'In the glove compartment,' Nick replied.

The man found the small roadmap in there; it had some drug company logo on it. He looked at the index and turned to the local area. Elstree was not far away but the map was next to useless. It was not big enough to show where the aerodrome was.

'Say, Nick, do you guys always rely on drug companies to give you crap presents? This is a piece of shit. Just head up the A1 until we turn off for Elstree.'

'I've got a bigger map in the boot. Do you want it?' Nick offered.

'Nope, you're really hoping these boys are going to blow my head off, aren't you? Keep driving.'

The man needed some thinking time as he tried to formulate a plan. In any military operation, he would quickly appraise the ground, situation, mission and plan of attack. He was in unfamiliar ground; the situation was frankly hopeless and his mission to kill the target had failed. There was no backup as this had been a 'deniable' operation. His only plan of attack was to take the initiative. He knew he could not leave the country through a commercial airport or seaport, but there was a remote chance of flying out in a small aircraft, perhaps heading towards France. His military training had included some rudimentary knowledge of flying small aircraft. It was more than likely the aircraft would be monitored by radar all the way to France and the Brits could ask the Royal Air Force to give chase.

However, once the plane was in France, he could fly low, lose radar contact and find a suitable field to land on. He could then simply disappear, unless they used sophisticated thermal imaging equipment. There was no other choice apart from giving up or killing himself, but he intended to do neither of those things.

Nick looked in his rear view mirror. He could see the police Volvo T5 pursuit cars following behind with more flashing lights up ahead. The man knew he was outgunned against the police's MP5s and Glock automatics; he couldn't possibly take them on, no matter how well trained he was. Nick was the only bargaining tool left. Shooting him would make no sense.

Nick had figured things out differently. He thought the man would kill him once they had reached the aerodrome and found an aeroplane. He kept his speed steady at around 40 mph. There was no rush to get there. The man also knew that a high speed chase would give him less thinking time. Fast moving action could lead to bad decision-making and he knew the police were capable of firing first without thinking properly. They had just shot some innocent guy in a tube train thinking he was a terrorist. It did nothing for the tourist industry. He could also see Nick getting tense about this whole thing and he didn't want him to do anything stupid either. He tried a little humour.

'Say, Nick, do you think these guys could escort us to the aerodrome? How about asking on your cellphone?' he suggested in a humorous way.

Nick pretended to concentrate on the road ahead and did not bother to answer. His mind was on other things. He quickly glanced to see where the gun was without moving his head. The weapon was in the man's right hand, resting on his lap. He was also aware the man did not have his seat belt on. It was a tough call and the adrenalin level was building up in him. His heart pounded away strongly as did his head from all the stress. The car even sped up as he subconsciously pressed the throttle. They were now on a piece of newly resurfaced road with just the police in front and behind them; traffic had been prevented from joining the North Circular. The man had not anticipated the next move.

Nick knew within himself that it was now or never. His sweaty palms made the steering wheel a little difficult to hold when his brain suddenly screamed 'now, now, now!' He slammed the brakes on as hard as he could. The car shuddered and skidded as the tyres struggled to grip the tarmac, generating a plume of rubberised smoke. Nick was thrown forwards by the sudden deceleration but was held back by his seat belt. The man hit his head on the dashboard but failed to fly out of the windscreen. Nick had neither gone fast enough nor braked hard enough. Perhaps the new thin road surfacing material had created less friction with the tyres. The car had taken longer to stop than Nick had thought, and the reduced deceleration had saved the man from fatal injury. He was stunned but very much alive.

Nick could only think about the bullet that was surely coming his way. In a panic to get out, his fingers desperately fumbled for the seat belt release button which seemed like an age to get off. In reality, it took no more than seconds. The seat belt finally slid away as it retracted back into the casing. He now reached for the door handle, concentrating on bailing out. A hand suddenly grabbed him and held him back. In a vague blur, he saw the man trying to bring his weapon round to bear on him. Instinctively, he reached out with his left hand and gripped the man's wrist, pushing the gun away from him. He then felt fingers clawing into his eyes. He tried to turn his head away but the fingers were too strong. With his free hand, Nick managed to grab hold of the man's little finger. With a sharp yank, he bent it right back until he felt it crack. The man's grip slackened briefly as he let out a low grunt. They were both now panting hard with the effort of fighting in the small car, but Nick was burning up extra nervous energy trying not to get killed. He just wished the police would hurry up and shoot the man.

The police had stopped and surrounded the car. The armed response teams deployed and covered every angle with their MP5s but did not want to rush in without evaluating the situation. Nick knew that the man would shoot if he had a chance but the police could not unless they had a clear view of the target inside the car. Right then, he felt the loneliest man in the world, despite the swarm of armed police outside. It was up to him now to sort out the problem. He desperately wished for some sort of a weapon he could use. Fending the man off with his left hand, he quickly reached inside his coat pocket with his free hand and found the pen, quickly clicking the tip out. Without giving the matter any further thought, he rammed the pen as hard as he could into the man's neck. He felt it go in until it stopped at something hard: the cervical spine. Along the way, the pen hit several important structures including the carotid artery. Initially, the man still held onto his grip but very slowly, Nick could feel his strength ebb away as the ruptured artery pumped the life out of him.

The car had started to look like an abattoir as the blood sprayed out in huge spurts. The roof and dashboard were quickly covered in the sticky fluid, just as Nick was. Some blood had squirted into his face, temporarily blinding him. He held on until the man died, giving a final shake in his death throes. Nick was drained by his emotions. It had all been a horrible nightmare. Tears welled up in his eyes until they became a flood. He had sworn on the Hippocratic oath to save lives, but now he had killed somebody. He just needed to get away from this carnage.

He pushed the dead man back into the seat; the gun fell onto the floor. He opened the door and stepped out into the fresh air, staggering away from the car. His mind was numb from the trauma and he barely registered the flashing lights all around him. Somebody shouted as he walked away from the car. More voices were now screaming at him. He could see several people pointing guns at him. They kept repeating their warning but it all made little sense to him.

'Armed police! Get down on the floor with your arms out! Do it.' A dozen submachine guns were pointing at him.

Nick no longer felt afraid, despite all the guns aimed at him. He just lay down on the ground and stuck his arms out. The police moved in and stood on his wrists, making sure he did not move whilst they searched him. Other marksmen pointed their weapons inside the car. They could see the dead body but still checked it for signs of life just to be sure.

Lying on the cold road quickly allowed the reality to sink in. His body hurt, especially his mouth, which had now got swollen from the punch earlier. His gums had been indented by his front teeth and they were starting to fester. He was annoyed by the unnecessary pain in his wrists caused by the police standing on them. He suddenly felt angry.

'I want you gorillas to get off me now!' he shouted.

A senior police officer appeared and ordered the men off. They had formally identified the body in the car. Nick now sat on the road, shaking from the emotional trauma. He was totally covered in blood but somebody had thrown a blanket over his shoulders. He figured sooner or later he would have to give another statement starting with his name, date of birth, occupation and qualifications. At least that part of the bullshit was routine.

He had a little more explaining to do regarding the dead man in his car. That would take place at the police station. Once there, he had to remove all his clothes in case forensic evidence was needed. As far as he was concerned, it was pretty straightforward. Somebody had wanted to kill him and he owed it to himself to save his life. At least the hot shower and the cup of tea, courtesy of the police, had made him feel reasonably human again. The spare clothes he was loaned were clean, unlike the blood-soaked garments he had to put into plastic bags.

Paul Lewis had given the police more information about the assassin. Nick was not going to be held up for murder and he was free to go. He felt quite relieved about going home.

31

The Aftermath

The police dropped Nick off at his flat. They had taken a statement and informed him there would be an inquiry. His car had been taken away by the police forensics team, despite it being quite obvious what had happened. It was a total mess inside and Nick doubted if he would ever drive it again. Right now, that was the last thing on his mind. He simply wanted to have a stiff whisky. The police had kindly offered to arrange psychotherapy for him but they could not undo what had been done. Post-traumatic stress affected people in different ways but Meg was all the therapy he needed at the moment. He quickly climbed the front stairs to the flat, impatient to speak to her. She had probably misunderstood his earlier cryptic phone call. There was an unexpected visitor sitting by the door.

'Bloody hell, what's that you're wearing?' Paul Lewis was there.

'Paul! Sorry about my appearance; they're not mine. On loan from the police,' Nick replied.

Nick quickly opened the door and was pleased to see that the flat looked the same this time, without a maniac waiting there for him. He actually felt remarkably calm and wondered what Paul was doing there. He wanted to change into his own clothes.

'I'll tell you all about it after I've changed. Just pour me a large whisky and have one yourself. I don't have any beers left,' Nick ordered. Paul kept quiet as he tried to understand what was going on. Despite all the trauma, Nick seemed relatively uninjured. As there was no beer, Paul poured two whiskies, although he hated the stuff. At least it contained forty-three per cent alcohol; all he could find was the eighteen-year-old MaCallan. He sat bemused in the lounge until Nick reappeared.

'Do you want to tell me about it?' he asked.

Nick grabbed the whisky and took a large swallow. He felt more human now but the alcohol burnt his lip.

'It has been one hell of a weekend. What do you remember about yesterday, Paul?' he asked.

'I remember the party until some big ape held a knife to my throat and made me inject heroin into myself. Thanks for saving my life by the way. But what happened to you? What's up with the clothes?' Paul asked.

'Let's just say I killed that ape. It got a little bloody,' Nick replied.

'Nick, say that again. You killed the guy who tried to kill me?' Paul asked incredulously.

'Yes, he was in this flat when I got back from Meg's this morning. In fact, he was sitting where you're sitting now. He wanted to kill you here because he couldn't get to you under police protection. I phoned you and Meg with a vague message hoping that one of you would twig I was in trouble. The police said it was you who told them what was going on. So how come you're at the flat?' Nick asked, after explaining what had happened.

'The police at the safe house said it was all over. I was free to go so I decided to come here. They wouldn't give me any details, so I just presumed you were at the flat. Your face looks a mess by the way,' Paul said.

'The lip feels a little bit swollen. He punched me when he found out you weren't coming. This whisky stings a bit but hopefully it should numb the pain.' Nick tried to smile.

'How did you kill him?' Paul was curious to know.

'Stuck a pen in his throat but I'd rather not talk about it,' Nick replied.

'Yeah, sorry, mate. Did this guy ever say why he wanted to do me in?' Paul asked.

'It was to do with the Paris incident. Apparently you gave the French police a statement,' Nick said.

'Are you sure it wasn't about the photographs, mate?' Paul asked.

'Think about it, Paul. He didn't try to find the photographs before he tried to kill you. They were irrelevant anyway. He couldn't possibly have known that you had them because Ricky didn't put them up for sale then. You were being stalked in the car park before then. He must have been ordered to kill you because whatever you told the French police could have been used as evidence if this inquiry ever goes ahead. What did you actually see in the tunnel that was so important?' Nick asked.

'All I said was I thought I saw somebody climbing into the crashed car on the driver's side and giving an injection to the man who I presumed was the driver. Maybe it was somebody trying to help, but it wasn't a paramedic. It was some biker who jumped on the back of another motorcycle which scooted off when we arrived. That was all I saw. At the time I was really confused about what I had actually seen, but thinking about it over and over again has made it a little clearer,' Paul said.

'So who do you think is behind all this, Paul?'

'I don't know, mate. It looks like there is something shady going on. Did this guy say anything else?' Paul asked.

'He just mentioned about the Brits who still think they have a big role to play on the world stage, but how it was now the Arabs who owned the oil and had the big money. He was also upset about his friend who killed himself because of Jeff's pictures and the whole business regarding the Afghanistan war. Somehow, I don't think he was a lone killer. This is probably something bigger than we could possibly know about. I can understand why the American special forces soldier came after Jeff, but why you?' Nick asked.

'Don't these people work with the CIA, just like the SAS worked closely with M16? There is a special link between the two countries. The Americans used the SAS to destroy the Scud missiles in the first Gulf War because they were the best unit out there. I think the Brits have asked the Americans to sort out some unfinished business here,' Paul said.

'The man also hinted that the Arabs were taking over the royal family. God only knew what he meant by that. The Queen may only worth a few hundred million pounds but apparently Saudi Arabia has three hundred billion dollars it wants to spend over the next few years. I suppose there are other oil-rich Arab states, such as Dubai, who are also investing heavily in other countries. Large UK institutions are selling up to foreigners so, in theory, this country could eventually be owned by them. I presume this Paris incident had something to do with the national interest. It's over, Paul. At least I hope so,' Nick said.

'And what about you, mate, how are you coping with all this nonsense?' Paul asked.

'I really don't know. I feel okay just now, but what happened today is something I really want to forget. The police suggested I saw their psychologist and I might have to if I crack up, but I'll let you know when I start to see monsters! I think I should give Meg a call.' Nick took another swig of his whisky. He noticed Paul had poured out the good stuff. It was just as well the 1961 Glen Grant was still in the box. The chances were high that Paul may have added lemonade to that.

'Yeah, you do that, mate. Look, I'm going to head off. You got my number, Nick. Give me a call anytime. I owe you one. I mean that,' Paul said.

'Let's just say we're quits. You got me out of this one today. I'll give you a call soon about a beer,' Nick promised.

'Yeah, good one, mate. Say hi to Meg for me. See ya.' Nick saw him to the door.

32

Headache

Meg had come over yesterday. Nick had explained what happened and had drunk the whole bottle on McCallan during the course of the evening. She'd stayed overnight but had to get away before seven to start the early shift. As predicted, Nick woke up with a hangover. The little clock on his bedside table said 8.10. He struggled to lift his head from the pillow. Little men with pickaxes were working away inside his skull, all striking in unison. The throbbing just speeded up when he moved. It was no use. He would have to phone in and say he wasn't well, thinking up all the excuses. After all, he had been held at gunpoint. The psychological trauma would have sent most people off work with stress for at least a year. He looked again at the clock; it was now 8.21. With a huge effort, he dragged himself out of bed. The anti-diuretic properties of the alcohol had filled his bladder up to the max. Now or never, he thought. The consequences would be too unbearable to contemplate. The last thing he wanted to do was think about work, but there was a large clinic on that morning. James Townell and the senior house officer could see a few of his patients but he really needed to be there. It would be unfair to cancel the clinic. It was going to be a long and hard day but he needed to dig deep into his mental reserves. Phoning up and putting on a pathetic voice by asking for a day off wasn't on his agenda. Doctors on average only took one day off a year on sick leave, compared to nurses who took seventeen. He didn't want to use it up.

Having shaved and showered, his body now needed fluid replacement and lots of paracetamol. A full-blown fry-up usually settled the hypoglycaemia and nausea, but he didn't have time for that. The sugar in the coffee would do for now, but it was a bad way to take in a carbohydrate load. He vowed never to do it again, until the next time. His head only felt half as bad now, but with a clean shirt and tie on, he didn't look too bad. Without a car, he had to call a taxi. It was just as well. He still exuded alcohol. The minicab tooted outside a short while later.

He arrived at the ward round long after it had started. Before joining them, he caught sight of the ward auxiliary, a big woman of Jamaican origin who always seemed concerned about him. She was a simple but big-hearted person who always seemed to say the right thing when it mattered because she cared. She was like a substitute mother to him.

'Nicholas, you look like shit. What have you been up to, child?' she said in her West Indian accent.

'I'll tell you later, Etti.' He was still trying to cope with the little men in his head. He never knew if Etti was her real name or shortened for something like Henrietta.

'Come into the kitchen after the ward round and I'll make you a coffee and toast before you do your clinic. You're a silly boy.' He felt better already for the telling off.

Nobody said much as he joined them. The ward round was unusually subdued, but it wasn't because of Nick. Turning up late didn't help, but everybody else was in a bad mood also. He had to speak to James Townell afterwards. As Etti had said, he did look like shit, despite having a clean shirt on. James had noticed his late arrival but thought better than to make any unnecessary comments in front of everybody. He waited until the end of the ward round.

'Nick, what the hell have you been up to now?' James asked.

'James, something happened yesterday. Sorry for the way I look,' Nick replied.

'Do you want to tell me?'

'Yes, I was taken hostage by a professional killer.'

'And?'

'I killed him,' Nick answered.

'Good God, Nick! What happened?' James looked shock.

'To put it very simply, this man tried to kill me and wanted to kill somebody else in my flat until the police turned up. He took me hostage and made me drive to some aerodrome in Hertfordshire. After a fight in my car, I killed him.' Nick said that in a matter-of-fact way.

'For heaven's sake! You've been in enough trouble as it is. So what are the police going to do about this? Please tell me this is not a joke!' James was getting exasperated by his wayward registrar.

'They are currently investigating various incidents. Other people have died. The police have said they will not be pressing charges against me but there will be an investigation. It's all a bit complex, James, and I can't go into details just now.' Nick suddenly felt tired and hung-over, wishing it was all a bad dream. It was not a good time to explain things right now.

'I'm concerned about you, Nick, particularly about your mental state after all this nonsense. I suggest you go and see a psychologist or a counsellor. You smell of alcohol and I don't want you to do the clinic today. Go home and get yourself sorted out. We'll have a chat tomorrow in my office after the ward round,' James said curtly.

He strode off, looking quite angry because Nick had let the side down badly. Orthopaedic surgeons had a duty to care for their patients and should not be leaving a trail of death and destruction behind them. Nick was still pondering the situation when he heard the familiar voice.

'Nicholas, get your backside in her and drink this coffee now.' Etti spoke with a sense of purpose. Nick didn't dare to ignore her.

'Yes, Etti,' he replied meekly, his voice sounded totally flat and depressed. He was just glad for the sweet coffee. Etti also produced a plate of freshly buttered toast, something even his mother had rarely done for him. He just loved this woman's kindness and gave her a quick squeeze on the arm to say thank you.

After struggling to take part in the ward round, Nick was relieved to be able to wander down to the doctors' mess room. It was somewhere familiar and he could read the newspapers until he had sobered up a little more. He was glad about not doing the clinic but that been James's decision. It would have been rather disconcerting for the patients to smell his alcohol-laden breath anyway. No doubt the hospital would have received more complaints, but at least he had turned up for work. He looked in the pigeon hole to pick up his personal correspondence. There was the usual drug company mail shot and a medical journal, but also a typed letter addressed to him. His name and the hospital address appeared through the clear cellophane window on the envelope. He took the mail and sat down on one of the easy chairs. The mess room was deserted as he knew it would be at this time of the morning on a Monday. He closed his eyes for a few minutes, wishing for the headache to go away.

In the relative tranquillity of the room, he almost fell asleep before the peace was shattered by one of the doctors making a noisy entrance. Nick opened his eyes and glanced at the envelope: it looked official. Right now, more bad news was just something he didn't need. He opened the letter with resignation.

Dear Nick,

You will know of me although we have not personally met. There is something I would like to discuss with you so I wonder if we could meet on Tuesday evening at 6 p.m. across the road from the main hospital gate. I suggest we go for a drink to talk about this and I will pick you up in my car. I will look forward to meeting you then but it would be better if you said nothing about this to anybody for now. Should you fail to receive this letter in time or are simply unable to make it, I will get in touch again.

With kind regards.

It was unsigned and could only be someone playing a trick on him. It had to be Meg. She knew he didn't have a car at the moment. Perhaps she was going to take him out somewhere nice. It wasn't a nasty letter after all, thank God. He also thought briefly about what James Townell had said about seeing a psychologist. What could a quack do that a person like Etti couldn't? She gave him all the feeling of comfort he needed just as she would have done for her own kids. She was the archetypal clucking mother hen whose concern always made him feel wanted and safe in the knowledge that somebody cared. Nick also had Meg at his side and Paul, at a pinch. In fact there were now enough people around him to give him all the psychological support he needed. The psychologists probably had enough on their plates dealing with the people who couldn't cope with their lives. Modern life was tough, despite the comforts of home. The extended family structure was no longer there and people led busy lives. The perceived lack of success in their lives drove neighbours to outdo each other. Cars could only get so big or so fast and the initial enthusiasm for washing and polishing soon became a chore. As Paul had pointed out, it was a dog eat dog world, but competing with the neighbours only led to discontentment. Nick was happy with what he had. He just didn't want other people to make a dog's dinner of his life all the time. He was tired and still in the aftermath of a hangover. Going home was the only sensible thing to do. Tomorrow would be a brand new day with a mystery tour to look forward to.

33

Nightmares

The nightmare kept returning, night after night. She could see her father standing at the end of the bed, cooing soft words in her direction. Before, it was mostly her mother who put her to bed after the usual night-time bath. She always got a story and loved to hear her mother's voice but sometimes Mummy hurried up the story because she said she was tired. Then Daddy started to take her upstairs. He was always funny and played games like submarines in the bath. He read her stories but it was not as good as the way Mummy did it. But he did make her laugh and she would giggle and squeal until her sides hurt or Mummy would tell Daddy off for winding her up before bedtime. There would be shark attacks or creepy crawly spiders coming to get her under the duvet. The creatures would run up her leg and sometimes it would stop 'there'. As she got older, the creatures always seemed to stop there. That was their little secret. It felt strange, but she wasn't to tell anybody. Then one night, the creatures started doing something really strange. Daddy was not so funny any more and looked different. He got angry when she didn't want to play any more. She was now more grown up and would soon be a teenager. That night would change her forever and it was the start of the nightmare. She vowed it would never happen again, but it did, time and time again for another three years. She tried to speak to Mummy about it but couldn't. There was no one to turn to; how could she possibly tell anybody? She felt dirty and worthless, withdrawing into herself. She struggled at school and had only a few friends, but none close enough to share her secret. The burden was too much, almost unbearable. She told herself all this would end one day. She wanted to do something good, to get away from all this evil. She would help other people by becoming a nurse one day.

After sitting her O levels, she applied for a nursing course at one of the district hospitals in Surrey. She needed to get away from London, especially from that horrible brute. Her mother could never understand and would never know. She felt let down by her parents, the very people who should have been there for her. Gaining her independence was the best thing in her short miserable life. The sudden overwhelming sense of freedom nurtured a profound confidence she'd never felt at school. She rapidly blossomed into a very striking young woman. The emptiness remained in her which could not be filled easily. She discovered men, real men and bad men, also women. There was a constant need for attention which she could not satisfy. Her numerous lovers never seemed to be enough. She had a greater need to feel used and abused, as if a dark force was driving her towards self-destruction. The warped psychology did not fit in with any conventional rules of life and she was now part of this twisted world. She needed rough sex. Pain was part of the pleasure.

Sex through the tradesman's entrance was perversely satisfying. Her sexuality attracted both men and women and the diversity made her feel alive, even wanted. The allure of sex never failed, drawing people into her net. The nurse's home became her kingdom, trapping lovers until they were spent and discarded.

She had forgotten about the ogre until the call came one day. She was told her father was in hospital with prostate cancer. Against her wishes, she promised to see him after the operation, to appease her mother. As a qualified nurse working in a surgical ward, she knew what was involved. A total prostatectomy was a major operation, but it was possible to remove the whole cancer unless it had spread to the other organs. She felt totally detached and could not care less if the cancer had spread. Perhaps he may even die and that could just be the balm she needed to erase the nightmares. Suppose he did?

She saw her father for the last time in the ward. The drive from Surrey had been uneventful and she was in plenty of time to catch the visiting hours. It was her day off. He was recovering from the operation and was still sleepy from the anaesthetic. She walked up to his bed and pulled a chair next to him, barely able to recognise his ageing face and the pallid complexion. It was an image which repulsed her and the memories came flooding back. The monster was now a shadow of his former self, lying there quite helpless with a drip running into his arm. For the next twenty-four hours, he would be kept alive on a drip of normal saline and dextrose until he could eat and drink again. He opened his eyes slowly, but it took a while for his muddled brain to clear.

'Oh, it's you. I never thought I would never see you again.' His speech was barely audible.

'It's okay, Dad. I'm here now. Don't talk if you're still feeling tired. I'll stay here a while until visiting time is over. Are you in any pain?' she asked.

'No, I'm quite comfortable. I just feel really tired so forgive me if I fall asleep,' he replied. He tried to look at his daughter through half-opened eyelids but could feel them getting heavier. The cancer and the subsequent operation had taken a big toll on his strength. He felt like an old man although he was only in his early sixties.

The hospital ward was designed to hold twenty-four beds. There were three bays with six beds each, plus individual rooms for the very unwell. The male and female patients were in different bays unless it was unavoidable. The man was in the end bed of the middle bay, which could not be seen directly from the nurses' station, situated at the top end of the ward. The bay only had two other patients there, but they were in the television room. Apart from a few visitors coming and going, the ward seemed calm and tranquil. It was usually quiet, ready for a new influx of patients the next day. The normal ward activities had stopped during visiting time and the patients had already been fed. It was only the night-time medication to be given later, once the visitors had gone.

The man was almost asleep again. The bag of saline hanging from the drip stand had emptied slowly at a rate of 500 millilitres every six hours, giving him two litres of fluid over twenty-four hours. The kidneys needed to make around fifty millilitres of urine per hour, so there was enough fluid to keep him going. The catheter bag was nearly full. She looked at her father and thought how vulnerable he looked just lying there. He would certainly not do that filthy thing to her again. An excitement crept into her thinking about it, not of what he had done but of what she was going to do to him. It was the sense of power, to be the arbiter of life or death, which suddenly gave her a heady intoxicating sense of euphoria. It was the ultimate aphrodisiac.

The ward was reasonably empty except for a few people walking around in the corridor, but the task would only take a few seconds. Her father would not know what she was about to do, let alone do anything about it. She stood up slowly and, seeing nobody around, quickly turned off his drip. From her handbag, she brought out a syringe filled with potassium chloride which had been acquired from her own ward. It was a simple matter of injecting the potassium into the saline bag through the injection port. The body needed potassium, but too much and the heart would go into an abnormal rhythm. It would finally fail and stop beating altogether. The high potassium level had to be corrected quickly if the patient was to be resuscitated.

She kissed her father on the forehead for the sake of saying goodbye and smiled. He briefly opened his eyes and could see what a beautiful woman she had turned into. The longing was there again but he knew that it would probably be impossible for that to ever happen again when his prostate had been ripped out. He felt contented that his lovely daughter was next to him but he didn't see her switch the drip on again. That night, the curtains were all pulled around the beds. The porters wheeled in the metal container to retrieve the body. The cause of death on this occasion was post-operative myocardial infarction.

Murder by Night

The taking of a human life had been an incredible journey into the moral abyss, a journey from which there was no turning back. Like a drug, it drew her back time and again but the trick was never to get caught; it had become the ultimate game.

She was working night duty on the ward. Her vocation for nursing, to help others, had been replaced with an overwhelming sense of being the giver of life or death. She was fed up of seeing the decrepit creatures lying on the bed, forever asking for bedpans only to soil the beds instead. Age was not kind to the human body. As the giver of life or death, she would help them on their way, to leave this awful world by the last act of kindness. Nobody lived for ever so what was so wrong in ending a miserable life prematurely? That would now be her new vocation, her purpose. It was exciting to watch the aftermath. Her heart had pounded loudly when she'd left her father's bedside, conscious that the drip was slowly killing him. Her mind had screamed at her to stop the drip, but the devil had pulled her away, like some giant hand tugging at her soul. That night, sex with a complete stranger had been totally exquisite, out of this world. The opportunity to do it again arose without much difficulty. The next victim was also recovering from an operation when she injected the potassium into the drip bag. The junior house officer was persuaded to sign the death certificate with bronchopneumonia as the cause of death. The patient had had a slight cough after the operation.

He was a young doctor, barely into his first job since qualifying, and it did not take him long to be smitten by her charms. The sex was incredible and she would let him do anything to her. It had all started with a pinch on his bottom during a ward round whilst presenting a case history. He had temporarily stammered before recovering his composure, much to the hilarity of the others. A sideways glance had showed him the culprit. She had had a little smirk on her face, before surreptitiously giving him a wink.

During his six months as a surgical house officer, he signed thirteen death certificates. The cause of death for nine of those was obvious, but the other four were doubtful. The consultant in charge felt a little unhappy about these, but had allowed the junior house officer to sign the death certificates without asking for an autopsy. The cause of death had a probable cause. It was good enough. She had got away with it, but the game had to stop for now. Somehow, the thrill had got a little less intense with each time. Unknown to the young doctor, he had been complicit in her acts and she felt a bond with him, more so than with any of her other lovers. When he left for another job in London, she followed, getting a staff nurse's post at the same hospital. They still saw each other on a casual basis, more for the sake of sex rather than a true love affair.

She could not be satisfied by just one man but she was jealous when the other nurses made a play for him. The jealousy got worse when she realised the competition was getting younger. Her sexuality would hold out a little longer, but with maturity came responsibility. She had to leave her past and also her reputation behind in Surrey if she was going to go up the nursing ladder. Ambition now took over as the new driving force. She was determined to make it to the top.

The post of Casualty sister came up at one of the hospitals and she got it. The young doctor had also climbed the greasy pole and was sitting his membership exams for the Royal College of Physicians. After gaining his MRCP, he was on course for a career in hospital medicine. She suggested they set up home together but he refused. The hatred swelled within her, but the bond was too strong. He was addicted to her body whilst realising she would never make a good wife. Throughout their careers, they had remained in contact, meeting for secret trysts in various hotels in London, even when he had married. During that time they had worked at different hospitals, but fate had brought them together one last time and they now worked at the same hospital. Her ruthless ambition had taken her to the top and it had been enough to stop the urges, until now. The overwhelming need to kill again had reared its ugly head. The devil was calling to her once more. The preoccupation ate away until she could stand it no more. The voice within her commanded her to do it. Kill him. Kill him. Kill him.

35

The Meeting

Nick went back to work the next day feeling much more alive. The alcohol had long since been metabolised and he was no longer ketotic; the faint smell of acetone had now gone from his breath. The day went by quickly and he was looking forward to the mystery tour, something which had played on his mind all day. The only fly in the ointment was Meg. They met up for lunch but she could see Nick was cagey about something. The more she asked him about it, the more elusive he became. It was obvious it wasn't her who had written the note. He innocently strung her along by saying nothing about the letter. It made her more suspicious. She wanted to know what he was up to and her jealous streak had started to become intolerable. Nick told her he had to do something after work and he could not see her tonight. The red flag really dangled in front of the bull this time. She stormed off from the canteen without saying a word. Nick was left with a stupid grin on his face, torn between reading the situation as a joke or a serious rift between them. If so, that would be their first one. He had no idea how mad she could get, but that would have to wait until later when he had a chance to explain things.

He finished up just after 5 p.m. With nearly an hour to kill, he went to the doctors' mess for a coffee. At 5.50 p.m. he put on his jacket and walked out into the chilly winter evening. It was now dark as he made his way across the hospital compound, heading towards the main entrance. The pavement was lit by the orange glow from the lighting but he hardly noticed anybody walking around as his mind remained focused on the rendezvous. The letter had been typed so it was impossible to even recognise if it had been written by a male of female, which would have given some clue at least. Doctors' handwriting was notoriously bad, simply because of the sheer volume of words and abbreviations they used to document everything in the case notes. At least that was the excuse. Doctors also had to document the negative findings to show that they had excluded certain diseases from their clinical examinations. Even illegible handwriting was a document of sorts.

Nick had no idea who wanted to see him but as the time drew nearer, he felt more and more apprehensive. Why not just arrange to meet at some well-known location, like the pub just down the road where most of the nurses went to? He walked out of the main gate and crossed the road. At a suitable area just further up, he waited for his lift. He was still concerned about Meg stomping off. That had spoilt what should have been a good afternoon. He had already seen how easily she could fly off the handle when he dared to suggest that her nursing staff had not done their job.

After seeing Nick at lunch, Meg was annoyed by his childish behaviour. Sometimes he just appeared like some big kid thinking that life was one big joke. He was obviously hiding something from her and the curiosity had now got the better of her. The events on Sunday still made her very wary that Nick was still involved in some major incident. She even wondered if the mental strain had got to him, making him unbalanced in a disturbing way. She had started to worry about how their relationship was developing. Perhaps he was seeing another woman. Her new-found confidence was still at a fragile stage, especially when she was going out with one of the most eligible surgeons in the hospital. Her shift was not due to finish until 7.30 p.m. She felt compelled to tell a lie by saying she had a terrible migraine and needed to go home. Instead, she sat in her car near to the hospital entrance. It wasn't long before she saw Nick crossing the road. Perhaps he was going to walk home after all, as it was just a couple of miles to his flat. Rather than walking away, he just stood there as if waiting for a lift. She decided to drive across and offer him a lift. Her feelings for him had grown too strong to just drop the matter, even if he was doing something suspicious. She simply had to know.

Nick was still hovering on the pavement as she started her car. He had not seen her at all. In fact he had no reason to think she would be following him. Meg was still thinking about an excuse to give when a car suddenly pulled up and stopped. Nick opened the door and the interior light came on, silhouetting the shape of a woman inside. She appeared to be smiling as Nick clambered in. They drove off together.

The wave of anger hit her with a sickening thump. The pit of her stomach tightened as the irrational feeling of jealousy gripped her. What was Nick doing with another woman? She quickly turned into the main road, almost hitting another car going by with its horn blasting away. There was just enough time for her to see the car turn left into the busy main road up ahead. She drove quickly to catch up with them but it was already busy at that time of day. Despite the traffic, she pulled aggressively into the flow and could just make out the car as it made its way along the outside lane. It indicated right and headed up the A10 going out of London. She was now reasonably close behind and managed to follow without much difficulty. The car continued on up the A10, which was filled with speed cameras. It went past the turnoff for Enfield and headed past Cheshunt towards Hoddesdon. By now Meg was the only one behind them and didn't want to get too close in case Nick saw her. They drove into Hoddesdon, a small market town in Hertfordshire, before taking a left turn at the next roundabout. She followed them through the next roundabout before taking a right turn, which headed out towards Ryehouse. The small railway station was situated on the right just after the humped back bridge over the railway line. A second bridge spanned the River Lea a few yards ahead, heading towards Rye Meads and the countryside. Remnants of the old rye house remained on the left, adjacent to the Rye Meads nature reserve. The road ahead was dark except for the pub on the right by the river.

The car drove into the car park at the side of the pub and slotted into a parking place. Meg didn't want to drive in after them until she could think up of some excuse to be there. She carried on a little further up the road for about a mile before turning round. It was totally desolate there. The RSPB nature reserve centre was closed and the whole area was completely eerie. Driving very slowly this time, she approached the pub but drove straight into the car park. She could see the other car there. They had obviously gone in. How cosy! She parked and thought about the next plan of action. The temptation would be to walk right in and confront Nick about the other woman. She was in a mood for a bloody row, but partly felt she had no right to do this as they still hardly knew each other. The events of the past few days had still not quite caught up with her yet, but she desperately needed to know what else was going on in Nick's life. It was just a gut feeling that something was not right about any of this. She sat for another ten minutes before deciding to go in. It was too cold to hang about.

36

Femme Fatale

Nick saw the Jaguar signalling as it approached; the car stopped and the woman inside looked at him with a pleasant smile. He opened the car door and was intrigued by the amiable woman asking him to step in. Almost immediately he could smell her expensive perfume and felt totally relaxed. She didn't appear to pose any threat and he felt quite safe. The Jaguar was nicely kitted out with wood and leather, something he quickly noticed, being a typical man. As they set off, his thoughts turned to the woman next to him. She had started off by saying something about knowing him and his recent troubles, which she was sorry to hear about. He must have gone through so much and obviously he was very strong to cope with all this. Her flattery and sympathy had made an immediate impact on him but there was something very familiar about her which Nick could not put his finger on. She had not wanted to say anything about herself until they had reached the pub she was taking him to. Nick was totally amused by the whole thing and felt flattered by being picked up by an attractive woman in a Jaguar. It all added to the mystery, but hopefully nobody was going to shoot him today. His recent life could not have been more eventful, but this was exciting in a totally different way.

He could see she was probably in her late forties and had obviously kept in great shape. She had short dark hair with a strong purposeful, but attractive, face. She wore a knee-length skirt and Nick could just make out her shapely legs. Some women simply exuded sex appeal despite their age and it was quite evident she had it in spades. Thank you, Mrs Robinson, for making young men drool in anticipation. The young bimbos in low cut jeans and knickers showing had as much going for them as a soggy kipper in a sandwich.

The Jaguar glided smoothly along the road until they reached the pub. It had taken twenty minutes to get there, which seemed a long time to spend in a car just to go for a drink. Nick was desperate to know what this was leading to. He could see the pub was nicely located by the river on the outskirts of the town, but there were other equally nice pubs closer to London. As he was not doing the driving, he would be the perfect gentleman and not ask too many questions. They got out of the car and walked into the pub. Their senses were immediately assailed by a mixture of noise and cigarette smoke. Pop music played in the background and the telltale slot machines were present in a corner, which totally destroyed the image an English country pub, which it had been once been in gentler times. Even so, they found an empty table and took off their jackets. Nick offered to buy the drinks but she gently touched his hand and insisted on having the honour. The world had moved on. He asked for a pint of IPA; lager was for those who didn't appreciate real ale. After five minutes, she returned with the drinks. Nick took a couple of large swallows of the frothy liquid, already forgetting about the state he had been in yesterday.

She looked at him closely before speaking, running her well-manicured fingernails along her wine glass. Nick could just imagine them running down his back. Whatever she wanted to say to him, she had all the time in the world.

'Nick, you must be wondering what all this is about. I hope you won't be upset or offended when I tell you who I am. I presume you have not recognised me,' she said.

'No, I am sorry if I didn't. So who are you?' he asked, raising the beer glass to his mouth.

'I'm Sheila Hawkins, Brenda's mother.'

He nearly choked on his beer but got it down in time. He looked at the smiling woman in front of him and suddenly felt angry. It was short lived. He also remembered that Paul Lewis had come to see him after they had fought each other and admired his courage for coming. In a similar way, he was impressed that his current enemy had the courage of getting him here under false pretences, except she was a little more charming than Paul was. She saw his flash of anger and waited for the outburst.

'You were the chief executive?' He deliberately used the past tense.

'Yes. I wanted to say sorry for what happened but I also want you to know the truth. That was why I needed to see you. Picking you up outside the hospital was a little bit risky, but it was dark and people are usually more concerned about getting home at that time of the evening,' Sheila said.

'Why did you have to bring me all this way here? Surely we could have met up somewhere closer to the hospital?' Nick asked.

'That is just the point. I didn't know if you would turn up if you knew it was me and also I did not want anybody to see us together. It had to be far enough away from the hospital and this seemed to be the simplest way,' she explained.

'I suppose so. What is it you want to tell me?' Despite the very strange situation, Nick started to feel unusually relaxed and was enjoying the beer with no thoughts of his handover yesterday.

'You should know that it wasn't me who reported you to the GMC. It was the medical director,' she said.

'Why did he do it?' Nick asked.

'It was his job. There was a sudden death and you were involved. He had no choice.'

'But it was your daughter who made the mistake and tried to cover up by blaming me,' Nick replied.

'Listen, Nick,' she said sincerely, 'Brenda told me it definitely wasn't her who made the mistake. If it wasn't her, then it must have been somebody else.'

There was instant confusion in Nick's mind. He thought everything had been resolved but this just opened up the case again. If Brenda hadn't done it and he hadn't, then who had?

'I don't understand. We showed how the mistake was made. It was a genuine error and hopefully it won't happen again. Brenda must accept that,' Nick tried to explain.

'I have lost my career over this incident regardless of whose mistake it was. Have you considered the possibility that somebody could have engineered this whole thing?'

'No, I didn't. You are making this all very confusing,' Nick replied, staring at his pint.

'Just think, Nick, who else had the key to the DDA cupboard that day.' She spoke softly and seductively,

'Sister Wallis was the only one I can think of.'

'Well, how much do know about her?' Sheila asked.

'A little, I suppose.'

'I believe she is not married,' she said.

'I cannot see the relevance of that,' Nick replied.

'Perhaps you're right. I just want you to consider the possibility that Brenda did not use the wrong vial, that's all.'

Outside, the night was definitely getting colder and frost was sure to set in, even for November. Just sitting there in the cold car was enough to force Meg into the pub. Her mind was made up; she was going to go in and confront them. She piled out of the car and slammed the door shut with a bang. The pub, by contrast, was filled with a warm fug as she walked in, seeking out Nick and his companion. They were sitting by themselves at a table and looked quite friendly. She calmly walked up to them and smiled, despite feeling mad inside. Sensing somebody next to him, Nick looked up and was surprised to see Meg standing there. He hit the charm button.

'Meg! What a surprise to see you!'

'Hi, fancy meeting you here,' she replied, trying very hard not to fly off the handle.

'How come you're here?' he asked.

'I'm meeting one of my friends. She lives in Hertford, just up the road. We sometimes meet up here. It's halfway.' She did have a friend in Hertford, the rest was a lie.

'Meg, this is Sheila. Can I get us all a drink first?' he offered.

'No, I'll get these, Nick. Are you having IPA? What can I get for you, Sheila?' Meg asked, remembering that Nick liked IPA because it was like Scottish 80 Shilling, a creamy smooth beer. That was during a Casualty night out a long time ago, before she 'knew' him.

'Nothing for me thanks. I'm just sticking to one.' She smiled sweetly.

Meg went off the bar without appearing to recognise that name. Sheila certainly knew who she was and, despite smiling at Meg, was fuming at her presence. The conversation she was having with Nick was all but over. She wanted to finish telling him something before Meg reappeared with the drinks.

'Look, Nick, there is something else you should know. The medical director is not all he seems.'

'What do you mean?' Nick asked.

'Brenda is his daughter. He had to protect her by referring you to the GMC.'

Nick had become speechless with all this information, but thankfully Meg appeared with the drinks just then. She joined without being asked. The second pint was totally necessary as he digested the information. He enjoyed the first but the second was even better. The whole evening then suddenly become quite strange and surreal in a short space of time. He tried to concentrate on the two women talking but struggled to understand what they were saying. Meg seemed to be on the offensive as only a jealous woman could be. Meg clearly hadn't realised who she was.

'Can I ask if you are one of Nick's friends?' she asked bluntly.

'No, we have just met this evening.'

'This is a strange place to meet.' Meg had lost any pretence of being friendly.

'I just needed to talk to Nick in private. I don't really think it is any of your business,' Sheila replied, in an equally frosty manner. The gloves were off.

'Is it so private that you had to come out to a pub all this way?' Meg asked.

'Where I choose to go is none of your business. Nick came here quite happily. I didn't force him,' Sheila replied.

'So you just picked him up?'

'No, I asked him to meet me.'

'Who are you?'

'Sheila Hawkins. I think you know my daughter Brenda.'

'Good God. So that's what all this is about. Whatever you have to say to Nick, say it to me too. You really have a nerve to do this.' Meg was furious, but her manners stopped her from starting a bun fight. 'What do you want from him?'

'What has this do with you?'

'I want to know what you are up to. Was it because you wanted to save Brenda's career? You were obviously quite prepared to see Nick's go down the pan,' Meg said angrily.

'I am not going to answer that. I have just lost my career! Don't you dare accuse me of trying to destroy Nick's career. I offered to help relocated him to another hospital,' Sheila answered just as angrily.

'I want you to leave Nick alone and get out of our lives,' Meg hissed.

Nick had tried to follow the conversation whilst sipping away at his beer. He drained the second glass but now felt very light-headed and was struggling to think properly. It was quite unusual for him to feel this way after only two pints, despite not having eaten anything since lunchtime. His brain somehow felt detached from the rest of him, like an out-of-body experience. He thought about what Sheila had said earlier. Before he could stop himself, the words just came out.

'Meg, did you switch the diamorphine vials?' he asked.

Both the women stopped talking and stared at him. Despite the haze sweeping through his mind, he could see the corner of Meg's mouth twitching away. She now looked down at the floor as if in guilt or shame. The silence was palpable before she stood up and walked out, with tears welling up in her eyes.

'Oops, think I said the wrong thing.' Nick thought it was funny. His mind was definitely cloudy.

'Nick, I'm going to go away now. There's a train station just down the road so you'll be able to get back to London.' Her warmth had suddenly evaporated. There was no smile.

'Okay. Cheers my dear.' He slurred his words.

Nick was past caring. In fact, he didn't even know where he really was but felt totally unconcerned at the same time. He watched Sheila stand up and walk out, just as Meg had done. He struggled to stand up and felt disorientated. He needed some fresh air badly; the beer must have been stronger than he realised. With the remaining powers of any lucidity, he headed for the door and staggered outside into the cold. To all intents and purposes, he appeared totally drunk. Looking to the left and right, he could see that one direction was in the light but the other was totally dark. Simple logic dictated that the railway station must be in the direction towards the light. He placed one unsteady foot in front of another, heading for the first humped back bridge over the River Lea. He thought to himself, Nick, you're pissed as a fart.

He approached the narrow bridge and was vaguely aware of car lights coming from behind him. In his corner of his mind, he knew it would be tight for both him and the car to cross the bridge at the same time but he didn't care or appreciate the danger. He carried on walking, staggering as he struggled to find his feet and did not hear the car speeding up. Suddenly, there was a massive thump on his right hip before he was thrown through the air. The car roared past as he hit the road. Initially, there was no pain, just a dim recollection of flying through the air. It had all seemed to happen very slowly, despite taking only seconds. He could feel something hot seeping into his trousers before the dull pain started. Somewhere, a woman was screaming hysterically. Mercifully, he passed out.

37

The Patient

The searing pain in his hip woke him up and he could see the male paramedic looking down at him. This all felt very familiar, with a flashback of when he was knocked down as a child. An oxygen mask had been strapped to his face and his neck had been immobilised in a hard neck collar. At least he was receiving some attention this time. His trousers now felt cold and uncomfortable. He wanted to speak but couldn't get the words out. His mind was still very confused. The paramedic kept asking him questions but he didn't how to answer.

'Hello, mate. How much did you have to drink? Is there any pain in your neck or head? Can you move your toes?' Questions, questions, questions. Just give me something for the pain! his brain screamed. The paramedic carried on.

'Won't be long now until we get you to hospital. You're going to Hertford County General. Hang in there, mate.'

The ambulance rushed through Hertfort town with the siren on, going around the numerous roundabouts until Nick felt he was going to throw up. Lying down on the stretcher had made him dizzy and he wanted to sit up, but was not allowed to. The paramedic would have a major job on his hands if Nick threw up whilst he was lying on his back. With a suspected neck fracture, he couldn't be moved very easily, especially at the back of a moving ambulance but, thankfully, his stomach contents stayed down. The ambulance eventually slowed down and came to a standstill. Cold air now wafted into the back of the ambulance as the door was opened. The stretcher was unclipped from its safety mooring before it was lowered onto the ground. Nick was wheeled into the A & E department. The staff there took over. The paramedic rattled off a brief history, having got some of Nick's details from his driving licence in the wallet.

Thirty-year-old male by the name of Nick Forbes, hit from behind by a car which failed to stop. Possible fracture C spine and right femur. We found him lying facedown with a twisted neck. Current GCS thirteen but appears to be inebriated. Obs stable. Minor laceration to head and legs. Also incontinent of urine.'

GCS stood for the Glasgow Coma Scale, fifteen being the top score for normality. Thirteen meant he was a little sluggish in some of his responses. It gave a quick assessment of a person's cerebral function; the lower the score the more likely a serious brain injury had occurred.

'Thanks. We'll sort him out. Let's get him over onto the trolley. Okay, people, possible fracture C spine and right femur. Do it gently. Ready? One, two, three, over,' the charge nurse called out.

Nick felt himself being transferred over onto the trolley in a controlled fashion. He could see the fluorescent lighting on the ceiling and was conscious of the normal sounds in A & E, including the blip blip blip of an ECG machine which had been attached to him.

'Hi, Nick, I'm Sarah, the Casualty doctor. Can you tell me what happened?'

He still couldn't answer properly and his head was fuzzy. He was aware that his clothes were being cut away from him in order for the Casualty team to properly assess his body. At least they were getting rid of the cold wet trousers, but he wanted to tell them to keep his underpants on. His pupils were reactive but sluggish. Clearly the Casualty doctor wasn't going to get much out of him.

'Okay, I'm going to need FBC, U & E, LFT, glucose, drug toxicology screen and alcohol levels. Also cross-match four units and run in some saline. Get a catheter in and check for any blood in the urine; make sure there is no kidney damage. He needs x-rays of his cervical and thoracolumbar spine, pelvis, right hip and femur. Let's get to it.'

Despite his condition, his mind was awake enough to know what was going on. He groaned at the prospect of all this, especially the urinary catheter. The pain in his right hip was the worst bit, but he would not get any painkillers until they knew exactly what damage had been sustained. He was now in their hands and there was nothing he could do except to be a good patient. Getting a catheter through his penis was definitely the oddest thing he had experienced in his life. It was the easiest way to monitor his renal output.

Despite having various things happening to him, he was drifting in an out of sleep, rather than consciousness. His various aches and pains only throbbed when he moved. The next time he woke up, the room was very dark and quiet, unlike in the A & E department. A small desk light was shining from the nurse's station which just gave enough light for him to see where he was. The ward was like any other in a hospital; they were all very similar. Whilst lying there, he tried to think back about what had happened; he could not remember much at all. At least the bed was warm and comfortable and he didn't have to get up to go to the toilet. He closed his eyes again and tried to think of Meg.

He woke up to the sounds of a busy ward but his senses had not fully come to. He knew he had been injured and gently tried to find out which part of his body had been affected. Very gingerly, he tried to move his toes, neck and arms by wiggling them slowly. Everything seemed to be working. The drip was still attached to him, as was the catheter. One of the nurses approached him.

'Hello. How are you today?' she asked.

'Okay, I think. What happened to me yesterday?' Nick asked.

'You were knocked down by a car. It's okay, nothing broken or badly damaged. I'm sure we can get those things off you today,' she said, referring to the drip and catheter.

'Thanks. Look, can you phone my work to let them know I won't be in today?' Nick asked politely.

'Sure. Give me the details.' Nick told her. She then told the rest who he was.

The ward round was conducted by an orthopaedic consultant who knew James Townell. He introduced himself and told Nick that he had not sustained any major injuries and he would be free to go home later. He also told Nick about his blood test results. Traces of the date rape drug Rohypnol had been found. Normally it was females who were drugged with this and then raped without even being aware of it. Drugging a man was useless unless it was by another man who was going to rape him. Getting drugged by a woman made no sense at all as Nick would have been incapable of performing. The consultant tried to make a joke of it but Nick wasn't ready for that just yet, still feeling rather fragile. He was left alone again as the ward round moved on.

He could remember going to a pub with the ex-chief executive and then Meg had walked in. That was the strange part. It was too much of a coincidence for her to be there. They had both bought him a drink so either of them could have slipped the drug in. Sheila had also said something about a set up and that Brenda was the medical director's daughter. What if it was Meg who switched the diamorphine vial? Did she have a grudge against Brenda because of who her parents were? Also, who had run him down in the car? Could Meg have done it? His thoughts were interrupted by the nurse who drew the curtain around the bed.

'I've got to remove the catheter now.' She said that in a cold clinical way.

'Okay,' he said.

He felt her cold fingers on him, despite the disposal plastic gloves, but it was a relief to get it out.

'Thank you,' Nick said it with as much dignity as he could.

'It was my pleasure. Take care, Nick.' She was gone, with a big cheesy smile on her face.

It was time to go home.

38

Honey Trap

Nick took a taxi home which metaphorically had cost him and arm and a leg. He could have caught the train into London from Hertford station just up the road from the hospital, but he would still have had to make his way back up to Palmers Green. Going by taxi was far easier. He also didn't have any clothes apart from what the hospital could provide, as his own ones had been cut away from him. He still had his wallet and keys plus a massive bruise on his right buttock and hip which made sitting down a painful experience. The police had no idea who the hit and run driver was and the only witness available who had seen the car hitting him could not give a description of the car itself. The police were not going to oblige by giving him with a lift home this time.

There was a lot to think about. Meg had been the one person he would have trusted with his life, but what Sheila Hawkins had said was now playing on his mind. It seemed unlikely that Meg would do anything wrong but, in reality, he knew nothing about her. Sheila, on the other hand, had seemed genuine enough and her story about the medical director was a complete revelation. They must have had a long-term relationship despite being married to other people to produce a daughter who was in her twenties. Jeff the paparazzo had uncovered their love affair, but she must have changed her hairstyle because Nick didn't recognise her from the press photographs. Bob McLean had done what he could to save his daughter's career at the expense of Nick's. The only person who knew the real truth was Brenda Hawkins herself. Maybe she was just as innocent as she had claimed to be but he had to find out for himself. He would try and speak to her directly. First he had to find her and her mother's house would be a good place to start. He easily managed to get the address and phone number from Glampic, the paparazzi people. The girls there were only too happy to hear from him. He phoned the house and it was answered by Sheila, who sounded extremely surprised to hear from him.

'Nick, it's you!' she said.

'You sound surprised,' Nick replied.

213

'I didn't expect to see you again after last night.'

'I was hoping you could tell me where Brenda is?' Nick asked.

'Why do you want to know?' Sheila replied.

'I think I know who changed the diamorphine vial but I just need to speak to her,' Nick said.

'Oh I see.' Her voice had regained the warmness again. 'Were you okay when you left the pub? You seemed a little drunk. I didn't want to make things worse by offering you a lift home when your girlfriend was obviously upset,' she said.

'Actually, I was knocked down by a car after you had both left.'

'Oh no, were you hurt, Nick?' Sheila asked.

'Nothing broken. It was probably my fault.' He did not mention the date rape drug.

'Well, Brenda is not here just now but she may be back later. By the way, how did you get my phone number? It's ex-directory,' Sheila asked.

'I asked the medical director,' he lied. There was a pause as she obviously tried to figure it out.

'Nick, why don't you come round later today?' She sounded very inviting. 'Brenda should be back around 4 p.m. Do you have the address?' she asked.

'No, but I'm sure you're going to give it to me,' Nick replied.

'Okay, Nick. Here's the address.' He didn't have to write it down; he already had it.

'Thanks, I shall see you later,' Nick said.

It was going to cost him another small fortune to get to her house by taxi; the sooner he got his car back the better. He needed to shower and get into some decent clothes but he also wanted to phone Meg and get her story. He decided to skip it for now as she was probably at work. It was just too ridiculous to even think that either she or Sheila would have run him down yesterday and not stop. Then again, who had put the drug in his drink? It was know for men to slip in the drug when the women weren't looking. It was a long shot that somebody at the bar had slipped it in when either Sheila or Meg went up to buy the drink, but spiking a pint of beer was still a strange thing to do.

There wasn't much time before he had to phone for a taxi. In some perverse way, he felt a little excited to see her again. He believed her story about the medical director shopping him to the GMC and bore her no grudges. It was a thirty minute ride by taxi to Buckhurst Hill at that time of day. The evening had already drawn in and the lights were on around the house. Nick paid the cab driver and walked up to the front door. He waited for half a minute before Sheila appeared.

'Come in, Nick. How nice to see you again.' She had a warm smile.

'Thanks.' He could smell the lovely perfume again.

The house was modern and built to a high standard. Good quality carpets covered the floor and the leather furniture looked expensive. The decor was in good taste so she obviously appreciated the good things in life.

'What would you like to drink?' she asked.

'Just water, thanks. I've had a very rough few days and I don't think my liver can cope with any more alcohol just now,' he answered.

'Are you sure I can't tempt you with something?' She had said that very well.

'I'm quite sure. It's a lovely house you have.'

'Thank you. Why don't you have a seat?'

'Thanks.'

'You were saying something about being run down yesterday? You must be hurt because I can see you're limping.' She appeared concerned.

'I was hit from behind and my right hip took the brunt of it,' Nick replied, trying not to be too macho about it.

They both sat down, Nick rather uncomfortably so. Sheila crossed her delicate legs and Nick could see she had suspenders and stockings on under her black skirt. She knew Nick was looking although he tried not to.

'So what do you remember about last night, especially when you were run down?' she asked.

'Not much at all. I woke up at Hertford hospital with a drip in my arm. I can't even remember what we had talked about in the pub. I must have been drunk having had nothing to eat before I went out,' Nick answered.

'We could have gone for something to eat if I had known. I'm sorry I left you in the pub but the situation with Meg was a little fraught so I hope you understand. She is a good-looking woman. How long have you been together?' Sheila asked.

'Oh, we only met up just recently although we have been working together for several years.'

'I believe you are at the end of your training?'

'Yes, that's right. Sheila, could I possibly ask you something?' Nick smiled nervously.

'Yes, of course, Nick.'

'Whose idea was it to ask me to leave my job?'

'I think you know the answer to that already. Bob thought it would be best for both the hospital and your career if you moved on quietly. Now why don't you have a little drink? It won't hurt, I promise! The drinks are in the kitchen. Would you mind, Nick, if I changed into something more comfortable?' She had used all her feminine charm to avoid the question and had quickly changed the subject.

'No, not at all.' It would have been rude to press the point but she had answered his question.

He decided he would have a small drink, just to be sociable, as he watched her get up from the sofa. For a woman clearly older than him, she wasn't in bad shape. He didn't need another drink right now, but a small whisky may help to ease his pain a little, especially when he wasn't driving. The kitchen was just off the living room and again, it was beautifully finished with stainless steel units and an American style fridge-freezer. He looked around and found a small wine rack on the worktop but could not find the whisky. He opened a few cupboard doors and only found crockery and other utensils. Perhaps the whisky was kept in the utility room, a common storage area for alcohol.

He went into the small utility room just off from the kitchen. Apart from the usual washing machine and tumble drier, he didn't find any drinks there either. A door lead to the garage and curiosity made him take a quick peek. The garage was in darkness until he flicked the light on. The Jaguar was there, but no stash of alcohol. The car and gardening equipment seemed to take up most of the space. Something about the car also caught his eye; the bonnet was dented. It had definitely looked in pristine condition when he saw it yesterday. He switched off the light and closed the door.

Sheila was standing in the kitchen when Nick came out of the utility room. He could see that her feet were still covered in stockings but she was now in a silk dressing gown.

'Oh hello, I couldn't find any whisky. There was nothing in the utility room.' He didn't say he had looked in the garage.

'Sorry, Nick, I should have told you to look in the cupboard beneath the wine rack. What would you like? I've got some Johnny Walker.' It wasn't a malt but it would do.

'That's fine.' He could just about get the words out as she poured him a generous measure.

'Ice?' she asked.

'Yes please.'

'Cheers!' She handed him the glass.

'Indeed.'

'Tell me something, Nick. Do you find me attractive?' she suddenly said.

He swallowed his whisky a little too quickly and felt the urge to cough.

'Yes, but …,' he didn't finish the sentence.

'Come to bed.' She pulled his arm and led him to her bedroom. He was still clinging on to his glass.

This was all wrong, he had to tell himself. He found it hard to fight against the flow of events. She was using him, no matter how attractive she was. Her dressing gown had now opened to reveal only her suspenders and stockings. He could see her full breasts, tantalisingly close to his touch. She was smiling at him, willing him on.

'What about Brenda?' he asked, trying to find an excuse to break the spell.

'She'll be here later.' Sheila grabbed his head and planted an intimate kiss in his mouth, her tongue exploring his. Nick pulled away, fighting against his natural instincts to just let things happen.

'Wait, please wait. Tell me why your car bonnet is damaged,' he asked.

He could see an instant transformation in her demeanour. The seductress had suddenly turned cold, and Nick was the cause of it. She quickly moved back into the kitchen. He followed her, waiting to hear an explanation but instead found himself facing a large cook's knife waving in his face. She was obviously annoyed about the rejection but there was more to it than that. Nick had just figured out what happened yesterday. He was a total fool to have let himself walk into a situation like that.

'It was you who ran me over! I suppose you drugged me too! Why did you do it?' He was angry with himself for being so stupid.

'Damn you! It took me years to build my career and now all that is gone! I hated you from that very moment. I hated the press for poking their noses in but why didn't you just go away when you had the chance! I would have got you another job, even made sure you became a consultant next year,' she screamed back at him.

'Because, it wasn't my fault all this happened! Your daughter screwed up and all you and the medical director could do was try to save your skins. How could you try to seduce me after trying to kill me yesterday?' Nick asked.

'You'll never understand! It would have meant more to me to have you first before killing you. It would have been fun. After all, isn't that what some men do to their victims before killing them? This would have been payback for women. Did you know my father raped me time and again? Well, did you?' She became hysterical.

The anger within her had turned to rage, as if all men were somehow guilty of sex crimes. The knife wavered in front of Nick's face, just inches away. Somehow, rather than being scared, he was just starting to get a little fed up with twisted psychopaths trying to kill him, even if this one was good-looking and half naked.

'You're mad. Have you been to see a shrink?' he asked her. It was the wrong thing to say.

'Don't mock me. You won't be the first to die. It was a shame I didn't kill you in the countryside after you had that drink. Now you know what it is like to be given a date rape drug. Isn't that what you men do? Your luck has run out, Nick. I'm only sorry you survived yesterday.' The venom in her voice had become evil.

'Sheila, it doesn't have to end this way. Why don't you put the knife down? You need help and I can try and help you,' Nick said.

'I don't want your help. I want to enjoy killing you. It gives me pleasure.'

'Can I have another drink first?' he asked quietly.

'What?' she asked incredulously.

'I need a large glass of whisky if you're going to kill me. Surely you won't grudge me that?' It was Nick's turn to take the initiative.

She was taken aback. Nick held the whisky glass in the air as he slowly walked towards the whisky bottle, watching the tip of the knife at all times. She followed him closely, as he poured more neat whisky into the glass until it was almost full. She was smiling at the audacity of the man, the person who had destroyed her career, rejected her advances and who had cheated death twice yesterday. Nobody had ever done that to her before. She watched him raise the whisky to his lips, and then in a flash felt the fiery liquid hitting her face as Nick threw the contents of the glass at her; the alcohol burned fiercely into her eyes. With her guard down, she felt a smack square on the mouth before seeing the darkness descend on her. The knife tumbled out of her hand as she collapsed on the floor. Her legs were spread-eagled, offering Nick a glimpse of her nakedness before he restored her dignity by pulling the dressing gown over her. There was nothing else to do but phone the police and wait for their arrival. He knew the form. This time he poured a small whisky just for himself, before the relative calm was shattered.

39

Make Up

Meg arrived at the house in Buckhurst Hill after Nick had phoned her to collect him. She had not heard about the deliberate attempt on his life until now. Seeing the police with Nick was becoming a regular event. Sheila had put some clothes on by now and was escorted out by two female police constables. Her lips were bruised and swollen, just as Nick's had been. Somehow Nick felt guilty for doing that to her despite what she had tried to do to him. He would have a lot of explaining to do to Meg.

They didn't say much in the car on the way back to Nick's flat. It was only after they got in and sat down in the living room when he received a broadside from her.

'What the hell were you doing with that woman? Yesterday you accused me of being complicit in killing the patient and today you were out to see her again! What is the matter with you, Nick? Have you lost the plot or what? Please tell me! I could scream at you.' He could see she was mad.

'Hey look, I'm sorry. She asked to meet me yesterday and I had no idea who she was until I got to the pub,' Nick explained.

'So you would just saunter off the pub just because some woman asked you to? Is that it, Nick?' Meg asked.

'Hey, you're missing the big picture here. She asked me out for a drink in order to kill me. My drink was spiked. If you hadn't gone to meet your friend I would be dead today. As it is she tried to run me down,' Nick said.

'I didn't go to see a friend. I followed you! I just know when you're up to something because you're a bad liar!' Meg was still very annoyed.

'Who the hell gave you permission to follow me?' He just realised the stupidity of what he said. 'Don't answer that.'

'Just tell me why she wanted to kill you,' Meg said.

'Something to do with destroying her career, I suppose,' Nick replied.

'But you didn't do that deliberately!'

'It just goes to show what a mad world we live in.'

'Now tell me why I should have anything more to do with you,' Meg wanted to know.

'Because I'm a nice guy and I'm really sore all over.'

'Does that mean you want me to stay tonight?' she asked.

'Yes.'

'Okay, so long as you promise me there is to be no more nonsense.'

'Yes.'

'Do you love me?'

'Yes.'

All the emotional assault on him had totally drained his mental reserves. Nick felt so incredibly tired and falling asleep was just too irresistible. Even big boys can only take so much excitement in the space of a few days. His eyes felt heavy as he drifted off. Meg cuddled into him, resting her head against his chest. She just wanted a sensible man who knew a good thing when he saw one. Nick had got to learn how to trust people who loved him. The demons inside his head would not be easy to deal with, but she would be there for him. Maybe he was just too confused about everything. She loved him so much.

40

The Medical Director

Bob McLean had managed to keep his marriage intact and also his consultant post, but the medical directorship had been taken away from him. The affair with the chief executive in itself was not a crime as far as the NHS was concerned. It was a moral decision which no one was qualified to make apart from himself. As a clinician and medical director, he had done a good job for the hospital. He had also heard about Nick's recent involvement with Sheila and was glad that he had managed to figure out for himself about her psychopathic nature. There was something he wanted to say to Nick and he asked him to come along for a chat. His office was now in the medical block rather than in the administration department, as he had reverted to his previous role as a hospital consultant. He was seeing patients once more rather than pushing paper around behind a desk. It made a nice change from the medical politics. Nick met him as arranged but Bob seemed very subdued, which Nick put down to the recent events.

'Thanks for coming, Nick. Please don't say anything for now as there are some things I need to say to you. This matter will remain confidential, I hope. You should know that I am sorry for putting your career at risk and for what you have been through. You must also know that the ex-chief executive and I have had a relationship for many years and that Brenda is our daughter. Sheila became pregnant when we were just starting out on our careers but I didn't want to marry her. It is a little hard to explain this to you but I realised a while ago that she was mentally unstable and suffered from pathological jealousy. She would lie or say anything to save her reputation or her daughter's career. There was an episode in my own career when I was too innocent to realise what I was involved in. Sheila persuaded me to sign several death certificates which in retrospect I should not have done when she was a working as a staff nurse in a surgical ward. Nurses obviously have no power to dictate what goes on a death certificate but they, as you know yourself, have a great deal of experience and often give helpful advice to the young house officers. Some of the deaths were probably suspicious and they should have gone for a post-mortem. I think she may have deliberately killed several people and I essentially helped her get away with it. There will probably be no evidence left to prove any of this, so she will never be found guilty. I have kept silent all these years because both our careers would have finished long before now. You should know that I have tried to be a good clinician and I would never hurt anybody. When the young man died in the A & E department, I immediately wondered if Brenda had taken on her mother's mental illness. Her mother forced me to take action against you so that Brenda could avoid the blaze of publicity. We don't know how the press got onto our relationship but from then on the game was up. I have questioned my own fitness to practice medicine for many years and I have now made up my mind to inform the GMC about all of this. That is all I have to say to you, Nick.' Bob finished his short speech.

'Thank you for telling me this, Bob. I think you're being too hard on yourself. Did know that Sheila tried to kill me?' Nick asked.

'I didn't know the details but I think she rather blamed you for destroying her career which meant everything to her. I would not be at all surprised,' Bob replied.

'And what about you, Bob? Will you carry on here?'

'At my age, there is nowhere else to move on to, unlike you, Nick. I wish you well in your career. Something tells me you're a survivor and that you will go far in the profession. But you also need some luck to survive in the murky world of medical politics, especially when you become a consultant.' It was good piece of advice.

'Thanks for that. Perhaps we'll meet up again,' Nick said.

'Perhaps,' Bob said, giving a sad, knowing smile.

Nick shook the ex-medical director's hand before leaving the office. Somehow he knew he would be seeing a lot less of Bob from now on. There was something different about the man which Nick could not explain. He had seen this often enough in his patients who had simply resigned to their fate.

Several days later, Nick picked up his newspaper and saw the headlines:

'Hospital consultant found dead in hotel room.'

Nick never did see Bob McLean again. At least he had the decency of not causing a spectacle at home in front of his wife. Enough was enough.

Epilogue

The two men had decided to have their lunch at the club in St James. They both chose the grilled Dover sole, accompanied by a perfectly chilled bottle of Chablis which had been placed in an ice bucket next to them. The senior man spoke first, as usual.

'I've heard that our American friend was killed the other day. Was it necessary for him to have taken a hostage, especially when the cat was out of the bag regarding the photographs?'

'Apparently he had made a bad job of things and wanted to resolve matters.'

'Yes, he certainly did make a hash of things. Did you have much of a problem to persuade our friends to resolve the situation?' he asked.

'No, your suggestion of a second set of photographs was all it took. They let their man off the leash. He had also been part of the four-man hit team in Paris.'

'The same chap who was involved in Afghanistan?'

'Yes, he was a specialist in Arabic matters. We let them take care of the Paris situation in return for a favour we did for them in South America.'

'I think the inquiry may not go ahead. Some people are extremely keen to see that it doesn't. I suppose we ought to let sleeping dogs lie, but how on earth did this whole thing end up in such an awful mess?' the senior man asked.

'I believe he had made an error in Paris by crashing his motorcycle and was then caught administering the injection to the driver. The paparazzi have certainly done him no favours. He made a second mistake in Afghanistan when he failed to remove the photographs from the photographer who captured the incident, as we have seen. The photographer had pulled a fast one on him by switching the memory card in his camera. Our suggestion of a second set of Afghan photographs made the Americans re-evaluate their position and they wanted a clean sweep, to make sure they had them all. We didn't think there were any other photographs but, rather by coincidence, the paparazzo involved in the Paris incident had managed to acquire a copy. The dead man had joined the same paparazzi company after returning from Afghanistan and, presumably, the other chap pocketed the photographs prior to selling them to the newspapers. It was a rather unfortunate coincidence.'

'I thought the mission would have been called off once the photographs had been published, leaving the Paris situation unresolved, which it still is.'

'Yes, let us hope the inquiry does not happen.' The other man raised his wine glass and savoured the Chablis.

'Quite an unfortunate coincidence for their man to be involved in both situations, but fingers will naturally point in our direction. We shall deny everything, of course.'

'Were we ever sure the target in Paris posed a major threat?'

'Ours is not to question why, dear chap. It had all seemed rather sloppy on their part. Would the SAS have made a similar mess?'

'I can think of Gibraltar. They shot three IRA suspects in broad daylight despite having no bombs on them. It can happen, even to the best. By the way, the new government had just got into power shortly before the Paris incident. Was this sanctioned by somebody higher up?'

Just then the lunch arrived. The Dover sole looked wonderful, served with crisp mange tout and gratin dauphinois. The senior man lifted his knife and fork before pausing for a second to think about the answer.

'Tell me about this chap Nick Forbes. I think he should be batting for our side. It would certainly be safer, wouldn't you say?' He chuckled, avoiding the question.

The end.